DANGER CLOSE

KAYLEA CROSS

Danger Close

Copyright © 2014
by Kaylea Cross

* * * * *

Cover Art by
Sweet 'N Spicy Designs

* * * * *

ISBN: 978-1496126221

Author's Note

This is the fourth book of my Bagram Special Ops series, and I'm so excited to finally bring you Erin and Sandberg's story. I really love the villain in this one, he's so complex, and I thoroughly enjoyed showing Wade's transition into life back home. Hope you enjoy the book.

Happy reading!

Kaylea Cross

Chapter One

One day. Just one more day and she was out of here.

Erin stood up straight to stretch the stiff muscles in her spine. She was ten hours into a twelve hour shift and she was looking forward to finishing up so she could crash until it was time to get up and pack. Then she'd be on her way home for some much needed R&R. Two weeks of peace and quiet on her parents' ranch outside of Billings. She couldn't freaking wait to get out of this warzone and recharge for a while.

She checked her watch and bent to add more notes to the chart she'd been working on at the nurse's station. *07:10 hours. Heart rate: 74. BP: 110/70. Patient alert and oriented, resting comfortably, has declined further pain meds.*

"Lieutenant, the doctor wants to see you after he's finished with Sergeant Thatcher."

Erin glanced up and nodded at the other nurse. "All right. Be there in a minute." She put down her pen, repositioned her stethoscope hanging around the back of her neck and headed down the hallway to the room she'd put Sgt. Thatcher—Jackson, he'd told her to call him—into half an hour earlier. Staff members bustled past her. Bagram's Craig Joint Theater Hospital was a flurry of activity this morning, even busier than usual because of the new load of patients she'd accompanied on the flight up from Kandahar less than an hour ago. She pushed open the door, expecting to find the doctor in there as well, but he wasn't.

Jackson turned his dark head on the pillow and smiled when he saw her. "Hey."

She smiled back. "Did the doctor come to check on you yet?"

"Yeah, he just left a minute ago."

She'd track him down later then. "How are you feeling now that you've had a chance to settle in? Change your mind about those pain meds yet?"

"Nah, I'm good." He shifted slightly, his slow, restricted movements telling her just how sore his abdominal incisions were. He'd refused meds before and during the flight here, too.

"Well if you change your mind, let one of us know. Promise we won't judge you for taking them. And it won't jeopardize your superhero status."

He grinned at her, a slash of white against his bronzed skin. "Will do." He paused a second, a slight frown tugging his eyebrows closer together. "Any update on Maya at all?"

Erin's heart went out to the guy. He, Maya and the Secretary of Defense had all gone through hell out there during their captivity and escape back to friendly forces. And though Maya had previously been annoyed by Jackson's obvious interest, Erin knew they'd bonded deeply during their ordeal. Apparently Maya had refused treatment for all her injuries until she'd been able to see

Jackson for herself and verify that he would be okay. "No, sorry. I already asked my CO to see if he could find out anything, but everything's blocked by security clearances."

"Yeah." He placed one hand gingerly on the blanket covering his abdomen and didn't elaborate on what had happened out there. Erin was dying to know, but wouldn't ask because she already knew he wouldn't— couldn't—tell her. "So I hear they're transferring me to Landstuhl in the morning?"

"That's the plan I was told, unless something changes before then."

"You'll let me know if you hear anything about her?"

Oh yeah, he was definitely head over heels. And from what she'd observed on her own, the feeling was reciprocated. "Of course. I'll come check on you at lunch, but call if you need anything."

"Thanks."

She returned to the station to finish up her paperwork. At movement in her peripheral vision a few minutes later, she glanced over and saw one of her remaining roommates, Ace, striding toward her. The tall, blonde gunship pilot had her hair pulled back in a bun and she was still wearing her flight suit. Fresh from a night of hunting, Erin guessed. At the concerned look on Ace's face, she set down her clipboard. "Hey, what are you doing here?"

"Heard you'd brought in some patients from Kandahar," Ace replied, stopping at the other side of the desk. "How's Maya? Is she okay? I can't get details from anyone."

While Erin couldn't divulge the extent of Maya's injuries or treatment for privacy reasons, she could certainly tell Ace the basics. She and Maya were tight, which was saying something, because Maya didn't let anyone get close to her. "She had some minor surgery yesterday, but she'll be fine. They've flown her to Qatar for a few days before they send her stateside."

Ace's brown eyes searched Erin's. "Yeah, but how *is* she?"

Erin hesitated before answering, and when she did, she answered Ace as a friend, not a medical professional. "Physically she'll be okay. But whatever happened out there, it was tough." In fact, after she'd read the injury report on Maya while waiting for her to be taken to recovery, Erin's throat had tightened at the thought of what her roomie must have endured.

Ace nodded, pain flashing through her eyes. "And Jackson?"

"Same deal. I just checked on him and—" She trailed off when she spotted a man dressed in civvies heading down the hall toward where Jackson was. "Gotta go. See you later," she blurted to Ace, and rounded the edge of the counter to follow the man. How the hell had he gotten in here? He didn't look back at her, but headed straight for Jackson's door and put out a hand as though he was just going to walk right on in.

"Hey," she called out.

He paused to look over his shoulder at her, his hand resting on the door. His dark eyes locked on her, and in the midst of the thick, nearly black beard he wore—even longer than most of the SOF guys she'd seen around base—his mouth tightened in annoyance.

Erin did a visual sweep and kept coming. He looked like a local. His hair was way longer than regulation allowed, but he had a muscular build and confident bearing that spoke of time in the military. Given his very relaxed grooming standard, the cargo pants and black T-shirt seemed out of place. He was tall, a little over six feet if she had to guess, and maybe in his mid-to-late thirties. Not a bad looking guy. Except he had no business being in this area. "What are you doing?"

His dark brown gaze flicked over her with a mixture of surprise and wariness, his expression cool and remote. "Going to see a friend of mine. He was just brought in." His deep voice was pure American, which surprised her. Not a local, then, and not military either. A contractor of some sort?

She walked right up to him, stopping only a few feet from him to stare up into his face. A hard, weathered face. His skin was darkly tanned, with deep crow's feet fanning out from his eyes. Whoever he was, he hadn't lived a soft life. "Who are you?"

"A friend of his."

I don't think so. "This is a restricted area. How did you get in here?"

He gestured behind her with a slight frown. "The front door."

Smart ass. She folded her arms over her chest, letting him know that his height and size didn't intimidate her one bit. He wasn't getting into Jackson's room until she was certain he wasn't a threat. "You're not supposed to be back here."

He sighed, dropped his hand from the door and faced her fully, even though she knew from his pained expression that this was the last thing he wanted to be bothered with. "Look, I already spoke to one of the docs here. I was in Kandahar with Sergeant Thatcher. I saw you at the hospital down there."

Well she didn't remember *him.* "You got any ID with you?"

He gave her an are-you-for-real look. "No, but—"

"You're standing in a restricted area of a military medical facility, dressed in civilian clothes, you don't have ID and you're trying to get into see one of my patients who needs to sleep. See the problem?"

5

He shut his mouth, that frown reappearing, this time edged with annoyance. "I just need to…" He trailed off as he looked at something over her shoulder. Erin glanced behind her to see the doctor she needed to talk to about Jackson striding toward them.

The middle-aged surgeon raised his eyebrows at her. "Problem?"

"He wants to talk to the patient, but he doesn't have authorization or ID," Erin explained.

"I gave him authorization. Let him in, Lieutenant."

Surprised, Erin turned her attention back to the stranger. She half expected to find a gloating smirk on his face or a triumphant gleam in his eyes. Instead, he swept her with a lingering, curious gaze before nodding at her once in acknowledgement, then pushed the door open and stepped inside.

Expelling a breath, Erin turned back to the surgeon. "Who *was* that?"

He smiled and adjusted his surgical cap as he turned away and motioned for her to follow. Erin trailed after him. "Today you're on a need-to-know basis, Lieutenant. And that, you don't need to know."

****

Shutting the hospital room door behind him, Wade met Jackson's stare and grinned. "You're looking a helluva lot better than the last time I saw you."

"Amazing what some rest, fluids and having a few chunks of metal taken out of your gut will do," the PJ responded in his Texas drawl, a twinkle in his dark eyes. "Won't be doing any core exercises for a while though."

"No, guess not." Wade stuck his hands into his pockets. It felt weird to be able to do that again, having lived in native garb for so long. The cargo pants he wore

6

felt oddly restrictive, foreign. Felt weird to still be speaking English out in the open like this too.

"So Erin gave you a hard time, huh?"

"Who's Erin?"

"The nurse." Jackson nodded toward the door. "I heard her arguing with you."

Wade waved a hand. She'd only been doing her job. "Just a misunderstanding. Who is she?" She'd certainly caught his attention with her directness and looks. It felt really weird to notice a woman that way and feel that shot of attraction after all this time being forbidden to do so.

"Roommate of Maya's."

"Ah." That explained a lot, actually. He'd first seen her leaving the recovery room in Kandahar after Maya had been brought out of surgery to repair her fractured wrist. "Speaking of Maya, I wanted to check out something with you." When Jackson's gaze sharpened, he continued. "Word is, she saw Rahim on the battlefield as the Chinook lifted off."

"Yeah, she told me just before we took all that incoming fire."

Wade's heart started to beat faster. This could be the break they were looking for. "Did you see him too?"

"No."

"Did Maya say anything else? About where he was exactly, or what direction he was headed?"

"No, sorry."

Wade nodded even as his heart sank, disappointed by the response even though he'd known walking in here that finding out anything more of use would be a long shot.

"What about you? I guess now that your cover's been blown…"

Wade sighed. "Yeah, I'm done over here." Probably forever. And knowing that fucking sucked. He'd worked so hard, sacrificed so much, both for his country and to execute this ongoing secret mission. For three years he'd lived deep undercover, most of that spent out in the mountains of the tribal region straddling the northern part of Pakistan and Afghanistan. It had a bitter irony to it. He spoke flawless Urdu and Pashto, was an expert student of the Quran, knew all the customs and how to blend in with any of the local populations on either side of the border, knew every major player in the insurgent game over here and a lot of minor ones too. He'd handled his job seamlessly, played his part to perfection...

Right up until the moment when he'd seen the U.S. Sec Def locked in a cage back in that cave in the Pakistani mountains. As of that moment, his fate had been sealed. He'd had no choice but to sabotage everything he'd worked for. Wade was still reeling from it all. "Looks like I'm off the case, for now at least." He hoped it wouldn't be for long.

"Sorry, man. That's rough."

Wade shrugged. Even if he could go back and do it all over again, he knew he wouldn't change a thing. He'd done his job well, and that was something he could be proud of. "They're sending me stateside until they can capture Rahim." Who would be doing everything in his power to find and kill him right now. "Security reasons."

A man like Rahim wouldn't get over the insult and betrayal of learning that his most trusted man, a man he'd relied heavily on for the past two years, was actually an undercover CIA operative. No matter where he went in the region now, Wade did so with a permanent bull's eye on his back. Every hour he stayed here put him at further risk. He'd only taken the chance of coming to Bagram rather than head stateside immediately from Kandahar in the hopes of talking the

CIA staff here into letting him stay on the case. Of course they'd flat-out refused him. His last hope had been that Jackson might know something that would help lead to a break in the case, something that might make him still necessary to the hunt. He'd grasped at that last straw and come up empty.

"When's the last time you were home?" Jackson asked.

Wade had to think about that for a moment. "Almost four years, I guess." At least a year longer than he'd been undercover.

Jackson's brows shot up. "Then I'd say you've earned an extended holiday anyhow."

A holiday. Right. More like a sentence handed down to him by Uncle Sam.

"Yeah, guess so." He rocked back on his heels, pushing aside the anxiety that kept spiking every time he thought about what lay ahead. What the fuck was he going to do with himself now? Not just in the interim, but long term. Go back to babysitting VIPs in the States and Europe as a security contractor? He wouldn't last a week doing that kind of work now. Over the past few years he'd shed the last of his civilized veneer, and with it, the ability to fit into western society. He'd left it somewhere out in the harsh, snow-capped mountain peaks he could see to the east out the small hospital room window right now. This felt like home now. There was nothing left for him back in the States, no one waiting for him except the estranged siblings he hadn't had contact with in almost five years, since before he went to Afghanistan this last time.

"They have any leads at all? About where Rahim might be?" Jackson asked.

The CIA wasn't telling him jack at the moment, but there was one piece of intel Wade did know. "He was wounded. Blood samples on some clothing found in the general area where Maya reported seeing him last came back as a match for him. The amount of it suggests the wound was serious, but probably not fatal if he got the right treatment in time. Assuming they stopped the bleeding and dosed him with antibiotics..." He shrugged, knowing he didn't have to spell it out for Jackson. The guy was a PJ, after all, a much better trained medic than Wade had ever been, even back during his SF days. That all seemed like another lifetime ago now, however.

Jackson's gaze hardened. "Well, let's hope they find the asshole. Not gonna lie, I'd love to see the bastard hanged for what he did to Maya."

Wade noticed he didn't say anything about the beatings he and the Sec Def had both suffered during their captivity. Or that fucking twisted game of Russian Roulette that would have resulted with one of them putting a bullet in their brain if Wade hadn't been there to intervene at the last second. Wade's conscience hadn't bothered him at the time, because he'd been in character as Jihad. Now that he was suddenly back to being Wade again, little flares of guilt pricked at him.

"I hear you." The beatings and torture had been rough. Although Wade had seen Rahim do and command others to do far worse to people who crossed him or got in his way. Another reason Wade could never fit back in to life stateside. He'd been forced to do things in the line of duty to maintain his cover identity that no one else back home would ever understand, but strangely, the enemy here would. What the hell did that even say?

But there was nothing more he could do for the time being. He'd taken up enough of Jackson's time and the guy needed to sleep. "Well." Wade pulled a hand free of his pocket as he stepped close to the bed. "Good to see you on the road to recovery. All the best to you and Maya. Say hi to her for me when you see her."

Jackson shook his hand, held his gaze. "I will. Take care, man."

Wade was at the door when the PJ's voice stopped him. "Hey." He glanced over his shoulder at Jackson.

Jackson nodded once, a show of respect. "Thanks for everything you did for us. Not that it probably means much to you now, but I know how much you sacrificed to get us all out of there, and I want you to know I appreciate it. All three of us owe you our lives. Make sure you keep that in mind when you get back stateside."

Jackson had correctly guessed that transitioning into life back home in the States wasn't going to be easy for Wade. Not knowing what to say to that, he inclined his head and left. When he turned the corner in the hallway, he spotted Erin standing at the nurse's station, doing paperwork. She looked up and met his gaze, her pen halting in the middle of whatever she was writing on the chart. "He still doing okay?" she asked, all traces of hostility and suspicion gone.

"Fine." She was a pretty little thing, especially now that she wasn't scowling at him. Her chocolate-brown hair was pulled up into a tidy bun at the back of her neck, and her bright green gaze met his unflinchingly, which was a shock in itself. Aside from Maya, he couldn't remember the last time a woman had looked him dead in the eye like this, but he was pretty sure it must have been before he'd gone undercover. Muslim women were forbidden from making eye contact with men outside their family. He hadn't realized how much he'd missed it until now.

His gaze trailed lower, to the smattering of freckles that marched over the bridge of her nose and spilled across her cheeks. Even disguised beneath those shapeless green hospital scrubs he could make out the shapely curves of her body. Curves that would fill a man's hands as he stroked them over her naked skin.

Christ, it had been a fucking long time since he'd done that, too. He jerked his attention away from the swell of her breasts, but not before he saw the nametag on her chest. *Kelly.* Lieutenant Erin Kelly, he mused. Parents must be Irish or something.

She straightened, looking at him expectantly, and he realized he was standing there staring at her like a total fucking moron. But after living for so long in what amounted to the Stone Age and having little to no contact with women the whole time, being at Bagram was proving to be one hell of a culture shock. Meeting a hot, confident woman like her on his first day back was yet another surprise. *Stop staring and say something polite.* "You have a good day, Lieutenant."

"You too, Mr..." She raised her eyebrows in question.

"Sandberg."

She nodded, gave him a pleased smile that made an adorable dimple appear in her left cheek. "Mr. Sandberg. See you later."

He nodded and walked toward the exit, fully aware that he'd never see her again. Because by this time tomorrow he'd be halfway to Kabul, where he'd catch a flight back to civilization.

He should be feeling excitement or even relief at the prospect of finally going home after all this time overseas. Except all he felt was an increasingly familiar sinking sensation in the pit of his stomach. He didn't know where the hell home was anymore.

Chapter Two

Rahim sat very still on his pallet in the main room of the elder's mud brick house as the doctor they'd brought in from Pakistan checked the wounds in his left arm. One bullet had passed right through the back of his upper arm; another had pierced the flesh of his shoulder before the ballistic vest had stopped it from plowing into his chest. The left side of his ribs were bruised all to hell, making breathing painful. A cough or a sneeze made him break into a sweat. If not for the Kevlar barrier over his torso that he never went anywhere without, he would have died on that battlefield two days ago.

"You're not going to be able to do much with this arm for the next week at least," the doctor told him in Urdu as he injected him in the hip with another dose of antibiotics. His third, and still the fever raged as his body tried to kill the infection.

Rahim suppressed a shiver, aware of how hot his face was, of how badly his skin hurt and his bones ached. All he wanted was to sleep, but he couldn't afford to rest now. And probably not for the foreseeable future, either. He'd have to leave this place soon. The pressure was on. "Will I need more antibiotics?"

"Yes, but I can give them to you in pill form if you need to travel."

"Good. I won't be here much longer." Even here surrounded by friends and supporters in the remotest part of the Hindu Kush Mountains, he knew he couldn't let his guard down. Not when he'd just been betrayed by the man he'd trusted more than anyone else since he'd joined the mujahedin and became a soldier of Islam rather than a brainwashed pawn of Uncle Sam's. Loyalty in this region shifted as quickly as the winds did, and Rahim knew that only too well.

He was still reeling from the blow. He'd suspected there was a mole leaking intel to the Americans, but he'd never for a moment considered it might have been Jihad. Youssef had vouched for him as a reliable informant for the Pakistani ISI. Whatever his real name was, Jihad had played his part to perfection.

The doctor finished and Rahim nodded his thanks. One of the villagers escorted the man outside as Rahim struggled back into his clothing and put a new vest back on beneath his tunic. By the time he was finished he was covered in a film of sweat and the pain in his arm had his stomach churning. The burn of betrayal stung far worse.

He'd made a grave mistake in placing all his trust in a man who'd in reality been a spook for the CIA. But Jihad had served him so faithfully over the past three years, the last two as his second-in-command. It was incredible, actually. The man had never once slipped up. Ever. Not even to accidentally slip into English when he'd overheard Rahim speaking it. No, nothing about him had ever given Rahim a single moment's suspicion or pause. He planned to rectify that mistake and avenge that humiliation by whatever means necessary.

And yet, although they were now on opposing sides of this war, Rahim couldn't help but admire the man's dedication to his cause, all the sacrifices he'd made to give up his old life and transform himself into Jihad so seamlessly. Having guarded Rahim's life with his own for the past three years, Jihad was now his most dangerous threat.

Rising from the pallet, he swayed a moment and wiped the cooling sweat off his face with his sleeve before calling to the man waiting outside. "Safir."

A moment later the heavy rug covering the doorway shifted and the twenty-year-old stood in front of him, his dark eyes scanning Rahim's new bandages. "Shall I assemble the men?"

"Not yet. What did you find out on the phone call?"

Safir stepped away from the door and walked into the center of the room to face him. He had finished school in Islamabad before rejoining his family in the tribal region. Rahim had known the family for more than three years and owed them a great debt. Of all his remaining followers, Safir was the only one whose loyalty he didn't question, though he'd never fully trust anyone again. Lessons learned the hard way tended to stick in a man's head. "Our contact got a call from an American source less than an hour ago. Very reliable."

Rahim paused in the act of sliding his sidearm into the holster at the small of his back. "What did he say?" They'd been looking for information about Jihad. Who he really was, where to find him. Fortunately, Jihad's betrayal had pissed off a lot of the locals, who in turn were more than willing to pass on the information they heard.

"He gave a name and a possible location."

Rahim's fingers tightened around the grip of the pistol. "Who is he?" It enraged him even more to think of the name that traitor had taken. Jihad. Must have loved the irony of that, the bastard.

"Wade Sandberg."

Rahim stared at him as the name registered. A Jew? A fucking American *Jew* had done this to *him*, a devout Muslim and soldier of Allah? Not only betrayed him, but helped the U.S. Sec Def and the others escape and compromise every operation he'd had in the planning stages? A wave of rage rushed through his bloodstream, so strong it stole his breath.

When he calmed enough to be able to pull in a rough breath, his mind was already racing. The only saving grace about this entire catastrophe was that even Jihad hadn't known the exact details of the last operation Rahim had been working on. He could still go ahead with it once he made a few last minute changes, but he'd have to move the timeline up considerably. "What's the location?"

"The American said Sandberg is flying out of Kabul International late tomorrow morning. Apparently he's at Bagram right now."

"He's flying out on a commercial flight?" That didn't make any sense, given that he had to know Rahim would be hunting for him. "Did the contact say how he was getting to Kabul?"

"No, but if he couldn't get a military flight, he might be driving there."

Rahim frowned. Maybe Sandberg and the CIA weren't expecting him to be a threat now that he was wounded and in hiding. But not on the run, he reminded himself vehemently. He would never *run* like a cowardly dog, not from anything or anyone. "And the American just offered up all this information, why?" If this so-called "source" wasn't just feeding them false information or trying to lead him into a trap, that is. Rahim was far more wary today than he had been even a few days ago, and he wasn't about to do anything stupid. He could act from out here in the middle of nowhere without placing himself in direct danger and do what he could to avoid enemy drones and satellites out looking for him.

Safir shrugged. "I don't know. But it's worth checking into, don't you think?"

Oh yeah, very worth it. He gestured impatiently with his right hand, determined to ignore the pain and fatigue pulling at him. "Bring the senior commanders in. I need to coordinate everything immediately." Starting with placing people at the Kabul airport and the checkpoints on the roads leading from Bagram to Kabul by morning.

If Rahim's wish came true, the only way Wade Sandberg would be leaving Afghanistan was in a pine box.

****

Erin woke with a start when the alarm on her phone buzzed in her hand. She'd fallen asleep holding it again. Stifling a groan as she rolled over in her bunk, she smiled as her sleepy brain realized what day it was. In a few hours she was going home.

Sitting up, she took a look around. The other four bunks in the B-hut were empty. Maya was now in Qatar, of course. Devon had long since been back in Washington State recovering from injuries sustained during a medevac mission gone terribly wrong, Ace was no doubt out hunting in her gunship again, and Honor was—

The door to the hut swung open to reveal the woman in question standing there. The aviation maintenance sergeant's cheeks were pink and she was breathing hard as though she'd run all the way here from the hangar. She was still dressed in her grease-stained utilities, and strands of her strawberry-blond hair had come loose from her tidy bun. Her pale blue eyes held an almost frantic light as she met Erin's gaze.

"What's wrong?" Erin demanded.

Honor stepped inside and shut the door behind her. "I just came from the hangar. They flew a damaged Chinook in from Kandahar this morning. It had bullet holes all over it. There were bloodstains in the back all over the deck, and on the pilot-commander's seat. I know it was Liam's bird, and no one's telling me anything."

Oh, shit. Erin pushed the covers off her and stood up. As a pilot with the Army's elite Night Stalkers, Liam often flew the kinds of dangerous missions like the one to extract Maya, Jackson and the Sec Def yesterday. No surprise that Honor had seen the damage and put two and two together on her own. "Are you—"

"Have you seen him?"

Erin shook her head. "No, but—"

"Have you heard anything?" Her face was pinched.

Hating to see her so upset, Erin waved her over. "Come here."

Honor tightened her jaw but did as she said, stopping a foot from Erin. The smell of oil and hydraulic fluid drifted in the air between them. "Just tell me."

Erin set an arm around Honor's tense shoulders and drew her down to sit stiffly beside her on the edge of the bunk. She understood how tough this was. Three years ago she'd gotten the call that her boyfriend David was KIA and it had been devastating. "I didn't see him personally but I know he was admitted to the hospital in Kandahar yesterday and that his injuries were minor. He was treated and released after a couple hours."

At that Honor turned her head to stare directly into Erin's eyes. A don't-you-dare-bullshit-me look, capped off by a sheen of tears that made Erin's heart clench in sympathy. "You're *sure*?"

"I'm sure." She squeezed Honor's shoulder, rubbed her palm over it in a show of comfort. "He's okay."

Honor swallowed and looked down at her hands, clasped tightly in her lap. "Okay as in he's well enough to still be on active duty? Or okay as in he'll be fine once he recovers from whatever happened to him?"

"I'd say the first, but maybe only a few days if it's the second."

Honor searched her eyes again for a moment, as if she was trying to decide whether Erin was telling her the truth or just giving her a bullshit story to calm her down. She must have decided Erin was being real, because at last she dropped her face into her hands and took several slow, shaky breaths. Erin rubbed a soothing hand over her friend's back, not knowing what else to say. At least Honor knew Liam was all right.

She knew they'd been engaged until a few months ago, before Honor had come here on her most recent tour, but that was all. It was clear Honor still cared very much for him despite the breakup. What the hell had happened to make them split when it was so obvious that Honor wasn't over him?

"Better?" Erin asked softly a minute later.

Honor nodded, face still resting in her hands.

"Can't you send him an e-mail or something, just to put your mind at ease?" Erin assumed she wouldn't want to actually speak to him over the phone or anything like that.

"No, it's...no." Honor straightened with a sigh then stood. She frowned as she glanced around and noticed the packed bags Erin had stowed by the head of her bunk. Those pale blue eyes flashed up to hers. "Is it that day already?"

Erin nodded, feeling a pang at leaving Honor here. Of all her roomies, she was closest to Honor. "Leaving for Kabul in forty minutes."

"Oh." She glanced around the hut, taking in all the empty beds. "Getting kind of lonely around here. Now it'll just be Ace and me."

And Ace's night shifts meant she'd be mostly sleeping during the day, so not much company for Honor. "I'll be back in two weeks. You'll barely even have time to miss me."

Honor put on a smile, but it was less than convincing. "Yeah. You take care, okay?"

"I will." She reached up to return the hug Honor offered, patted her back, but she could tell her friend was still upset. "Maybe have someone pass on a message to him for you at least. I know you, you'll drive yourself nuts without at least hearing something from him, even if it's passed on from someone else."

"Maybe," Honor said evasively as she pulled away and straightened. "See you in two weeks. Say hi to the horses for me."

"You bet."

As soon as she was alone, Erin grabbed her toiletries and rushed across to the shower facility through the cool March morning air. Scrubbed, dressed and fed, she gathered her bags and headed toward the main gates where the truck she'd be riding in was waiting. After verifying everything with the driver, she loaded her gear into the back of the Hummer, slid into the backseat and fastened the chinstrap on her helmet. They were all required to wear body armor outside the protected confines of the base, and the roads to and from Kabul could still be dangerous for anyone wearing a military uniform. Especially if said uniform had a U.S. flag anywhere on it.

The usual noises of Bagram came through her open window: the pulse of rotor blades, the muted purr of engines, the bustle of personnel moving around the base. Tomorrow night she'd be hearing nothing but crickets and maybe the occasional howl of a wolf or coyote out on the ranch. The thought made her smile in anticipation.

Approaching footsteps sounded to her right. As she turned her head the opposite door opened and a man started to slide inside. When she saw his profile a tiny shock ran through her. He reached for the door handle, glanced over and froze in place when he saw her, those dark eyes filled with startled recognition.

Sandberg.

He'd shaved, she thought inanely, unable to tear her gaze away. The long, thick beard from yesterday was now trimmed to a very sexy heavy stubble that made him look rugged and intensely masculine.

For a second she floundered for something to say. His big frame seemed to crowd the interior of the Hummer. She was suddenly aware of just how broad his shoulders were, how ripped the muscles in those arms were beneath the sleeves of his snug T-shirt that hugged his powerful chest and flat belly. He was lean though despite that obvious strength, and more than what being in phenomenal shape would do. The slight hollows beneath his cheeks told her he'd been living on a very restricted diet for a long time. She remembered the way he'd watched her yesterday. Stared, actually. With way more than average masculine interest. It had damn near bordered on fascination, like he hadn't seen a woman in forever. Just where the hell had he been living, and for how long?

"Are you going to Kabul too?" she finally asked
when he didn't say anything, a little discomfited by the
unexpected pull of attraction she felt toward him. He
was hard and remote, and he had dangerous written all
over him. The exact opposite of what she wanted in a
man.

"Yeah, the airport. You?" He was doing it again.
Staring at her with a mixture of awareness and...veiled
interest. As though he was fascinated by each feature on
her face and wanted to memorize them. She wasn't sure
if she was flattered or if it made her really damn
uncomfortable.

"Flying out at eleven hundred." Because it was
cheaper for Uncle Sam to send her back home on a
civilian aircraft out of Kabul than take up valuable room
in a military aircraft when it could be transporting
supplies or equipment instead.

"To Heathrow?"

She blinked. "Yes."

"Huh." He settled back against the seat and broke
eye contact, and she noticed he didn't have a helmet with
him. He was wearing a military-issue armored vest
though. "What are the odds of that?" he murmured as he
stared out the passenger window, effectively ending the
brief conversation.

Pretty slim. She turned her attention back out her
window, acutely aware that for the next few hours she'd
be stuck beside a man who had her internal female radar
pinging like a freaking pinball machine, yet had no
interest in talking to her. Yay. Her leave was off to a
fantastic start.

Chapter Three

The Humvee Wade sat in was the last in a line of five vehicles. Another one was up front in the lead, with two big supply trucks sandwiched between it and the Humvee directly in front of theirs. They all rolled out together through the main gates, past all the razor wire and the secure perimeter and started out toward Kabul.

It still didn't feel like enough protection.

Other than his increased vigilance now that they'd left the relative safety of the base and being conscious of the SIGs snug against the small of his back and strapped to his right calf, Wade was vividly aware of the woman beside him. And of the slightly awkward tension in the vehicle now that the initial small talk was out of the way. Behind the wheel the driver, a guy named Thompson, was completely tuning them out as he listened to rap or hiphop or whatever the hell it was he had going from whatever electronic device he'd plugged into the radio deck. Sounded like godawful noise to Wade.

"So, where's home?" Erin asked him a few minutes into the drive, apparently uncomfortable with the lack of conversation.

"Wyoming." Technically. The word *home* evoked memories of the house he'd grown up in as a kid, but that was long gone, torn down nearly fifteen years ago. He didn't have anywhere in particular to go now, so he'd probably rent a cabin or something up in the Blue Ridge Mountains once he was done in Langley, to reacclimate for a while. It was going to take time to fit back into society and he wasn't sure if he'd ever feel comfortable in it again. When Erin kept looking at him he realized he was being rude by not extending the basic courtesy of lobbing the conversation ball back over the net to her. "You?"

"Montana. Just outside of Billings. Where are you from in Wyoming?"

"Near Jackson Hole." Not that far from Billings.

She was quiet for a moment, then picked up the thread of conversation when he let it lapse for too long. "Do you ride horses?"

He turned his head to look at her again. She was watching him, those expressive green eyes full of curiosity. "Yeah, practically grew up in the saddle."

Her excited smile made her eyes sparkle, and something about the sight damn near mesmerized him. She wore her emotions right out there in the open, something that was as foreign to him now as fast food and booze. "Me too. I can't wait to get home and take my horse out. He's at my parents' ranch."

Wade nodded to show he was listening, actually enjoying the sound of her voice, which surprised him, since small talk had always bugged the ever living shit out of him. He thought back to the last time he'd been in the saddle, when he'd been riding an ugly-ass mule in the Kush back in his SF days. Before that, it'd been years before when he'd worked as a ranch hand prior to joining the Army. Sometimes he missed those days, the freedom he'd always felt on horseback, out roaming the hills and coulees by himself. Still made some of his fondest memories.

They lapsed into silence after that, but it felt less strained this time and he was glad, because this time she seemed content not to fill the quiet. As a nurse, she'd be used to working with and handling people all day. He'd once been a people person too, for all his introverted nature, which was why he'd done so well in SF, because a good chunk of his career had been spent training indigenous forces. Since going undercover, that had all changed. He'd sometimes gone weeks without interacting with anyone other than Rahim, and even then a lot of the time it had been over the phone. Somewhere along the way he'd lost that engaging part of his personality. He was harder now, more remote, but he'd had no choice because it had been either adapt or die.

That was another reason why he wasn't comfortable engaging in small talk while they were out here in no man's land. He didn't like letting his focus wander even that much, and doubted he'd ever get used to western social norms ever again.

Grateful for the quiet again as the minutes ticked by—the damned rap music coming from the radio notwithstanding—he peered through the windshield and saw the first checkpoint coming up. Eventually the convoy slowed and ground to a halt. Wade kept his attention on what was happening around them, ready to act if his gut told him they were in any sort of danger. He also knew the others in the vehicle were oblivious to his hyper vigilance and the reasons for it.

While security made up of Afghan police and military inspected the forward vehicles, a guard came over to collect their travel documents. Wade watched the man's face carefully as he checked the photo in his passport and glanced up to study him. When he handed it back and moved on to Erin's without further investigation, Wade allowed himself to relax a little. The guard finished his check and waved them forward. Once they passed through the gate without incident, Wade eased back against the seat and placed his hands on his thighs, away from the grips of the concealed pistols. He watched in the passenger side mirror just to assure himself there was nothing funny happening behind them and no one following them.

"Something wrong?" Erin asked him.

"No." He didn't want to worry her, but he couldn't let his guard down until that plane lifted off the tarmac in Kabul. Rahim had an extensive network and there was no telling who might be a threat out here.

She studied him for a moment longer, as if she wasn't sold on the denial, then went back to staring out her window. Wade stole a glance at her profile. The curve of her cheek looked so soft and smooth, and that dusting of freckles across her nose was downright adorable on her. When she turned her head and caught him staring, he felt himself flush, but she didn't seem annoyed or offended. Rather, she let her gaze travel over his face for a moment before meeting his eyes, and if he wasn't mistaken she seemed to like what she saw.

"Can I ask you something?"

He might be rusty when it came to making conversation, let alone with a woman, but in his experience when a female phrased a question like that, it was gonna be really damn personal. Since he was going to be trapped beside her for the next long while, there was no escape except to be rude and shut her down, which he didn't have the heart to do. Digging deep for the forgotten social niceties his mother had drummed into him as a kid, he answered. "Sure."

"I assume you're not current military, so what are you? A contractor?"

Close enough. "Yeah."

Those intelligent eyes kept cataloguing his features and he knew she was studying him from the perspective of both a soldier and a medical professional. He was pretty sure she'd already figured out far more about him than she was letting on.

"Bet it's been a while since you ate American-style food, huh?"

Yep, definitely putting it all together in that pretty little head. He nodded in acknowledgement and braced himself for more questions, the inevitable lies he'd have to feed her to protect his identity, but she surprised him by letting it go to stare out her window once more.

They rode in silence for the next forty minutes until the convoy began to slow when they reached the next checkpoint, the last one before they hit Kabul. Wade watched as the military guards approached the vehicles. This time a few of the soldiers climbed into the back of the supply trucks ahead to inspect the cargo. He could see two other guards talking to the driver and passengers of the lead Humvee. The taller of the two guards sent to inspect the first vehicle talked to the occupants for what seemed a lot longer than necessary, and by the time he and his partner turned and headed toward their vehicle, Wade's instincts were already humming.

"Passports," the guy said to Thompson in heavily accented English as he scanned the interior. His gaze fell on Wade and he paused for just a fraction of a second before taking their ID from Thompson. Wade kept his attention riveted on the man as he perused the documents and glanced up at Erin before swinging his eyes back to Wade. "Wait here," he told Thompson, and motioned for his partner to come over. They stood far enough back from the truck that Wade couldn't hear what they were saying, but it was clear from the surprise on the second man's face that whatever the first one said meant bad news. Ahead of them, the first Humvee and both supply trucks started through the checkpoint.

"Taking their sweet fucking time clearing us, aren't they?" Thompson muttered in annoyance. Being isolated from the rest of the convoy was definitely cause for concern.

The first guard said something into his radio that Wade didn't catch, then turned and headed for the guardhouse. When the second guard stared at them and held up a hand to make sure they stayed where they were, the alarm in Wade's head started blaring. Something was definitely wrong.

Move.

He cursed in Pashto and jerked forward to grab Thompson's shoulder. "Get us outta here." Erin stiffened and shot him a disbelieving look but Wade didn't take his eyes off the second guard.

Thompson cranked his head around to gape at Wade, opening his mouth to say something, but Wade cut him off. "Right fucking *now*," he snarled, just as more guards exited the little building and started toward them, weapons at the ready. Erin sucked in a breath and froze in her seat. Wade didn't look at her.

"Holy shit," Thompson blurted as he realized what was happening, then started the truck and gunned it in reverse. His whole body tense, Wade stared through the windshield as the guards burst into a flurry of activity. Swinging them around in a hard J-turn, Thompson stomped on the accelerator and tore back the way they'd come, already on the radio to the lead vehicle, now trapped on the opposite side of the checkpoint. "They're coming after us—getting us outta here."

"Oh, shit," he heard Erin breathe as she ducked down and put a hand on the weapon strapped to her thigh.

Looking back through the passenger window, Wade saw two black pickups tearing after them, a gunner in the back of each manning the mounted rifles there. He whipped around to check their six o'clock. Beyond the barricade, the soldiers in the rest of the convoy were all being hauled out at gunpoint and ordered onto their stomachs on the ground. Over the radio Wade could hear the shouts and confusion going on, and the message was clear: they were on their own.

Wade faced front and leaned forward a little to peer out the windshield as they tore down the two-lane highway. "Get us off this road," he snapped at the driver.

"And go where?" Thompson demanded, jaw tight, fingers clenched around the wheel.

"Where they can't follow. More of 'em will be coming at us from the northern checkpoint now too."

Swearing, Thompson glanced once in the rearview, saw the trucks coming at them, and veered off the main road. The big vehicle bounced and bucked as it tore across the dry, open plain. Over the radio, the response from Bagram came back. *Stand by.* "Got any ideas?" Thompson demanded.

The only two options were left or right. "Head for those hills." Wade pointed left, to the northwest.

"What about mines?" Erin said in a tight voice, her body tense. She had her weapon in her right hand, her left one gripping the door handle so hard her knuckles were white.

Wade took in her pinched expression, how pale she was. A foreign feeling of guilt settled in his chest. He'd done some fucked-up things in his time undercover, but knowing he'd put her in this potentially lethal situation because Rahim was targeting him made him feel badly.

"Shouldn't be a problem here." Unless they ran over an IED buried in the ground.

"So, toward the hills. And then what?" Thompson jerked the truck to the side to avoid a clump of boulders.

"We see what happens."

Erin cranked around in her seat, mouth thinned as she stared out the rear window. "I think they're gaining on us."

Wade swung around to look. Yeah, and at this speed, in another few minutes those gunners would have them within range. He turned back to search in the distance ahead of them, scanning the terrain for a better, faster route. There wasn't one. The Humvee plunged and groaned as it hit a shallow gulley then heaved up the other side. Thompson steered them out at an angle. "Shit, there're fucking rocks everywhere," he grumbled. They bounced and rattled over the ground as he swerved them around rock clusters. "Hold on," he warned.

Beside him, Erin grabbed the upper handle above the doorframe with her left hand and holstered her weapon to grip the edge of the seat with her right while Wade flattened a hand against the seat in front of him. A second later the Hummer slammed into something. The bone-jarring impact jerked them forward against their seatbelts amidst a loud bang and a groan of metal. When the vehicle evened out once more, a telltale thumping sound came from beneath it.

"Just blew out a tire, and maybe an axel," Thompson said, face grim as he kept maneuvering them forward. Already the vehicle was beginning to lose speed.

"They're still back there," Erin reported, "but it looks like they're not gaining on us now."

Yeah, but it was only a matter of time before they blew more of the self-sealing tires on this terrain. Wade searched the base of the foothills for someplace they could go until backup arrived.

"What's the story on our backup?" Thompson demanded over the radio.

"Unknown at this time. Stand by," came the response.

"Yeah, I'll fucking stand by," he grumbled derisively under his breath before giving a terse acknowledgement.

"Over there," Wade told him, pointing a little ways to the north where a trail cut up the hillside to where a small village lay nestled in the shelter of a ridge high up. "Get us to the base of that trail."

"Why?" Thompson's voice was laced with stress.

"Just get us there."

Cursing under his breath, Thompson aimed for the base of the hill. They jostled and rattled over more rocks and the thumping sound became louder. At least one more tire was blown, but the big beast kept on rolling anyhow. When Wade checked behind them again, the pursuing trucks had slowed enough to buy them some time to ditch the vehicle and disappear before the enemy caught up.

He glanced around the interior for weapons. Thompson had an M4 up front with him, and a sidearm. Wade looked at Erin. "That your only weapon?" he indicated the holster on her thigh.

She hadn't let go of the door handle. "Yes."

"Any spare mags?"

"Two."

Better than none, and with any luck they'd be up and out of range before the chasing force arrived. The Hummer limped its way over the last few klicks to the bottom of the hill Wade had indicated. "Kill the engine," he said to Thompson. "We've gotta hump out of here on foot." He didn't need to tell them that staying with the truck would guarantee them getting killed.

"*Shit*," the guy muttered, but did as Wade said, shoving the keys into one of the pockets on his web gear.

"Grab whatever water, weapons and ammo you've got, and let's go," Wade ordered as he slid out of the vehicle. He ran around back and hauled out his duffel while Erin and Thompson grabbed their rucks and hurriedly put them on. He looked up the trail that switch-backed up the hill. The village appeared to be a quarter mile or so up, but with the trail winding like that, the hike was going to be a hell of a lot longer. He glanced at Erin. She stood at the foot of the trail, helmet on and ready to go, watching him tensely. "Come on."

He took point, leading them up the trail at a rapid clip. The air was cool, but the morning sunlight bounced off the hillside in waves. Between that and the relatively steep grade of the trail they climbed, he was sweating within minutes. They were only a few hundred yards up the loose dirt pathway when the sound of the approaching enemy engines reached him. Wade glanced upward, hoping to find a place where they could scale the hillside from one level of the trail to the next. They had to make headway, fast. "Up here."

The others followed him to a short incline. He grabbed Erin by the arm and towed her to the spot he had in mind, then took her by the hips to push her upward as she scrambled her way up to the top. Soil and rocks slid down the side as she moved, but soon she was at the next level. She dropped to her knees and extended a hand down to Thompson, who ignored it and clambered up after her. Wade went last, clearing the lip just as a rifle round buried itself into the rocks about twenty feet below them, the report echoing in the air. Erin snatched his hand and dragged him to his feet, her eyes wide. Together they started running up the next leg of the trail, moving away from the shooters.

When Wade glanced over his shoulder a few seconds later he saw one of the pickups stalled too far away from them to be any threat, its occupants already moving out on foot. The other truck was only a few hundred yards from the Hummer. In the back of it the gunner opened fire with another short burst. Rounds impacted the hillside in an explosion of dust. Ahead of him, Erin was in the lead. She'd picked another spot to scale the hillside and was clawing her way up it when another burst rang out, this time close enough to their position to raise Wade's heart rate.

"Gimme your rifle," he shouted to Thompson, who glanced back at him for a second as if he thought Wade was crazy before handing it over. "Go. Stay with her." Thompson ran to catch up with Erin as Wade dropped to one knee behind a boulder and took aim at the gunner in the back of that truck. The range on the weapon wasn't the greatest but it was close enough so he fired and a high-pitched metal ping rang through the air a second later. He'd missed the gunner but hit the big mounted rifle in back, and for the moment the return fire stopped. To conserve what ammo he had, Wade slung the M4 and raced to catch up to the others. The enemy truck was almost at the Humvee now.

No sooner had he clambered up the incline Erin and Thompson had just scaled than the bark of more rifles broke the stillness. Ahead of him Erin ducked and instinctively threw her hands up to shield her face as a round plowed into the dirt a few yards in front of her. The enemy was well within range now. Wade whirled and took aim again, this time at the guy in the lead, and fired. The guy fell back with a cry, blood spurting from a wound high up in his shoulder. One of his buddies picked up the fallen rifle to return fire along with someone from the group farther back. Wade fired at the closest man at the bottom of the hill, winged him in the thigh.

Then he heard Erin's shout. "Thompson's down!"

He glanced up the trail to see her kneeling over Thompson, who had his hands pressed low over his belly, his teeth bared and his eyes squeezed shut in an agonized expression. Erin already had his ruck off, was trying to drag the much larger man by his web gear toward safety, behind the cover of some nearby boulders.

Wade swore under his breath in Pashto. There was no way they could make a run for it and escape now. They'd have to stay and fight.

Chapter Four

Erin was focused solely on getting Thompson behind cover. He was bleeding badly from the wound in his lower belly. She had to get them both to safety before they had more GSWs to deal with. She gritted her teeth and hauled him along the path, the muscles in her arms, legs and back burning. Rounds pinged off the rocks below them. Sweat trickled down her face and under her arms.

Thompson let out a throttled growl as she towed him behind the nearby hip-high boulders. She squeezed behind the pitiful shelter with him and dropped her ruck to rummage through it.

"Why the fuck are they attacking us?" Thompson muttered, already shaking from shock.

"No idea." Though she was fairly certain it had something to do with Sandberg. He'd picked up on the threat before she and Thompson had even realized what was happening. Before that he'd seemed on edge, like he'd been expecting trouble.

Sandberg hurried over, lowered his rifle slightly and spoke to her without turning around. "Let's go."

He bent to put Thompson across his shoulders, his grunt drowned out by the wounded man's raw cry of pain as he hoisted him into the air and set off. Erin grabbed what ammo and water she could find in Thompson's ruck, stuffed it into her own, and tipped it onto her back before rushing to catch up with Sandberg. He moved at a steady pace despite the heavy burden he carried. Erin cast a nervous glance back down the hill, the quiet unnerving after the initial firefight. The wounded were being evacuated in the one functional truck, but she knew they'd bring more reinforcements at any time, and who knew when the backup Thompson had requested would arrive. Or if they even would.

"What's the plan?" she panted as she caught up to Sandberg.

"Get to the village."

"That's the first place they'll look for us!"

He just grunted and kept going.

There had to be something better. She glimpsed a trail winding up the hillside from the village, leading God knew where, but surely heading up that was better than sitting in a potentially hostile village when the enemy came hunting again. "What about there?" she asked, pointing at it. "We could—"

"The village," he snapped and she glowered at him. He wasn't her CO—he wasn't even freaking military—so who the hell did he think he was, deciding their fate for them?

"Why are they after us?"

He didn't respond and his silence put the match to her temper.

"Hey." She quickened her stride to come abreast of him, would have grabbed his arm to force him to look at her except he was clearly struggling under Thompson's weight and the grade of the incline. "What happened at the checkpoint? Were they looking for you?"

"Stop talking and walk faster," he growled without looking at her.

Thinning her lips, she shut up and picked up the pace, expecting to hear another engine or volley of shots at any moment. They covered the remaining distance to the village in about fifteen minutes, but by the time they arrived she and Sandberg were out of breath and sweating heavily. She was about to insist they keep going on the trail she'd seen fifteen minutes ago when a group of male villagers crested the rise. They were all armed with rifles, their expressions hard and distrusting. She faltered and reached for her weapon but Sandberg stayed her with another grunt and a terse shake of his head. Her whole body tense, she dropped her hand and waited. She never could have predicted what happened next.

Sandberg shocked her by calling out to the men in what had to be Pashto. They blinked at him in astonishment for a moment, then urged him forward. Erin followed closely in his wake, aware of her pulse thudding in her ears and a sick feeling of dread in the pit of her stomach. She watched the men's hands carefully, afraid to take her eyes off them.

They passed several mud brick homes and were approaching a slightly larger one in the center of the village when a man stepped out of the doorway. He was in late middle age, his thick beard liberally streaked with gray. His gaze swept over them with a cursory glance before he spoke to his men. One of them replied and the old man's eyes snapped to Sandberg in surprise. He said something, and Sandberg replied in turn. The hint of a smile warmed the old man's face, then he nodded and motioned for them to enter his home. Erin was right at Sandberg's back, all too aware of the curious and disdainful looks she was receiving. There were no other women in sight, all probably having been sequestered into their homes at the first sign of visitors approaching, as custom dictated.

Sandberg walked into the center of the dwelling and lowered Thompson to the hard-packed dirt floor. Even in the dim illumination from the lantern in the corner, she could see how pasty his skin was. She put on surgical gloves from the med kit, took his pulse and got to work assessing the wound more thoroughly, darting glances at Sandberg as he spoke to the elder. Thompson groaned when she revealed the bullet wound. She pushed his hands away and whispered for him to lie still while she worked.

The round had gone through his abdomen and out the side of his waist. Too low to have hit his kidneys, and too far to the side to have hit his bladder. With any luck it'd torn right through muscle and not much else. She poured in clotting powder and bandaged him up, wondering what the hell Sandberg was saying and how he'd learned to speak the language like a native. Had to be former Spec Ops. Who was he working for now?

By the time she finished and stripped her bloody surgical gloves off, Sandberg came over. "Bleeding slowed?"

"Nearly stopped. Hoping it's just a really bad flesh wound, but without further assessment and better lighting I can't tell."

"We need to move again, fast. Sorry, but has to be done," he said to Thompson as he reached down to haul him back atop his shoulders. Thompson gritted his teeth and let out a throttled sound, eyes squeezed shut.

Once again, Erin scrambled to get her gear together and rush after him. "Where are we going?" she demanded as they stepped out into the bright sunshine.

"Up the access trail."

She resisted the urge to snap at him at his clipped responses and followed him and three of the younger men up the trail. It snaked up the hillside in a winding route, but this time following wadis and dry streambeds that concealed them from anyone looking up from the bottom of the hill. Almost twenty minutes later another, smaller village came into view near the crest of a ridge. The faint sound of truck engines below in the valley floor reached them.

"Quick." Sandberg motioned for her to run ahead of him. She followed one of the villagers down a slight incline and into a shallow ravine, struggling to keep her balance with the added weight of her ruck. A minute later the first dwelling came into view. One of the men ushered them into the fourth house on the right, set against the hillside, and motioned them toward the back wall where a heavy carpet hung. He pulled it aside to reveal a passageway. Sandberg said something to him, received a reply, and motioned for her to enter what appeared to be a long tunnel. The carpet dropped over the opening, plunging them into blackness. In the sudden silence their breathing sounded magnified.

"What's going on?" Thompson rasped.

"Passage leads into a cave in the mountain," Sandberg answered. "Got a light?" he asked Erin.

She fished a slim flashlight out of her ruck and switched it on. The tunnel they stood in was narrow and small enough that even she would have to crouch to get through it. Staring ahead into the blackness beyond the beam of light, a sickening sense of dread filled her. The walls seemed to squeeze closer together even more, making the old panic rise up. She swallowed and forced herself to take a slow inhalation as she fought the old fear.

"I can't carry Thompson through here. You'll have to take point," Sandberg said to her in a low voice.

She nodded, doing everything she could to mask the terror trying to wind its tendrils up her spine. Keeping the light steady, she carefully picked her way down the tunnel. *Don't think about it, don't think about it*, she repeated to herself. "How far?"

"Until we get to the cave on the other end. Few hundred feet or so."

Great, she thought sourly. She pushed away the panicky sensation in her chest and kept going, reminding herself that she wasn't trapped in here. *Yet.* "You trust that guy?" she made herself ask.

"No reason not to. They'll keep us hidden and come for us once the soldiers leave the area."

No reason not to? "How do you know?"

"Pashtun tribal code. It's an honor thing."

"You believe him enough to risk our lives, waiting in here?" Being *trapped* in this tunnel with only two possible exits, in what could be a hostile village.

"Yes."

His immediate response surprised her. Since she didn't have a choice but to go forward now, she made herself walk on. The air in here was chilly, the stygian darkness ahead making her heart pound. Knowing Sandberg's and Thompson's big frames blocked the exit behind her intensified the fear. She was all too aware of the seconds ticking past, of the rock squeezing in from all sides, making her throat tighten more and more. Only she must not have masked her fear very well, because Sandberg's low voice broke the silence.

"You okay?"

Not even close. "Yeah." There was no help for it; she'd have to keep going until they reached the cave.

It seemed to take forever for her to inch her way through the rock tunnel, her heart pounding a painful rhythm against her ribs with every step, but finally she noticed a lightening up ahead. She picked her way over the uneven ground and the crushing fear began to recede as the tunnel finally widened a bit. The light ahead grew stronger and stronger until she was able to see well enough to turn off her flashlight. At last the tunnel took a slight turn. Their footsteps began to echo slightly, alerting her that a larger chamber lay ahead.

"Stop here," Sandberg whispered.

Without feeling like she was entombed in a rock sarcophagus, Erin was at last able to draw a full breath as she hunkered down and pulled off her ruck. "You hanging in there, Thompson?" she whispered.

"Trying to," he answered, his voice strained.

Sandberg shifted behind her and lowered the other man to the ground. "Aim your flashlight on him and let's check the wound."

She did, liking that he wasn't pulling alpha male bullshit and actually treating her like an equal in the process. In the beam of light, Thompson's bandages were soaked through with blood. Sandberg peeled the tape away from the edges to pull it back. The clotting agent was still doing its job, because the wound was only bleeding sluggishly despite all the stress just placed on it. Thompson was shivering as she added more Quick Clot gauze and re-bandaged the wound.

Once she was done she switched off the light, reassured by the faint natural light seeping in from ahead. "Now what?" she whispered to Sandberg.

"We wait for them to come get us."

Though she understood the basic tribal code and the sense of honor that ran deep among these people, she still thought it was a huge mistake to trust them with their lives. Honor was one thing, but she'd been over here long enough to know that allegiances here shifted as quickly as the weather. But if they left the cave now, they'd be exposed to the men now combing the hills for them. In the expanding silence she was aware of the thud of her pulse in her ears. "What happened at that checkpoint?"

He shifted but didn't answer.

"It was you they were after, wasn't it?" It was the only thing that made sense.

He grunted.

"Why?" she pressed, growing frustrated. After what they'd been through, she and Thompson deserved to know the truth.

A deep sigh filled the space. "Long story."

"Yeah, well, you've now got a captive audience with the two of us here. So what the hell's going on?"

He hesitated a long moment before answering. "Has to do with a job I was recently on."

She could just imagine what sort of "job" he referred to. "And?"

Another grunt and the sound of material shifting, as if he'd just shrugged. She opened her mouth to say something else but the distant sound of voices made her whirl to face the cave entrance. She could feel the tension radiating off Sandberg as he squeezed past her. Crouching in front of her, he reached back and put a hand on her shoulder, whether to reassure her or order her to stay put, she couldn't tell. Instinctively she backed up toward Thompson and withdrew her weapon from its holster.

Sandberg's wide shoulders all but blocked the trickle of light coming down the tunnel. The male voices grew louder, then came the sound of footsteps in the cave. Voices echoed off its walls, carrying to them. Erin couldn't understand what was being said, but the angry tones told her all she needed to know. Someone from the enemy security force was there, arguing with at least one of the villagers.

Her fingers tightened around the grip of the pistol as she waited, barely daring to breathe. Sandberg was still-as-stone in front of her. One man snarled a string of what sounded like curses at someone else, then the crash of what sounded like crates or boxes filled the air. Tension rolled off Sandberg at whatever they said, pulsing from him in tangible waves. Erin swallowed, fought to calm her racing heart as she strained to hear if anything was happening behind them in the tunnel. Were they being cut off? Surrounded?

The arguing continued for long minutes as the soldiers searched the cave. Then, finally, one man gave a terse command and everything got quiet. Real quiet.

Sandberg stayed poised ahead of her. After an unknown amount of time passed he began inching his way toward the cave opening. She stayed where she was, ready to grab Thompson and start dragging him back the way they'd come, or rush out shooting to defend Sandberg. He paused just out of view and remained there for a few minutes. Not long after that, a man called out softly. She was shocked to hear Sandberg answer him a moment later. Why had he just given away their position?

Shuffling footsteps came closer, and she relaxed when she recognized his big silhouette blocking the opening. "Come on," he said softly, reaching out a hand to her.

She hesitated for a heartbeat, then took it and allowed him to help her to her feet. His warm, sure grip helped calm her racing pulse. "What's going on?"

"They're gone. Looking for us up the mountain. But they won't be here long—backup's already on its way up. Should be here within a half hour, the elder said, judging by their progress up the hill. We'll wait just at the cave entrance for them. Can't bring a helo in here without giving away our position and there's no good place for one to set down, so we'll likely have to hump it out to an extraction point for them to pull us out."

Erin eyed him. She might not trust Sandberg fully, but he'd gotten them to safety and had put himself in front of her to protect her and Thompson. She'd follow his lead for this part of it too. "Well," she said into the darkness after a long silence. "Guess this means we've missed our flight."

Something close to a chuckle answered her, but it sounded rusty, as if it had been so long since he'd done it that he'd forgotten how. There were so many things she was curious about with him. Just what the hell had he been doing on this last "job" of his? She settled back against the rock wall, resigned to spending at least one more night at Bagram.

The man was still hiding something big from her, something that had almost gotten them killed. Once she got back to Bagram, she intended to find out exactly what had precipitated all this.

Chapter Five

E rin trudged back to her B-hut in the early morning
sunlight a few hours later, still trying to come to
terms with everything that had happened in the
last twenty-four hours. After staying in that cave all
night and hiking nearly four kilometers to the extraction
site with the rescue team, then the debriefing she'd just
come from, she was exhausted. And since she wasn't
going anywhere until at least tomorrow morning, she
was looking forward to some serious rack time.

Opening the door of the hut, Erin stepped inside to
find Ace standing next to her bunk, in the process of
stripping off her flight suit. "Hey."

Ace paused in the act of pulling down the zipper
and blinked at her in surprise. "Hey. What are you doing
back here?"

"Short version of that story is that I had quite a little
adventure yesterday on the way to Kabul that I can't talk
about. Except I *can* tell you that I got to spend some
quality time with Cam earlier this morning." Cam
Munro was a Pararescueman, and engaged to Devon, a

former roomie of theirs. He and the CSAR team had dropped in by parachute before hiking in to the rescue site to lead them to the extraction point. She'd never been so glad to see a familiar face when he'd shown up in the cave just before dawn.

Ace's dark eyes widened as she scanned her from head to boots. "Holy shit. Are you okay?"

"I'm fine. Just tired and shaken up." And pissed that no one would tell her anything about the incident. There was no way those guards would've just randomly targeted them. She knew this whole thing had something to do with Sandberg's "job" he'd mentioned, but he hadn't told her anything more. When she'd stopped to see Thompson at the hospital after he'd been stitched up—no surgery required other than a good debridement, thankfully—he'd told her he hadn't heard anything either. He was bad enough that they were sending him home though, and he was slated to be on a transport bound for the States in a few hours. Ironically, it now looked like he'd arrive home before she did.

Ace eyed her in concern, taking in the fresh scrapes and cuts on her forearms. "You sure you're all right?"

"Yeah, just tired." The only sleep she'd gotten was brief combat naps in that tunnel, until she'd at last succumbed and fallen fast asleep sometime before dawn. She'd woken to find her head resting on Sandberg's muscled shoulder rather than the rock wall when he'd shaken her slightly to alert her that the rescue force had arrived. Though she couldn't be sure, she suspected he must have settled her against him at some point during the night. And even though he was a virtual stranger who'd inadvertently put them in grave danger, she couldn't deny the magnetic pull she felt toward him. Waking up against his powerful frame had made her feel oddly safe and protected.

Ace sank onto her bunk, frowning. "Will you still get to take your leave?"

"God, I hope so. You just get in?"

"Yeah. Had a good night. Took out two targets."

"Perfect. We can crash together." And after everything that had happened, she'd feel better knowing Ace was close beside her while she slept. Erin dumped her ruck at the foot of her bunk, unlaced her boots and pulled back the fresh sheets she'd put on before leaving yesterday. Ace hit the lights and within minutes of crawling between the sheets, Erin was asleep.

A brisk knock on the door woke her sometime later. Still groggy, she lifted her head from the pillow and looked behind her at the other bunks. Ace was already up and gone, and she was alone. What time was it?

Another knock. "Lieutenant Kelly?"

She sat up, rubbing her aching eyes. "Yes?"

"I've been asked to escort you to a debriefing, ma'am."

Oh, God, another one? "All right. Hold on a minute." She got herself together, put her boots on, grabbed a bottle of water and opened the door to find a young sergeant standing there. "Where's the debriefing?"

"I'll show you."

Well, duh. Who wanted to see her this time? Already cranky due to lack of sleep and being deprived of what had really happened at that checkpoint yesterday, she fell in step with him and chugged half the water during the walk across base. He escorted her into a secure building and down a long linoleum-lined hallway to the door second from the end. When someone responded to her knock, she opened the door to find two forty-ish men dressed in khakis and button-down shirts seated behind a wide metal desk.

"Lieutenant Kelly, come in," the dark-haired man said.

She crossed to the chair he indicated opposite the desk. The man stood and reached out a hand. "I'm Agent Bertrand, and this is Agent Filiponi," he said, indicating the blond, balding man beside him.

"Are you with the FBI?" she asked as she shook hands.

"No." Bertrand sat and when it was clear he wasn't going to expand on that, Erin sat. She opened her mouth to ask something else, but the door suddenly opened. She glanced up to see Sandberg stride in and her belly did an annoying little flip. He was just so rugged and masculine, radiating all that quiet, controlled power. Coupled with that dark scruff on his face and those intense dark eyes, he was one hell of a distraction.

His irritated expression flared with a hint of surprise when he saw her, but he quickly turned his attention to the two men behind the desk as he sat in the chair beside hers. "Was it necessary to bring her here for this?" he asked, sounding annoyed.

Erin blinked, taken aback by the sharpness of his tone. Why didn't he want her here?

"Yes," Bertrand answered. He looked at her. "I'm sure you know by now what a shit storm this incident has caused with the Afghan government. They're refusing to admit that it could have been a planned attack, or that insurgents could have infiltrated the military and police personnel stationed at the checkpoint. And because of the firefight and the wounded they incurred as a result, they're not being cooperative with the investigation. But," he continued, and something in the way he paused sent a shiver of foreboding up Erin's spine, "we do know a few things."

"Like?" Sandberg prompted, sounding aggravated. Erin didn't blame him. As far as she knew he'd been awake the entire time they'd been in that cave and she knew without a doubt he'd been called to far more debriefings than she had since arriving back at Bagram. He had to be exhausted, especially after keeping watch all night.

"Like Lieutenant Kelly's passport and other ID has gone missing from the checkpoint, as has yours and Sergeant Thompson's."

"Is that it?" Sandberg asked in a clipped tone.

"No," the balding one, Filiponi, responded. "Recent chatter indicates that whoever took your ID at that checkpoint was working for Rahim." His pale blue gaze shifted to her. "Do you know the name?"

"I recognize it. Don't know much about him, though." Except that he was rumored to be a Taliban leader who operated in the mountains to the east, and that he was considered highly dangerous to U.S. forces in the region. She cast a questioning glance at Sandberg, but he was still staring at the two agents. Did his mysterious "job" have something to do with the terrorist leader?

Filiponi continued. "Your information has been passed up the chain of command, so it's likely already reached Rahim. Based on the chatter we intercepted this morning, he knows you and Agent Sandberg—"

Erin's eyes shot to the man next to her, and narrowed. *Agent* Sandberg. That shiver of foreboding was more like a full-fledged earthquake now.

"—were seen together at the hospital in Kandahar, and that you left Bagram together, arriving at the checkpoint a few hours later. And after the firefight Agent Sandberg told the village elder you were husband and wife—"

She stifled a gasp and threw an accusatory glance at Sandberg. He had his arms folded, that hard jaw clenched as he stared at Filiponi. The man could've been carved from granite from all the expression his face revealed.

"—so it's likely that's reached Rahim too," Filiponi finished.

Erin shot another glare at Sandberg, not that it did any good, since he wasn't looking at her. *What the hell have you done?* She understood that he'd told the elder that to protect her, but it had backfired big time. Instead of shielding her, apparently that lie had now embroiled her in the bigger picture unfolding around her. An incredibly dangerous one that had her stomach in knots.

"In short," Agent Bertrand said to her, leaning forward to lace his fingers together atop the desk, "you've been linked to Agent Sandberg three different times at three separate locations. By now Rahim will no doubt suspect you're working together."

She swung her gaze back to him, her hands tightening on the arms of the uncomfortable plastic chair.

"In short, Lieutenant, until we can prove otherwise, it's likely you're now a target of Rahim's network as well."

Erin absorbed the words in silence as they crashed through her with the force of a sledgehammer. *Holy. Shit.* For a moment she couldn't speak, could do nothing but stare.

"Do you understand what I'm saying, Lieutenant?" Bertrand asked.

She nodded, forced herself to swallow past the sudden restriction in her throat. Maybe she didn't know what Sandberg's history or involvement with Rahim's network was, but she understood just how deadly the possible threat against her was.

"Are you all right?" the agent asked her, frowning.

Sandberg snorted. "What the hell do you *think*?" he snapped, glaring at the two other men. "Is that seriously it? That's the best evidence you've got to bring her in here and tell her this shit?"

"It's protocol," Bertrand answered evenly.

"The hell it is," Sandberg fired back. "If you were following protocol, I wouldn't still be here at Bagram."

"Oh, you'll be out of here soon enough," Filiponi told him. "We've looked into how your travel itinerary might've been leaked to Rahim's network. Had to be someone on the outside. And as luck would have it, a tip came in about forty minutes ago."

Sandberg raised an eyebrow. "And?"

Filiponi stared at him for a moment. "And it's credible and serious enough that both of you will be going back to Langley to stay in a safe house until we get to the bottom of this investigation and neutralize the threat against you."

Erin exchanged a disbelieving look with Sandberg as her stomach dropped. CIA headquarters were in Langley. Safe house? She was going to have to spend God only knew how long in a freaking safe house because of this mess?

Pushing out a breath, Sandberg turned his attention back to Bertrand once more. "What tip came in?"

The man's dark gaze never wavered from Sandberg's. "We've got a few possible leads we're looking into. One in particular we find very…interesting."

Erin thought her stomach couldn't drop any lower, but the way he said it made it feel like she'd just swallowed a chunk of lead. Oh yeah, she definitely wasn't going home anytime soon, and even though she knew Agent Sandberg had no control over any of this or the terrorist after them, it didn't mean she wasn't still pissed as hell at him for involving her in this.

****

They weren't telling him shit because he was officially off the taskforce, Wade realized in disgust as Erin left the room. He couldn't believe they'd do this to him after all he'd done for The Company and his country during the past three years undercover, but agency bullshit was always a problem. It was why he'd always preferred work in the field rather than being trapped behind a desk and finding himself entangled in miles of red tape.

"You gonna tell me who you're looking into now that she's gone?" he said to Bertrand. Erin had been pale, clearly shaken when she'd left a minute ago. Wade wanted to go after her, but he needed to know this first. What exactly was he up against? Who'd set him up?

"You'll be alerted if anything comes of the probe. Your handler will update you when you get to Langley."

Wade's hands clenched into fists as he fought to curb the sharp spike in his temper. Blowing his cool here with these desk jockeys wasn't going to help his cause. He'd just have to wait until he got to Langley.

Dividing one last icy glare between the two of them, Wade stormed out of the room and into the hall. Erin was already out of the building. He hurried to the far door at the end of the hallway, scanning for her when he stepped outside into the bright sunshine. Shading his eyes with one hand, he spotted her headed toward the Exchange, and broke into a jog. "Hey," he called out.

She paused to look at him over her shoulder, her eyes shooting daggers at him. Not that he blamed her. If not for him, she'd be on her way to her parents' ranch right now. Instead, she'd been chased and shot at yesterday, forced to stay the night in a cave and was now stuck here at Bagram until they caught a transport back stateside to whatever safe house the agency had picked out for them. Where they'd be staying *together*, due to budget restrictions or some other shit Bertrand had explained.

He owed her an apology.

He loped up to her and stopped a foot away, trying to think of something to say. Her jaw was tight, her posture rigid, and the accusations in her pretty green eyes made him feel an inch tall. Transitioning back into civilian life was going to be hard enough for him, let alone while in the same house with a woman who couldn't stand the sight of him. "Look, I'm sorry you got caught up in all this."

She turned to face him fully, crossing her arms over her chest, which naturally dragged his gaze to the curve of her breasts beneath her BDUs. Small, firm breasts he'd bet would nestle perfectly into his palms if he cupped them. He dragged his eyes back up to her face as she responded. "I know it's not really your fault and you didn't plan for this to happen, but I just can't—" She paused to draw in a steadying breath, and he understood her need to vent her anger.

"Believe me, I never expected anything like this to happen." Not for someone to leak his travel itinerary to Rahim's people, anyway. Erin continued staring at him and he resisted the urge to drag a hand through his hair. He wasn't sure why it was so important for her to believe him and accept his apology, but it was. Usually he didn't give a shit what people thought of him or his actions, yet with her he did.

She shook her head in bewilderment, her eyes burning with resentment and frustration. "I don't even know your *name*."

He sighed, cast a glance around to be sure no one could overhear him before answering. "It's Wade."

"Wade *Sandberg*?"

He nodded, and, holding her gaze, offered his hand. "My real name, I swear."

Her expression was still wary, but she took his hand. "I'm Erin."

He nodded again, caught off guard by the invisible thread of attraction that wound through him at the simple contact. Her hand was small and soft in his own and he was struck again by how delicate and feminine she was. The overwhelming instinct to protect her swelled within him again, same as it had yesterday. When her head had lolled for the third time against that tunnel wall this morning he'd eased her down against his shoulder and something had twisted inside him at the feel of her sleeping against him so trustingly. In that moment he'd vowed to make up for the damage he'd caused.

He'd gotten her into this mess; he'd make sure she got out okay. It was the least he could do.

Realizing he was still holding her hand, he released it. "So what are—"

"Just tell me one thing."

That green gaze pinned him, needled his conscience. "If I can," he acknowledged.

"How were you involved with whatever's going on with this Rahim guy?"

Okay, most of that he *definitely* couldn't tell her. "I've been...undercover for the past few years." She was intelligent; she'd figure out the gist of what he was saying.

She studied him for a moment longer as if she was trying to decide whether or not he was telling the truth. His answer must have satisfied her, because after a pause she nodded once. "And you agree that I'm in enough danger now to warrant being put into protective custody when we get back stateside?"

"If he's identified you as working with me, then yeah." And shit, he was more sorry about that than he could say. Rahim's network extended farther than even Wade knew, so it was possible he had people activated in the States right now, waiting for them to arrive. Protective custody was the best option.

Erin looked away, her expression a study in weariness and resignation. For some reason Wade wanted to pull her into his arms and hug her tight. His sister was around her age, late twenties. He hated knowing she was feeling lost and scared because of him. It drove him nuts that he couldn't fix any of it right now.

Meeting his eyes once more, she swallowed. "And how do I know I'll be safe if I'm there with you?"

"Because I'll keep you that way." He owed her that much. He'd done many fucked-up things over the past few years in the name of duty, but this was one task that might balance the karma scales a little. Wade would do whatever it took to ensure her safety while she was with him. If Rahim was seriously thinking of targeting her, he'd have to get through Wade first.

His answer seemed to surprise her. "Why would you care? I don't even know you."

"You don't have to know me for me to promise that." Besides, she'd get to know him a hell of a lot more than he wanted her to in the days or weeks ahead once they got to Virginia. "I know this is a shitty-assed mess, and I know you have no reason to trust me, but—" He exhaled, wondered what the hell to say to put her at ease. "Just know that I won't let anything happen to you, okay?"

Holding his gaze, she let out a slow breath. "Don't have much choice, do I?"

No. They'd both been forced into this position of powerlessness. He hated it. Feeling helpless and powerless was not something he was accustomed to, and so far it fucking sucked. "Where are you off to? Want to grab something to eat?" He had no idea why he asked, since it was evident she wanted nothing to do with him. Still, part of him hoped she'd say yes. They needed to clear the air between them before they arrived at the safe house.

"Sorry, can't. Gotta go call my family and make up some excuse as to why I won't be home, then I have to meet with my CO about everything."

"You'll go home," he told her firmly. As soon as Rahim was brought in, the threat would be over. Shouldn't take long now, not with him wounded and half the U.S. intelligence services hunting for any sign of him. "I'll see to it." He'd make it happen, just as he intended to find out who the hell had set him up to die at that checkpoint, and to help nail Rahim. If The Company thought he'd stay on the sidelines of this investigation after everything he'd done for them the past three years, they were sorely mistaken.

She lowered her gaze. "Well. Guess I'll see you on the transport in the morning."

He nodded, but didn't respond. He stood there watching her confident stride and the sway of her hips until she disappeared from view around the corner of a building.

Between being removed from the investigation to nail Rahim and living under the same roof with Erin for the foreseeable future, it would be a miracle if his head didn't explode before this was all over.

Chapter Six

Erin stumbled around the corner into the kitchen of the safe house, only to stop dead at the sight of Wade standing next to the kitchen sink.

Whoa.

He was shirtless, checking something on the new cell phone he'd gotten a few hours before. Way fancier than anything he'd had over the past couple years. He looked up and met her gaze, and she couldn't stop herself from running her gaze over the sculpted planes of his wide chest and shoulders, the scattering of dark hair that thinned into a line that bisected his delineated abs. The man was sheer masculine power, his lean build showing off all those mouth-watering muscles she'd only imagined before now.

Realizing she was staring, she jerked her gaze back to his face and was taken aback by the odd mix of heat and embarrassment in his eyes. He set the phone down on the counter and folded his arms across his chest, as though she'd made him feel self-conscious. Regretting that, she would have reassured him that he had *nothing* to be self-conscious about, except she sensed that would make him even more uncomfortable.

"You get any sleep?" he asked.

"Some." She'd been so exhausted by the time the flight had landed and the CIA people had got them set up here, she'd crawled beneath the quilt of one of the upstairs bedrooms and crashed hard just after lunch.

He glanced away, cleared his throat. "Sorry, I uh, thought you'd sleep a lot longer once I finished my shower."

"Don't worry, it's no problem. I'm a nurse, in case you forgot." Yeah, and while she'd seen countless half-naked men in her day, she couldn't remember the last time she'd responded to anyone the way she did to Wade. The magnetic pull he exerted was ten times more captivating because he seemed unaware of it. Since losing David she hadn't dated much or been that interested in men as a whole, but Wade definitely interested her. An unsettling thought, as they had to live here together until the CIA let her leave.

Even more so because she'd sworn never to get involved with another military man again. After losing David she'd promised herself to find someone whose job didn't threaten their life on a daily basis. Wade Sandberg was everything she wanted to avoid in a man.

Try remembering that the next time you devour him with your eyes.

She crossed to the other side of the kitchen to grab some coffee—her favorite brand, which they'd bought along with some other groceries on the way here from the airport. The CIA had equipped and stocked the house ahead of time, but she'd wanted to pick up a few specific things and had received permission. The two-story white farmhouse with red trim sat in the middle of a gorgeous, six acre expanse of rolling farmland, with a thick stand of forest on the east side of the property. In the western sky the sun was already a glowing orange ball shining through the kitchen window above the sink that overlooked the gently curving terrain.

As she stood with her back to him, an awkward tension filled the room. She was acutely aware of him standing behind her in nothing but a pair of jeans that hugged his lean hips and muscled thighs, and of him not saying anything more. "So, what do you want to do about dinner?" She glanced back at him, had a hell of a time keeping her eyes on his face when half that gorgeous body was on display. It was weird, having to stay here with him when she knew hardly anything about him. "Do you cook?"

"Not really. You?"

"I'm decent, but it's already dinner time and it'll take me about an hour to get something on the table if I start from scratch now. Do you want to just do pizza or something? We could order in for tonight." Or could they, considering the security situation?

Wade frowned a little. "I haven't had pizza in years."

Erin's eyes widened. "Years?"

He nodded, rubbed a hand along his whiskered jaw. "Guess that would be okay. Be better if we ordered in, rather than go pick it up though. I'll let the security guys know."

This whole living under guard thing was totally new to her, so she'd follow his lead. "Okay, what kind do you want?"

"Doesn't matter, I'll eat whatever. You want me to order?"

"No, I'll do it. You want some coffee?"

A slight smile curved his lips, softening his rugged features, and something low in her abdomen did a somersault. "Love some."

She didn't ask how long it'd been since he'd had any coffee, Afghanistan being a tea drinking nation, but his reaction made her glad she could offer him that simple comfort. After a few minutes of silence that wasn't exactly tense but not completely comfortable either, the coffee machine finished brewing the pot and she filled two mugs with fragrant black liquid. "How do you take it?"

"I don't care—" His face brightened with anticipation. "Do we have any cream?"

"We do." She grabbed it from the fridge and poured some into both their mugs, then glanced back at him. "Sugar?"

His eyes lit up, and she knew he'd been deprived of that luxury for a long time too. "Sure, a little."

She stirred a spoonful in for him and held out the mug. He walked over and took it from her, and just having him stand so close in the quiet kitchen sent a buzz of feminine awareness through her. When his woodsy scent wrapped around her and their fingers brushed, a wave of heat prickled over her skin. Her body didn't give a damn that he was all wrong for her, it wanted him anyway. Badly.

Either oblivious of or not wanting to encourage the attraction between them, Wade looked down at his mug as though he wasn't comfortable holding her gaze at such close range, and took a sip. As he swallowed, one side of his mouth curved up and he let out an appreciative groan that seemed to reverberate right through her, heating her blood. Startled, she drank in the almost dreamy expression on his angular face and imagined that same look right after he'd enjoyed an intensely satisfying orgasm. Erin couldn't be positive, but if his reaction to a simple cup of coffee made him groan like that, she was pretty sure it had been a while since he'd had one of those, too. And man, the idea of being the one to end his dry spell was way too freaking hot for her own good.

Flushing slightly, she looked away and sipped at her own coffee as she tidied up and tried to think of something to say that would put him more at ease. "There's lots more here if you want any."

"Thanks. I'd forgotten how much I missed it."

The almost wistful note in his voice tugged at her. Her body was pulsing with arousal and having him so close to her without a shirt on wasn't helping matters any. "I'll uh, go put our pizza order in." She left the kitchen and pulled in the first deep breath since she'd stepped over the threshold. God, the man was pure walking sin and didn't even realize it. Pulling out the specially encrypted phone Wade's CIA handler had given her on the way from the airport, she found a pizza place that delivered on the list of acceptable takeout spots they'd been given and placed their order. "Food'll be here in about half an hour," she called out to Wade.

"Sounds good. I'll let the security team know." His footsteps retreated toward the back of the house where the stairs were and a minute later he entered the living room, dressed in a snug T-shirt and carrying his mug. A slight stab of disappointment hit her that he'd covered himself, but that shirt hugged every swell and curve of his muscular torso so she couldn't complain.

Without looking at her he set his mug on the coffee table and began searching the room, checking behind the TV and the paintings, objects placed on the bookshelf. "What are you doing?" she asked.

"Checking for bugs. I didn't find any upstairs or in the kitchen when I checked earlier, but there's probably at least a few in the house. Safe house or not, they'll want to know what's going on."

Oh. She sank onto the couch and watched him work, admiring the way he moved and the flex of muscle in his bare arms as he checked various things, shifting with each movement. The bugging thing didn't seem to bother him, more like he took it as a matter of course. He paused a moment, pulled something off the back of a book on the shelf and held up something the size of a grain of rice for her to see. "Transmitter."

She nodded and stayed where she was while he shoved it into his pocket and completed his sweep. Weird, to know someone might be listening to them right now, but she had nothing to hide, and if it kept her safer, she was all for it.

The two-way radio chirped from the kitchen. Wade went to answer it, spoke to the security guy on the other end, then called out to her. "Pizza guy's on his way up the driveway."

It was a long driveway, so she probably had another minute or two before he got to the door. She jumped up to grab her purse on the entry table by the front door, but Wade surprised her by taking her upper arm in one big hand to stop her. "Stay in the kitchen. I'll get this."

She did as he said, hating that her stomach was in knots over a pizza delivery. Even though she knew Wade was just being cautious, it was a grim reminder that her life wasn't her own right now, and wouldn't be for a long while yet. Once the pizza guy left, Wade called for her to come out. She brought the plates and napkins she'd gathered and set it all on the coffee table.

Wade placed the two large pizza boxes on top of a newspaper and raised a teasing eyebrow at her. "Hungry?"

"Starving, and I wasn't sure how much you'd eat, so I decided to err on the safe side."

"Back in a sec." He strode past her to the powder room near the foot of the stairs and a moment later the toilet flushed. "They won't hear anything from that one now," he said as he came back out and joined her, sitting cross-legged on the floor across from her rather than on the couch. "Can't guarantee I've found everything though, so just make sure you don't say anything you don't want overheard and recorded for analysis."

"I won't." Feeling uncomfortable with being perched on the couch while he sat at her feet, she started to slide off it but he stayed her with an upraised hand and a shake of his head.

"No, stay up there. I'm just more comfortable on the floor."

Okay, then. She watched him as they ate. He had to be as hungry as she was, but he took his time chewing each bite, as though savoring the pizza. And she guessed he was, after not having any for that long. "Good?"

"Weird," he replied, almost to himself, and when he didn't elaborate, Erin got busy demolishing half of the Hawaiian she'd ordered. She was halfway through her fourth piece when she glanced up to find him watching her with a hint of amusement burning in that dark stare.

She flushed and swallowed her mouthful. "Told you I was starving."

"Yeah, you did. Glad you're enjoying it." His lips twitched and she couldn't help but notice how full and soft they looked in the midst of that hard face. What kind of a kisser would he be? Rough and urgent? Or slow and seductive? Both possibilities made her insides flutter. His mouth and those big strong hands were insanely sexy.

She would have enjoyed something else besides pizza much more, but knew if she made a move that Wade would either shoot her down or avoid her during the rest of their stay, so she settled for finishing off the slice of pizza instead. He'd only eaten one, she noticed, and half of another. The remnants of the second sat on his plate, untouched. "You don't like it?" she asked with a frown. Surely he needed more than that to feel full.

He shrugged. "It was okay. I'm just not used to eating anything this heavy anymore, so I figure I'd better see how it settles first."

She should have thought of that. "Oh. Sorry, I—"

He waved her apology away. "Don't worry about it. There's plenty of other stuff in the fridge I can eat if I get hungry later."

She remembered the way he'd stopped and gazed around the grocery store when they'd first entered it. At first she'd been sure it was just his way of being vigilant, but then she'd realized he must be reacquainting himself with the overflowing cornucopia that was the American supermarket. He hadn't seemed overwhelmed, more like he'd been seeing everything with fresh eyes. It was a reminder for her to be thankful for the little things, the everyday conveniences she and most people took for granted. This had to be a huge adjustment for him.

Swallowing the last bite of pizza, she wiped her hands and face on the paper napkin and tilted her head. "So…how long were you undercover?"

When he didn't answer right away, instead lifting his mug for a sip of what had to be cold coffee by now, she thought he would ignore the question. But then he lowered his mug and responded. "Technically four years total."

Wow. A helluva long time to be cut off from everything and everyone. She chose her next question carefully before speaking. There were so many things she wanted to know, but she knew he either couldn't or wouldn't tell her most of them. She had to be careful not to be too pushy or he'd shut down, and that was the last thing she wanted. Considering they'd been forced into this situation together, he'd been nothing but considerate so far, and she found she enjoyed his company. He made her feel safe, and while they still had moments when they both felt awkward around each other, things were going pretty smoothly for the most part.

"And while you were undercover, that's when you met...you know," she continued, aware she was risking going too far.

A slight tension stiffened his shoulders, but he nodded. "Right."

She was dying to know more, could barely hold the questions back. "He captured my roommate, Maya, along with Jackson and the Sec Def."

Wade nodded and looked down at the coffee table. A thickening silence spread through the room and she knew she risked alienating him if she pressed any more. Her statement hung heavy in the air as the seconds ticked past.

Just when she thought he'd get up and make some excuse to leave the room, he surprised her by sighing and running a hand through his longish hair. He raised his dark eyes to hers, stared for a moment as though he was trying to come to a decision. "You're gonna find out anyway, so since you're involved in all this because of me, I'd rather you hear it from me instead of somebody else."

Erin tucked her feet beneath her and folded her hands in her lap, aware of the way her stomach tightened at his warning tone. "Okay."

He folded his arms across his chest, the gesture and his expression resigned, almost defensive. "I worked with Rahim."

She felt her eyes go wide. "*With* him?"

He nodded, his face set. "Closely."

"How closely?"

A long, tense pause. "I started out as his bodyguard and for the past two years served as his second-in-command."

Erin's mouth fell open. She didn't want to believe it. She stared at him, feeling as though she'd never seen him before as the implications slammed home. "But that means...that means you would have known about..."

Another nod, this one tight, defiant. "I was there when Maya and the others were being held captive."

The pizza she'd just inhaled seemed to turn into a ball of concrete in her stomach. She wrapped her arms around her middle and stared at him, heart thudding at the implications embedded in those words. "You were there?" she said hoarsely. "You saw what they did to her and you didn't do anything?"

He lowered his gaze. "Not initially."

So he'd stood back and watched her be tortured? Erin had seen the damage her friend had sustained. She felt sick knowing that Wade had been there and hadn't stopped it. She swallowed, suddenly not feeling so safe with him anymore.

Wade traced a line in the wooden table with one long finger, avoiding her gaze. "The CIA was waiting for the final bits of intel on other major players involved with Rahim's network before I could call in a team to bring him down. I was nearing the critical point in the last op when the attack on the Sec Def happened. One of Rahim's underlings had organized it. And when I saw him in that cell, I knew it was all over."

Erin waited for him to continue, for him to say something that would reassure her he was the decent man she'd thought him to be and not some cold-hearted bastard who put his reputation before American lives. Her hands curled into fists against her ribcage.

"I couldn't interfere right away without blowing my cover. The prisoners were all in pretty bad shape, Maya and the Sec Def especially. Because of the severity of the Sec Def's condition, I already knew my mission and cover were compromised. I contacted my handler. When the cell leader forced them into a game of Russian roulette, I took all the bullets out of the revolver when he wasn't looking then set up a diversion."

Russian roulette? As in, forced them to put a gun to their heads and pull the trigger to find out if the chamber was loaded or not? Erin unwrapped her arms from around herself and put her hands over her mouth, horrified by what he was saying, by what Maya and the others had endured.

"Once I did that there was no going back, so I did what I had to do and helped them escape back to friendly lines."

She swallowed again, the surge of relief so strong it made her feel queasy. He'd been the one to get them out. He'd saved them. But the sick feeling that remained in her gut was because she understood exactly what he *wasn't* saying. "So you mean if not for the Sec Def, you would have…"

Left them all there.

The words echoed between them in the sudden stillness.

To his credit, Wade didn't squirm or try to deny the silent accusation. Instead he nodded once, his jaw flexing beneath the dark covering of whiskers as he met her stare unflinchingly. "Yeah," he said in a low voice.

Chapter Seven

In the silence that followed his admission, Wade waited for Erin to react. He was ready for her to leap up and run from the room, prepared at least for her eyes to turn cold and a look of horror and loathing to steal over her face. But none of those things happened.

She merely sat there staring at him, weighing him for the longest moment, then nodded once. "Okay, I get why you did it."

Of all the things she could've said, that was the last thing he'd ever expected to hear coming out of her mouth.

She rubbed her palms over the thighs of her jeans, glanced down at her hands. "That must have been hard on you. Living that way for so long, I mean." She shook her head as if she had trouble imagining it.

Wade wasn't sure what to say to that, but he knew some sort of response was required so he cleared his throat and tried to think of something to say. "It was my job. And it wasn't all bad. There are things about living in Afghanistan that I loved. Aspects of the culture like the hospitality, living a simpler life than we do here, unplugging from everything. Many of the teachings in Islam. But mostly it was the villagers I got to know. They were good, hardworking people." He'd probably always miss those things, the friends he'd made there.

Erin raised her head, searched his eyes. She wasn't looking at him like he was a monster. No, she was looking at him as though she understood why he'd made the choices he had, though that was impossible, because who the hell could understand him and what he'd done? "I'm really glad you got them out, though," she added in a quiet voice. "No matter why."

Something eased in his chest. A pressure he hadn't even been aware of before now. He didn't want to like her more than he already did, but how could he not after those answers? "Me too." He was. When the specters from his past came back to haunt him in the years ahead, at least he had that to help balance the scales.

"Do you have any family?" she asked, watching him curiously. "I mean, that kind of work, for that long... It had to be really hard on your family."

"I've got an older brother and a younger sister."

"No parents?"

He shook his head. "They died in a car accident when I was sixteen."

"Oh, I'm sorry." She bit her lip, seemed to hesitate before continuing. "Do you still keep in touch with your siblings?"

"Not since going undercover." He knew how that must sound to her, when she was so close to her parents. But the truth was, in many ways, the undercover work had been a relief. An escape and a challenge, all rolled into one. "I was pretty tight with my sister, growing up. It'll be good to see her again when this is all over." Lot of lost ground to make up between them though. He wasn't sure why he was telling Erin this when he'd never told anyone else. Well, yes he did. Erin was kind and caring, and he'd already lied to her about so much he needed to at least be honest with her about whatever he could. And, she was so non-judgmental he actually felt relieved to tell her all this.

Rather than end the conversation or make some excuse to leave, she settled back into the corner of the couch and stretched her legs out, making herself more comfortable. He liked that she seemed relaxed with him again. "So before you started working for the CIA, what did you do? Something in the military?"

"Army."

The hint of a smile played at the corners of her mouth. "Not *just* Army though, right?"

"No." What the hell. Wouldn't hurt to tell her this part of it. "I did nine years in SF."

"Ah. That explains your fluency in Pashto and ability to blend in with the locals."

He inclined his head. "Yeah." He still dreamed in Pashto. Most of his inner dialogue was in it too. He'd spent so much of his adult life in Afghanistan, it felt familiar and comfortable to him.

"Any other languages?"

She was fishing for information, but in such an adorable, inoffensive way he couldn't help but answer just to keep her talking. If she was an interrogator, he'd be screwed. "Urdu."

"Of course," she murmured, almost to herself. "And when did you join the Army?"

"Right out of high school." Mostly so he could get as far away from his hard-ass brother and find adventure someplace far removed from the ranches he'd worked since his parents died. He'd found adventure, all right. And nightmares, too. "You?" he asked when she kept looking at him.

She shrugged. "I did a year of college after high school, but hated it and wasn't sure what I wanted to do.

There's a strong tradition of service in my family so I looked into the medical training I could get in the Army and decided to sign up."

"And this was your third tour at Bagram?"

"In four years," she said with a weary sigh. "Not gonna lie, I was ready for a break."

"Why nursing?"

She blinked at him for a moment, as though the question had startled her. "I like helping people. Always have. My mom's twin sister died of cancer just before I enlisted, so I spent a lot of time in the hospital with her. Some of the nurses were great, but others I wanted to strangle for their lack of bedside manner. I decided I wanted to be one of the good ones."

"I bet you are. I know for sure you're protective of your patients."

She grinned at his teasing comment. "I am, but I was feeling extra protective of Jackson that day because of his involvement with Maya and everything they'd just been through." Her grin faded at the mention of that.

Because she knew he'd stood back and let them be tortured to maintain his cover identity.

He rubbed a hand over his jaw, knowing there was nothing he could say or do to erase that image of him from her head, but wishing it was otherwise. He couldn't deny the truth, that he'd acted as both the hardened undercover operative playing a dangerous role, and a patriot who wanted to do his part to eradicate radical Islam from the world. "They held their own out there. I just led the way. Maya fought me tooth and nail before she realized I was helping her." He still had the tooth marks in his hand to prove it.

"Oh, I'm sure you did a lot more than just lead." The sparkle was back in her eyes. "I may not know you very well, but I've seen you in action already, and based on what I've seen since then, I know you're way too modest to brag about yourself."

He focused his gaze on the stack of paper napkins on the table, running his finger over the edge because he didn't know how to handle the compliment. Maybe because he'd had so few of them. The way he'd grown up, a man could assume he was doing a decent job unless he was told otherwise. Praise just never factored into the picture, not even back when he was a kid and his dad had been alive. "You handled yourself well," he said to turn the conversation away from himself. "Better than I expected." Maybe that was partly why he was so attracted to her. In a tight situation, she was someone you'd want at your back.

She raised an eyebrow in mock insult. "What's that supposed to mean? I'm a soldier, aren't I? What, did you think I'd curl into a ball and start crying when they started firing at us?"

He gave a grudging chuckle. "No. You were solid. Especially with treating Thompson." He'd been grateful for the extra pair of hands on that hill, let alone her medical training. Her bravery under fire had surprised him though. She'd started dragging Thompson behind cover immediately after he was shot without a second thought to her own safety.

In his experience, watching how someone reacted under fire was a great indicator of someone's true character. From what he'd seen out there, Wade knew Erin was good under pressure. She wasn't whining or complaining now or having a hissy fit about being cooped up in here with him, either. In fact, she seemed to be trying hard to make the best of it and was going out of her way to be friendly. He was thankful for that too, yet at the same time he didn't want to like her so much. Over the years—the past few especially—he'd built up thick walls to protect himself and keep everyone else out. And now after spending just two days with her, he could already feel cracks forming in them.

Erin nodded. "Thanks. And I appreciate the report you gave to my CO. You made me look good."

"I just told him what I saw."

"Okay, then I'm glad you saw it that way." This time she smiled enough for the dimple to appear in her left cheek. Between that and the way her eyes sparkled in the overhead lights, he had to tear his gaze away to keep from staring. Four years ago, before this last job, he would be on that couch next to her, stroking his fingertips over the softness of her cheek and gliding them over her lips just to see her pupils expand and the pulse in her throat accelerate. But he wasn't that man anymore.

He didn't answer her statement, because what he'd said was true. She was reliable and had kept a level head. The only time he'd seen her hesitate was when they'd been in the tunnel and she'd been on point. He'd sensed her fear, either of the dark or the tight space or the tunnel itself, he wasn't sure, but she'd pushed it aside and moved forward. He wasn't going to mention that though. And he hoped like hell she couldn't tell how damn awkward he felt trying to adjust to this new lifestyle.

"How old are you?" she asked with a tilt of her head.

"Thirty-four." He already knew she was twenty-six. Truth was, he was sitting on the floor only partly because he was more used to that, but more because it gave him an excuse not to have to sit close to her. If anything he was more attracted to her with every hour that passed, rather than leveling off. He'd been telling himself he was hot for her simply because it was a natural reaction for a man who'd been without a woman for four years to want one as beautiful as her, especially when they were staying alone in a house together. But if he was honest it was way more than physical attraction. Erin was kind and brave and sweet. She made him simultaneously want to gather her up in his arms to protect her and pin her to the nearest flat surface and kiss her until she melted and wrapped around him. The thought made his cock swell uncomfortably in his jeans.

Realizing she was watching him with a quizzical expression, he blinked. "Sorry?"

She seemed to smother a laugh. "I asked if there was anything else you knew about the situation that you could share with me. You know, before I go to the meeting tomorrow at Langley."

Well, that shot his arousal all to hell. Good to know in case it got out of hand again, which it probably would if he wound up spending more time alone with her. "How much do you know about Rahim?"

"Not much. Is he Taliban?"

"No, but he'll work with them when it suits his purpose. Or anyone else, for that matter." And he was far more dangerous than people outside of the intelligence community realized. "There's something else you should know."

At his grim tone she straightened. "Go ahead, I'm already sitting down."

The quick comment damn near made him smile, in spite of how serious a conversation this was. "He's American."

She blinked. "What, you mean born here?"

"In Michigan. Grew up there as Gary Dyer. Enlisted in the Army at twenty. Few years later he served two tours in Afghanistan, fell in love with Islam and decided he was fighting on the wrong side of the war."

Her eyes widened and she sat forward a little. "Are you kidding me?"

Wade shook his head.

"The CIA's number one high value target right now is an American. A *veteran*."

"Yep."

She blew out a breath and ran a hand through her hair. He liked that she'd left it down to swirl around her shoulders. Made him wonder if it would feel as soft as it looked if he stroked his fingers through it. "How the hell did that happen?" she asked.

He was on semi-shaky ground here. The CIA had bound her to a confidentiality clause, so she couldn't repeat anything she learned about the investigation—and he knew she wouldn't anyway, because she was smart and loyal—but very few people knew the details he was about to disclose. Still, she deserved to know now, rather than be taken off guard later.

"He was raised in a survivalist, doomsday-type cult, with an ultra-strict Christian upbringing. Sometime after high school he left his family, got involved with militant groups online and became interested in, if not outright sympathetic to their cause. He began to study the Quran. After he joined the military and deployed to Afghanistan, it solidified his belief that the U.S. and its allies were occupiers. Then he was wounded in a friendly-fire incident." He paused. "The damage to the area was bad enough that they never located his body and assumed he was KIA with the rest of his platoon. Crews went in to recover the remains but he was never accounted for and it was assumed he was vaporized in the explosion. DNA tests from some of the samples recovered confirmed he was in the area when the hellfire missile detonated. In reality he used the opportunity to fake his own death. Locals found him a few days later hiding at the bottom of a deep ravine and took him in. The military didn't know he'd survived until he turned up in an online video months later, as Rahim."

"Holy crap," she breathed. "What does he look like? I mean, he'd have to blend in well enough with the villagers to go unnoticed for so long, right?"

Rather than answer, Wade pulled out his phone, input the security code and searched through the encrypted files in his email account until he found a decent photo of Rahim. He pulled it up on screen and held out the phone to her.

She took it from him, her expression turning incredulous at the man on screen. "Holy shit."

Wade completely understood her shock. Rahim was descended from Scots-Irish ancestors. He had a pale, freckled complexion, bright blue eyes, strawberry-blond hair and a thick coppery beard. In the mountainous tribal region of Afghanistan, he would've stood out as much as an NBA player in a roomful of midgets. "So you can see just how devoted the people must have been to protecting him in order for him to avoid detection all those months before the video came out, and ever since. Until then, not even his family knew he'd survived the missile strike."

She handed the phone back to him, frowning. "Is he crazy?"

I wish. "Like a fox. One of the most brilliant people I've ever met."

"Great," she muttered, and sat forward to rest her elbows on her knees as she rubbed one hand over the back of her neck. He was tempted to push her hand aside and massage the back of her neck, try to ease her worries now that he'd landed her squarely on Rahim's hit list. She met his eyes, shook her head a little. "I know I don't know you well, but I still can't picture you living out there with him. Working with him."

Wade shrugged and made a conscious effort to relax the muscles in his belly as they tightened at her bewilderment. He wasn't going to lie to her about that, he couldn't. And he respected her too much to sugar coat this just to make her feel better. His SF training had made him an ideal undercover operative. "Until a few days ago I was closer to him than anyone else on the planet."

And that's exactly why she was in such danger now, being tied to him. Rahim would want his revenge. Knowing him, he'd want it to be delivered in person. But Wade didn't think even Rahim would risk trying to smuggle his way back into the U.S. If he was caught here he'd have no backup, and no way to break out of any holding facility.

Erin was quiet for a long moment. "Well, you'll have to tell me more about your relationship with him sometime." She let the invitation hang there, didn't push for more, and the tension in his muscles eased further.

"Maybe I will." He was astounded that she was taking all this so well and wasn't on the radio right now to the security guys, demanding they take her someplace else, anywhere else as long as it was away from him. He lowered his gaze to his cold coffee cup, searched for the right words. "I'm on the same side of this fight as you," he said, feeling the need to reiterate that in light of everything he'd told her.

"I know."

At that he raised his head and met her eyes, surprised at how readily she'd said it.

"I *know*," she repeated, and added a little smile that said she had every confidence in him. Which totally blew his mind.

How the hell did she know he was one of the good guys? How could she trust that he wasn't playing both sides and working with Rahim on the sly? No one knew the full details of what he'd done when he'd gone off the grid to infiltrate Rahim's network three years ago, not even his CIA handler. He'd killed to protect Rahim, done other ugly things he had to live with the rest of his life.

Still, he forced himself to nod. "Good." He didn't want her to be afraid of him, ever. He wanted—needed, for reasons he didn't understand—her to trust him, believe in him.

Clearing his throat, he stood, his knees cracking as he got to his feet. "Busy day tomorrow. We'd both better turn in."

"Yeah, we should." She gazed up at him, looking so soft and kissable he was tempted to close the distance between them and fist his hands in that shiny chocolate-brown hair while he claimed that tempting mouth.

Don't you fucking touch her, asshole.

He turned away with a gruff, "Sleep tight."

****

Mountains of northeastern Afghanistan

The runner came to him just after evening prayer.

Rahim stood to stretch his sore left arm, reaching his hand up toward the darkening sky. To the west the last, faint line of pink touched the horizon, bleeding into the purple twilight above. The muscles and tendons flexed grudgingly, sending jolts of pain up his arm until he at last lowered his hand to his side.

"Rahim. There's a message for you."

He turned to Safir, standing a dozen feet away. It still felt strange not to have Jihad with him, or at least close by. He'd grown so used to having that, Rahim felt totally exposed without him and his protection. Ironic considering he now posed the greatest threat to his life. "What is it?"

"Sandberg escaped the country."

Of course he had. The CIA had gotten him out, and likely the woman with him. "Any word on where he's going this time?"

"None yet. Do you have any ideas?"

"A few." Not back to Wyoming, where Rahim had learned Sandberg came from, because that would be too obvious. Washington D.C. maybe. CIA headquarters in Langley for sure, though he didn't know for how long. "Keep our people searching for something useful. I'll find him soon enough."

Safir looked uncertain. "But the plan...perhaps it's best to wait, or think of something else entirely. If Jihad knew everything—"

"He didn't know *everything*." Rahim would never tell anyone everything. He wasn't stupid. "And he doesn't know enough to stop what's coming. Not now." Taking a grim satisfaction in that, he peered out at the mountains to the west. The line of pink was gone, swallowed up by the darkness.

Safir shifted his stance, seeming restless. "Let me go in your place. I can do this."

"You likely could. But this is my destiny." By this time tomorrow he'd be in Karachi, ready to board the plane that would take him to Malaysia and then on to his final destination. "Besides, it's been far too long since I visited North America. I'm ready to go back."

And when he arrived, he had one hell of a homecoming gift planned for the land of his birth.

Chapter Eight

Wade hesitated in front of the coffee bar outside the CIA director's office. They had one of those fancy new coffee machines that made everything from plain coffee to cappuccinos, and they also had a huge variety of tea boxes to choose from. He'd gone through the whole readjustment thing multiple times back in his Army days when he'd come home from deployments, but he'd never experienced anything like this before. Having just come out of a long-term, deep undercover op, this was a whole new level of culture shock. The weirdest things seemed to jar him and he hated it.

This morning he'd been halfway through dawn prayers before he'd suddenly remembered he didn't have to pray five times a day anymore—or pray at all, for that matter. That was going to take some getting used to. And there were other little things. He'd once been a coffee addict, yet he was so used to drinking tea now that he preferred it to coffee—unless Erin made it, apparently.

Except the spicy chai he craved apparently wasn't one of the dozen choices in front of him. Figured.

Chalking his mental baggage up to sleep deprivation and jetlag, he went with the Earl Grey and stuck the teabag into a mug before studying the space age coffee machine, trying to figure out how to get it to pour hot water. If he could successfully maintain a cover identity on one of the most dangerous assignments on the planet for over three years, he could operate a damn coffee maker.

"You just press and hold those two red buttons at the same time."

He looked over his shoulder at Erin, standing in the doorway. The gentle smile she aimed at him told him she wasn't making fun of him, and he relaxed. He noted there were shadows under her eyes and she looked worn out. He didn't like the idea that what he'd told her last night had worried her enough to make her lose sleep. "You want some?"

"Tea?" She scrunched up her nose as she considered the idea, then shrugged. "Sure, I'll try some. Thanks."

He filled the cup and let it steep. "Anything in it?"

"Maybe some milk, please."

He took the teabag out, added the milk and handed it to her, acknowledging her thanks with a nod as he turned back to make his own.

"Guess you've been drinking your fair share of tea the past few years, huh?" she asked.

"Yeah." He tossed his wet teabag in the organic recycling bin set beneath the sink and caught the face she made as she sipped at the tea.

"God, it's like hot, weird-tasting dishwater or something," she muttered, but took another sip anyway.

He hid a smile. "It grows on you after a while."

She gave him a doubtful look and stepped up next to him to lean her lower back against the counter. The thin black sweater she wore hugged the pert curves of her breasts in a damn distracting way, and her sweet, clean scent went to his head. "I'm not sure I want to try it enough times to let it grow on me." She met his eyes. "How did that pizza sit last night, by the way?"

He wasn't sure if she was asking out of curiosity or out of concern as a medical professional. "Not the greatest." He was convinced his body thought he'd tried to poison it. He'd been nauseated for hours after eating just those one and a half slices, and had wound up making repeated trips to the bathroom during the night. It had totally been worth it to have the excuse to sit and talk with her during the meal though.

She nodded, took another small sip and managed to keep from scrunching her nose up this time. "Too rich, and too processed. We'll have to make sure we eat clean from now on."

Surprised by the *we* in that sentence, he just nodded. Damn, she looked really exhausted. He didn't like seeing her that way, wished he could make this all go away for her. "Go okay with Bill?" Wade's handler was one of the best in the biz, but could be a bit of an asshole. People skills weren't his strong suit and he was notoriously heavy-handed when he wanted something. Wade hadn't had much contact with him since going undercover, just the occasional check-in via satellite phone when he could manage it—until the Sec Def had been captured.

Erin shrugged. "I guess. I just feel like I'm caught in a whirlwind right now, you know?"

Yeah, he did know. He'd been in meeting after meeting since seven this morning, including several with the director, while Erin had been in a few debriefings and security clearance meetings, the last one with Bill.

"Should quiet down for you after today. The big concern was your security clearance, so once that's all taken care of the only thing left for you to do is lie low."

She nodded. "What about you?"

"More of the same." So far they were trying to keep him out of the loop about the investigation on Rahim, but Wade knew they needed him. Sooner or later, they'd have to let him back in the game again. With his intimate knowledge of how the man thought and operated, he was still the best shot they had at finding Rahim.

She opened her mouth to say something else but stilled as Bill came around the corner. "I need to talk to you again for a few minutes," he said to Erin without preamble.

Erin had stiffened when Bill first appeared, and she was watching him now like she was about to be dragged away into a full-on interrogation. Wade moved closer to her, until their shoulders touched, instinctively putting his body between her and Bill. He had to stay the impulse to wrap a protective arm around her.

Bill's hazel gaze flicked from Erin to Wade, not missing the gesture. "Alone," he clarified, but made no further comment about Wade's reaction.

"What's up?" Wade asked, though he already knew. Bill wanted to talk to her about *him*. Find out what he'd told her about himself and Rahim, the investigation. Wade clenched his jaw. Erin had been through more than enough already, she was mentally exhausted, and surely to Christ she'd already been asked everything Bill had in mind by someone else. Likely more than once, repeating the questions in various ways to ensure her story never wavered and that she was telling the truth.

"Just some more questions." He gestured impatiently at her. "Come on. Won't take long."

Erin set her mug down on the counter and straightened, flicking him a quick glance and the dread he saw in her eyes made him want to pull her into her arms.

"It's okay, he's one of the good guys," he said, putting his hands into his pockets so he wouldn't be tempted to reach for her as she passed by. After she left the room felt too quiet, too empty.

Shrugging off the strange thoughts, he turned his mind back to Rahim. Even with his substantial network overseas it still wouldn't be easy for him to move around, especially while wounded. The Company didn't know shit about his location at the moment. Wade had already told them he was convinced Rahim had crossed the border into Pakistan. The question was, where? Up to the tribal region to withdraw and heal up? To Peshawar? Karachi?

It all depended on how severe the wound was and how brave Rahim's contacts were feeling now that the heat had been turned way up. With the amount of money the U.S. government was offering through various back channels, it was likely some of Rahim's biggest supporters over there would be tempted to give a tip regarding his whereabouts.

He was still going over various scenarios in his head when Bill appeared around the corner and summoned Wade with a jerk of his head toward the hallway he'd just come down. Wade followed him to his office. Erin was seated opposite the wide desk, and the look of relief that flashed over her face when she saw him filled him with gratitude. He glanced at Bill.

"She can stay," he replied in a gruff tone as he seated himself behind the desk. "Close the door behind you."

Wade did and lowered himself into the chair next to Erin's. He was close enough that he could smell her clean, sweet scent, but more than anything he was glad his presence seemed to comfort her. "So? What's up?"

Bill opened a drawer and pulled out a file, placing it on the desk and pushing it toward Wade. "New intel just came in a while ago from Kabul."

Wishing he would just say whatever the hell it was he wanted to say, Wade reached forward and took the file. He opened it to find a report about the checkpoint incident. He looked up at Bill. They'd been over all this twice already. "And?"

"*And*, take a look at the name on the bottom of the second to last page."

Wade flipped to the correct page and looked at the bottom. The name jumped out at him like a neon sign.

Brayden Schafer.

He snapped his gaze to Bill, aware of a sudden tension gripping his muscles. "What the hell is this? You think he had something to do with it?"

Bill's stare never wavered. "That's what it looks like to us. All the signs point to him. He was in Kabul before and during the attack. He had contacts at Bagram who could easily have given him your travel itinerary. He had the means, the motive and opportunity. So yeah, at this point I'd say he had something to do with it."

Wade was already shaking his head. "No way. I know why you'd think that, but...no way." Bad blood and worse history between them, yeah. Schafer trying to have him killed? And using Rahim's network to do it? No fucking way.

"I figured you'd feel that way." Bill leaned back in his seat, dividing his gaze between him and Erin. Wade glanced over to find Erin watching him with a worried expression. "He can fill you in on the details later," Bill said to her, "since he's already told you so much about everything else."

Erin's face flushed and she flicked an apologetic, almost guilty glance at him. There was nothing for her to feel bad about. Wade wasn't angry with her for telling

Bill what he'd said to her last night. He'd never tell her anything classified or something that would put her in further danger anyway, and Bill had to know that.

"He's being transported here for questioning," Bill added. "Flight arrives tonight at twenty-one hundred."

"I'll talk to him," Wade said.

"No, you won't. Until we've questioned him and found out who set you up, you're staying at that safe house and you'll only be involved in the investigation on a consultant basis."

Wade set his jaw. "You need me on this one. You know it, and I know it."

Bill inclined his head in acknowledgement. "Not yet. We'll bring you in when necessary. It's for your own protection, Wade."

Yeah? Well it fucking sucked. He'd rather take his chances with Rahim and his network than stay stuck in one spot, waiting there like a sitting duck out in the country while the most important manhunt since the search for bin Laden took place without him.

****

Erin wasn't sure what the story between Wade and Bill was, but their relationship wasn't what she'd expected. When Wade had told her that Bill was his handler, she'd assumed they'd be on much friendlier terms than they actually were. Not outright hostility, perhaps, but an undercurrent of friction was there. Maybe it had something to do with Wade being off the grid for so long and having all kinds of rough edges, she wasn't sure. What she *did* know was that he'd been quietly seething all the way back during the drive from Langley. Now that it was just the two of them alone in the farmhouse again, he still hadn't relaxed. He was prowling around the lower floor like a caged lion and she'd been very careful not to say anything as she did her best to keep out of his way.

He stood at the window with his back to her, hands braced above him on the window casing, every muscle in his back stretched taut beneath the light gray T-shirt he wore. While she loved the view, she knew he was upset about the investigation and this latest development he'd seen in that file.

She took a few steps into the room and cleared her throat. "I was going to make something for dinner. You up to eating?"

He turned slightly to look back at her, and the anger in his eyes faded. "Not really hungry right now."

"You need to eat," she answered, the nurse in her taking over. The man already had no body fat on him. This wasn't the tribal region of Afghanistan. With a full refrigerator in the kitchen, he shouldn't be starving himself and making his body start metabolizing his muscle tissue.

He let out a deep sigh, visibly pushed his frustration aside, and nodded. "I'll help you."

Not about to argue, she turned back to the kitchen. "What do you feel like?"

"Whatever you want is fine."

She wasn't so sure about that. She could think of a *great* way for them both to burn off their excess frustration, but she doubted he was thinking along the same lines, or that he'd let his guard down that far. And it probably wouldn't be smart for them to cross that line while they lived here together anyhow. Just made things messier when it was all over.

From the fridge she pulled out a bunch of greens and veggies, some berries and goat cheese for a salad. "You want chicken or anything to go on the salad?"

"Sure." He stood there in the middle of the kitchen, looking awkward as hell, and Erin took pity on him.

"Can you grab a cutting board for me from the cupboard next to the stove?"

He found one and put it on the counter, then pulled a knife from the butcher block beside the stove and started to cut up a red pepper she'd just washed. She watched him work. His knife skills were good, but she knew he hadn't gained them by slicing up salad ingredients. To stop herself from thinking about him using that knife on human flesh, she turned back to washing the baby spinach leaves she'd placed in a colander. "So, whose name was on the bottom of that piece of paper?"

Wade paused for a fraction of a second before he resumed slicing the pepper into neat strips. "Brayden Schafer." He practically growled the name.

She turned off the tap and stole a sideways glance at him, noting the scowl on his face. "You know him?"

He nodded. "We served together. In SF."

Whoa. Betrayed by a fellow Green Beret? Erin stopped and turned to face him, incredulous. "And they think he's the one who set us—you—up?"

His jaw tensed. "Evidence looks pretty convincing so far."

"But you think they're wrong."

Wade lowered the knife to the cutting board, his fingers still wrapped tight around the handle. "It's way over the line, even for him."

She waited for him to continue, but he stared down at the knife, seeming lost in his own thoughts. Treading carefully, she asked, "What happened?"

He cut her a sideways glance, then back down as he resumed cutting, his strokes even and precise. "We had a kind of rivalry going in our SF days. Friendly one. But after, when we did contract work together, things changed. During one mission things turned to shit and he made a bad call. I stepped in to correct it, and after that…" He shrugged, the motion tight, stiff. "He blamed me for the smear on his reputation. And that guy holds a helluva grudge. But setting me up to die through Rahim's network? I don't think so. He's a piece of work, yeah, but he's a patriot and loyal to his brothers. He might hate my guts, but that still doesn't mean he'd do something like this."

She digested all that in silence, afraid to speak in case it made him clam up. He'd just strung more words together in the past minute than he had the entire time she'd known him, with the exception of the conversation about Rahim last night. "Well, I guess they'll find out the real story once they question him."

He nodded, and it seemed like his shoulders weren't as rigid as they had been at the start of the conversation. "Whaddya want me to do with this pepper?" He gestured at the neatly sliced pile of red cubes with the knife.

She grabbed a big bowl from the cupboard beside the sink and set it next to him. "Here, just toss them in there." She pan fried some sliced-up chicken breasts while he finished prepping the veggies. When it was ready she tossed the veggies in some dressing, plated the salad with some chicken and sliced strawberries on top, then added some crumbled goat cheese and chopped pistachio nuts. "Look okay?" she asked him.

"Looks great." He took the plates. "Want to eat in the living room?"

"Sure." She followed him in and took a seat on the couch. He handed her a plate and stood there hesitating a moment, but rather than sit on the floor as he had last night, he took the opposite end of the couch, sitting cross-legged with the plate balanced on his calves. She watched him fork up a bite and chew it, her gaze drawn to his mouth as he made a sound of pleasure. "This is good."

"Thanks." And way better for his digestive system than the pizza had been.

They ate in companionable silence and he took the dishes into the kitchen, telling her he'd clean up. Not about to argue, she turned on the TV and was half-engrossed in a show when he came back out. He stood in the entryway, as though unsure whether he should come in or not. "Want to watch a movie together?" she asked.

He put his hands in his pockets and gave a shrug. "Sure." He sat back on the far end of the couch.

She flipped through the menu and settled on an action flick. "This one okay?" she asked, glancing at him. He probably hadn't watched a movie in years.

"Sure."

She turned it on and tried to get into it, but with each passing minute she was more and more aware of the distance between them. He wasn't stiff exactly, though she could tell he wasn't completely comfortable, either. She wasn't sure if it was because they were sitting on the couch alone together, or whether he was still thinking about Schafer's possible involvement in all of this. "You want me to go?"

He looked at her in surprise, eyebrows drawing together. "No, why?"

"I feel like I'm making you uncomfortable."

He huffed out a rueful laugh. "You're not. It's just...everything," he said with a wave of his hand. "Weird sitting here watching a movie when I know he's still out there, that's all."

That wasn't all, and she knew it. They both knew it. He was attracted to her too, she was pretty sure, and didn't want to acknowledge that. She didn't want him to feel uncomfortable around her though. "I bet. But I'm okay going upstairs to read or something if you'd rather be alone. Or we could—I dunno, play cards or something for a while." She mentally rolled her eyes at herself. *Cards, Erin? Really?*

His mouth quirked. "No, this is fine. Thanks, though."

They resumed watching the movie. Partway through she lost interest and started to fade. It'd been a long couple of days and she was smoked. Only the corner of the couch wasn't very comfortable to rest her head in. She shifted around to find a better spot and closed her eyes. Sometime later she felt her head droop and she stirred, still half asleep. A moment later a gentle hand curved around her shoulder. Her eyes snapped open to find Wade right beside her, drawing her up and toward him.

She went willingly, a little shocked when he actually drew her head down to rest against his hard shoulder and draped an arm across her shoulders. She stayed very still for a few seconds, but when he didn't move and didn't seem tense, she sighed in contentment and shut her eyes. His clean, soapy scent wrapped around her and his body heat soothed her. She was affectionate by nature and loved to cuddle, and he made her feel so safe. But feeling all that hot, hard strength up against her... Arousal bloomed inside her, a slow, heavy throb warring with exhaustion, but exhaustion won out.

She surfaced briefly sometime later when he shifted her again. Blinking in the darkness, she realized sleepily that the TV was off. He eased her onto her side to curl up lengthwise on the couch, and drew the throw blanket over her. Already sliding off to sleep as he stood up, she felt the gentle stroke of his hand over her hair before his hushed footsteps moved away.

Chapter Nine

Rahim pulled the hem of his T-shirt over the weapon tucked into his waistband and pushed his sunglasses up on the bridge of his nose as he exited the rental SUV. He had a backup strapped to his ankle, hidden by his jeans. The heat hit him the moment he stepped out onto the gravel parking lot. Central Mexico had a different sort of heat than he was used to, more humid, but still a shock after being in the air-conditioned vehicle. That kind of luxury had been a shock on its own, and not an unwelcome one.

He ran a hand over his closely shaved beard and tugged the brim of his ball cap down lower on his forehead as he walked to the concrete building. He'd dyed his hair, eyebrows and facial hair dark, but it wouldn't be enough to fool facial recognition software if any intelligence agency got a good shot of him. Three other vehicles were parked out front. He rapped on the steel door and pushed it open, one hand on the butt of his weapon at the small of his back.

"In here," a familiar voice called from the back room.

Rahim stepped into the darkened interior of the warehouse and shut the door behind him, the thud echoing in the cavernous space. Male voices speaking Spanish floated out to him as he crossed the concrete floor, alert but relaxed enough. The doorway led to an auto shop they'd converted for their purposes. Two Mexican men looked up from the blueprints they were going over when he entered. He nodded at them and shifted his attention to the tall man emerging from behind a pallet of crates.

"Paul, how are you?" Rahim asked him in English.

The twenty-six year old American shrugged his bony shoulders and ran a hand through the jaw-length brown hair he'd grown out in a half-assed attempt to disguise his identity. "Fine. How was your flight?"

"Smooth as silk." The private luxury jet had landed at an air strip an hour outside of Mexico City. No one had even checked his passport. He was paying for everything in cash, and so far not even the Mexican authorities knew he was in the country. "What've you got for me?"

Paul motioned into the small office behind him. "There are two designs I wanted to show you."

Rahim placed his hands on the small desk and bent over the schematics. Both compact devices, both good designs as far as he could tell. He looked up at Paul. "Which one do you think's our best shot?" It still rankled that he'd been unable to secure the Strontium-90 he'd originally planned to use, but a less potent material would have to suffice now that the timeline for the attack had been moved up by several weeks.

"This one," the younger man said, tapping the second design. "The configuration's better, simpler and will decrease the chance of glitches."

"Let's go with it then." He straightened, nodded toward the two other men beyond the office door. "They speak English?"

"Not really, no. I thought you'd prefer it that way."

"I do. Good thinking."

Paul smiled, seeming pleased with the praise. "I've got pretty much everything I need, except for the…material."

"I've taken care of it. It's in transit." He asked a few more questions about the design for the device and the crew in place, and right on cue, his burner phone rang. Checking the number first, he answered. "You got it?"

"*Sí*, just left Mexico City," the man answered in a thick Spanish accent. "Where do you want us to bring it?"

"I'll let you know. Transfer the load and disguise it, then find a place to wait overnight. I'll call you tomorrow with the details." He ended the call and smiled at Paul. "Got it. I can have it here by tomorrow afternoon."

"Okay." Paul ran a hand through his hair again, a nervous gesture. "What kind of timeline are we looking at? It'll take me a day or two to assemble everything and—"

"I want it on the ship two days from now."

Paul gaped at him. "But that's…"

Rahim raised an eyebrow. "What?"

The other man pushed out a breath. "I'll do my best."

"I know you will." He smiled a little, clapped Paul on the back, and Rahim was pleased to see the other man wasn't relieved by the gesture. The engineer knew how closely Rahim would be watching this whole process. He also knew how easily Rahim could do away with Paul so that no one would ever find his body should he fail to complete the bomb or do anything to jeopardize the operation. He was being paid well for this, maybe too well, but then, nuclear physicists willing to work on this kind of project weren't easy to come by.

"Better get started," Paul muttered and brushed past Rahim to talk to the other men waiting outside the office.

Rahim kept an eye on them as they began to assemble the parts, and did a thorough inspection of the warehouse. He looked for cameras and checked for wires, even though the likelihood of anyone knowing what they were up to was minimal. Another call came in, this one from Safir, who was back in Karachi.

"Is everything in place?" Safir asked him in Pashto.

"So far. We're still on schedule."

Safir let out a relieved sigh. "I also have some good news."

Rahim's attention sharpened. "What?"

"I got a call from someone in our network. Apparently they found some interesting information that was leaked into the chatter stream, and when he checked it seems it's from that American informant who contacted us before."

Rahim kept his voice low, watching the men as they worked. "Go on."

"The informant gave a possible location for Sandberg. And the woman."

Something stilled inside him and his heart picked up speed. "Where?"

"In a small town in rural Virginia. They're staying together in a house."

Rahim frowned. Had Sandberg really been married all this time? Or was Erin Kelly merely a fellow agent? "How reliable is this source?"

"Ours? He's reliable. And the American contact was accurate the last time. It's worth checking out."

Yes, it was. "Give me what you have and I'll look into it." Safir detailed everything, including the farmhouse in the country. "If it's true, they'll have security on them."

"Of course. Shall I gather a team together and get them to Virginia?"

"No. I'll check everything and take care of this myself." Because it was personal. So personal Rahim was tempted to be part of the assassination himself, if the location was real. "The equipment will be on the ship in two days' time and I'm accompanying it."

"I wish you'd reconsider. I'd be honored to go with it instead—"

"No. It has to be me." He didn't trust anyone else to oversee this first, most critical move in shifting the war to American soil. Carried out correctly, it would cause mass panic. The stock market would flounder. Fear and chaos and panic would rule. Everyone would be afraid to stay in the city. Local medical facilities would be overwhelmed. The cleanup alone would be insanely expensive. Infrastructure would grind to a halt, at least temporarily. Tourism would decline sharply as well in the days and weeks after the attack, having profound impact on the economy that would last for years.

He couldn't wait to watch the dominoes begin to fall.

"I'll take care of everything and get back to you once I know more," he said to Safir, anticipation and excitement running hot in his veins. Ending the call, he stood off to the side and formulated a plan as he watched the men assemble the metal frame of the device. A slow smile spread across his face at the thought of what was coming and the revenge he would exact on Sandberg.

I'm coming for you, Wade.

****

Waiting in a lounge area just down the hall from the director's office, Wade paused in reading a file and glanced up at the TV mounted on the wall. The news anchor was reporting on some breaking news about a missing truck carrying nuclear material from a lab in California to Mexico City.

Instantly he tossed the file aside and grabbed the remote to turn it up. The truck was transporting material from a medical facility in San Diego and had been stolen sometime within the last six hours after crossing the border at Tijuana. Officials were scrambling to locate the truck and security agencies were concerned about what could happen if the material fell into the wrong hands.

Wade had a sinking feeling that he knew exactly whose hands were involved.

He shoved to his feet and strode down the hall to the director's office. The secretary looked up at him but waved him on back when she saw the look on his face. The door was shut. He knocked briskly. Robert always kept it locked. A few moments later it opened and Robert let him in. Three other men Wade recognized sat around the desk, including his handler, Bill.

Wade shut the door behind him. "A shipment of nuclear material just went missing south of Tijuana."

Robert nodded as he crossed to his desk. "I just heard twenty minutes ago." He lowered himself into his chair and studied Wade. "How likely is it that it could be Rahim?"

"Pretty damn likely. He'd been looking into getting a shipment of radioactive material out of a reactor in the Ukraine, and some Strontium-90 from Russia but he would've scrapped that plan the moment he found out about me and moved up the timeline. You know his end game is to attack here in a big city, probably on the eastern seaboard to garner the most attention and maximize collateral damage. Could be he's got a hand in this. Helluva lot easier and faster to move it across the border from Mexico than get it here from the Ukraine, especially once he's hidden it." And they all knew there'd been increased chatter amongst people in Rahim's network. Something big was in the works, they just didn't know when or where. This missing nuclear shit had Wade's internal radar going crazy.

Robert was in his late fifties and had been a four star general before coming to work for The Company, rising through the ranks before being appointed. It wasn't easy to rattle him. But the tension around his mouth now and the way his eyebrows drew together spoke loudly of just how scary a threat this might be. "Let's get our teams on this," he said to them all. "I want you to pull whoever you need and get them searching for that shipment. Wade, Bill and I will get people hunting for Rahim south of the border. Everybody report back to me when you find anything."

The moment he finished everyone stood up and got moving. With the threat potential they were looking at, the sense of urgency was clear. They had to find Rahim and locate that shipment immediately, and Wade would do whatever he could to help in the hunt.

He was in another office with someone from the taskforce when his cell beeped with a text alert. When he pulled it out, he was a bit startled to see it was from Erin.

Will you be home for dinner?

He blinked at the message, but didn't have time to respond before another came in.

Ha! I sound like a wife ☺. I was just curious. Was going to make something.

Smiling, he typed a response. *Not sure when I'll be back. You go ahead.*

A few seconds later, she answered. *Okay. See you later.*

He put the phone into his pocket, aware of a curious warmth spreading inside him. It felt strange to have someone check in on him about something as simple as whether or not he'd be home for dinner, but he liked it, because it was Erin. He also liked knowing she thought about him when he was away, and that she cared. Even with everything that was going on, he'd been thinking about her too.

As he glanced back up at the middle-aged woman across the desk from him, he realized she was staring at him, a little grin playing around her mouth. "What?"

She shrugged. "That's the first time I've seen you smile. It looks good on you."

He looked away, muttered something in reply and got back down to business. But that lingering warmth remained throughout the afternoon, easing the worst of the dread and anxiety about Rahim and the missing shipment. They were doing everything they could to stop the unthinkable from happening, and hell, he'd be going home to Erin at the end of the day.

When he'd contacted everyone he could think of who might be able to help and sent another report to Robert, it was nearly eight o'clock. Two guys from the security team were waiting for him in the lobby and drove him back to the safe house. The kitchen light was on and as he climbed out of the car, he could see Erin moving around by the sink. He checked the perimeter just to be sure all was secure in spite of the all clear given by the security team, then let himself in the back door with his key. The smell of something spicy and delicious wafted from the kitchen and his stomach rumbled, reminding him how hungry he was since he hadn't eaten all day.

"Honey, I'm home," he called out as he took his boots off. Her soft laughter drifted to him, and he found himself smiling again. After the long day he'd had and the increased threat going on, it surprised him how much he was looking forward to her company tonight. Hell, he was craving it.

"I'm in the living room," she called back.

Wade strode through the entryway and past the kitchen to the family room. In the doorway, he stopped dead and stared.

She'd shoved the coffee table off to one side of the room and laid a blanket out on the floor in front of the fireplace, where a cheery fire crackled. On the blanket were several pillows and throw cushions, along with various plates and bowls filled with food.

He glanced up when Erin came into view carrying another bowl in her hands. She was smiling at him, her long chocolate-brown hair tumbled around her shoulders, catching glints of the firelight. She wore a snug green top that hugged her breasts and a pair of dark jeans that molded to her shapely hips and thighs. "Hi. Hope you're hungry." She set the bowl down and seated herself cross-legged on the blanket, smiling up at him expectantly.

Wade stood there for a moment, totally at a loss. He'd told her to go ahead without him, but he'd sure as hell never expected anything like this. After a few beats of stunned silence, he found his voice. "You did this for me?"

She shrugged as if it was no big deal. "I know you're more comfortable sitting on the floor, and I was alone all day so I just puttered in the kitchen. I found some Afghan recipes online and fiddled with those. Apparently the supermarket was fresh out of goat though, so I had one of the security guys pick me up some chicken instead. Hope that's okay." She shot him a teasing look.

He suppressed a chuckle. "It's fine." It was more than fine, it was unbelievable. And she'd not only made all this, she'd waited for who knew how long until he'd gotten back so they could eat together. "I wish you hadn't waited for me. You must be starving."

"Nah, I snacked a bit here and there, and besides, I wanted to wait to eat with you. I had a couple of the security guys run into town and get me some ingredients I needed. Bet the CIA's never paid for that kind of service before," she said in a wry voice.

Wade lowered himself to the blanket and sat opposite her, still blown away by her thoughtfulness, her kindness. She knew some of what he'd done during his undercover assignment, that he'd stood back and watched her friends get beaten, yet she'd still wanted to do this for him. "Thank you," he said simply, even though that felt totally inadequate under the circumstances.

Her smile widened, the firelight reflecting in her eyes. "You're welcome. Now let's dig in before it all gets cold." She held out a hand. "Pass me your plate."

He did, feeling like he should be serving her instead of the other way around, but he didn't argue. She filled his plate and passed it back to him. She'd made a rice dish studded with what looked like dried fruits and chopped pistachios on top. The fragrant steam rose up, scented with cinnamon from the curried chicken dish she'd spooned on top. There was also a chopped salad and toasted pita bread with hummus.

Remembering the manners he hadn't used in a long time, he waited for her to begin eating before he did.

"So, how was your day?" she asked between bites.

He had to drag his attention away from her mouth as she chewed, his head filled with fantasies of tasting those pink lips, learning the shape of her naked body with his hands and tongue. "Busy." They'd kept him on the periphery of the investigation, not letting him in on new intel that came in unless the director had okayed it first. It drove Wade nuts. He couldn't tell Erin about the new developments, and couldn't prove the missing material had anything to do with Rahim, except that his gut told him it did. Pushing that aside, he focused on the beautiful, sweet woman before him. She made him fucking *ache* inside. "If you're not comfortable we can sit at the table—"

"No, I'm good. I kind of like this. Feels more authentic, anyhow. How does it taste?"

"Awesome."

Her eyes gleamed with pleasure. "Good. I like it too. And wait 'til you see what I made for dessert."

He looked up from his plate. "You made dessert, too?"

"Yeah, but it doesn't exactly go with the menu. It's my mom's recipe. I used to love baking with her, and now we only get to do it at Christmas. When I'm home," she added. "You'll love it, trust me. Everyone does."

"Can't wait to try it." He watched her as she ate, his gaze drawn once more to her mouth. Her lips were a soft pink and they glistened in the firelight when her tongue passed over them. Staring at the tempting display, he was reminded yet again of how long it had been since he'd kissed a woman. He also couldn't remember ever wanting to kiss a woman this badly before. She made it damn hard for him to keep his distance.

Once they'd eaten she started to gather the dishes but he stopped her with a hand on her arm. "No, you sit. I'll get this."

"Thanks, that's sweet of you." She gave him another smile, the gratitude and pleasure in her face hitting him like a sucker punch to the gut. He wasn't sweet, but she made him want to be, at least for her. It was all he could do not to take that pretty face between his hands and kiss the freckles that ran across the bridge of her nose and across her cheeks, then taste those inviting lips that tempted him so mercilessly.

Shit.

Tamping down the urge to reach for her, he cleared the dishes, put away the leftover food and washed up. He was just finishing loading the dishwasher—God, sometimes he loved modern conveniences—when Erin came in and opened the fridge. Her back was to him, but he had an incredible view of the way those jeans hugged her rounded ass as she bent over to retrieve something off the bottom shelf. He stared at it, he couldn't help it, and had a sudden image of her bent over for him, naked, her mouth parting in an erotic gasp as he fisted one hand in her hair and held her hip with the other while he plunged deep into her body.

He tore his gaze away from her ass and shook himself as she straightened, feeling guilty. She'd done something special and thoughtful for him and all he could think about was fucking her.

"Take a look at this thing of beauty," she said proudly, holding up a chocolate-frosted cake. "When's the last time you had something like this, huh?"

"Years." And his mouth was already watering. He'd probably pay for eating all that butter and sugar later, but right now he couldn't wait to dive in and he would savor every bite of it because she'd made it for him.

He followed her out to the blanket again and accepted the slice she served him. "Dig in," she said, already forking up a mouthful. Her quiet moan of enjoyment as she chewed reverberated inside him, going straight to his swelling cock. His hand tightened around the fork as he pictured her making that very same sound as he stroked and tasted her breasts and the soft flesh between her thighs.

Damn. Wade forked up a bite and savored the rich, moist chocolate cake with a groan of approval. Erin's mouth quirked. "Good, huh?"

"So good." He devoured the rest of it, glancing up when she scooted around next to him and set another slice of cake on his plate.

"You look like you enjoyed that so much that I think you need another piece," she said, so close he could see each individual freckle on her nose and inhale her sweet, clean scent. The pulse in his cock and the need unfurling inside him were too strong to ignore.

Unable to stop himself, Wade let go of his fork and wrapped his hand around her forearm. She froze, her gaze darting to his in surprise. He saw the exact moment when the heated awareness flashed in her eyes, her pupils expanding as she recognized his intent. The air around them seemed to vibrate with sudden sexual tension. He tightened his fingers slightly, savoring the silky texture of her inner forearm and the warmth of her skin. She was so soft and feminine she seemed delicate next to him, yet she was also strong. The combination fascinated and drew him more strongly than he'd ever have thought possible. She wanted him. Wasn't pulling away.

Her tongue darted out to moisten her lips and Wade couldn't help but track the gesture. And when her gaze dipped to his mouth, he couldn't hold back any longer.

Blindly setting his plate down on the blanket, he reached out to cup the side of her face with one hand and leaned in to cover her mouth with his.

Chapter Ten

Startled by the abrupt move, Erin gasped against Wade's mouth and dumped her plate aside so she could grasp his shoulders. All her senses were magnified around him, sharpened. She was vividly aware of the hard warmth of the muscles beneath her hands, his clean, crisp scent as it wrapped around her, the feel of his callused palm against her cheek and the soft prickle of his whiskers against her skin. And his lips. They were firm but tender against hers, and the kiss was so gentle—much gentler than she'd imagined.

He moved his lips over hers carefully. Not hesitant, but as though he wanted to learn and memorize the shape of them. And holy hell, was it hot. She'd fantasized about this many times over the past few days, but her imagination hadn't come close to reality. With all his rough edges and having been undercover in austere conditions for so long, she'd expected a raging hunger from him. The care and consideration in his hands and mouth shook her to her core, but it also made her crazy. She wanted to see that need and passion unleashed, wanted to feel what it would be like to be pinned beneath his hot, hard body as he let himself go. Parting her lips, Erin leaned in closer and rubbed her breasts against his chest, gasping at the bolt of sensation that rushed from her nipples to between her legs.

In answer Wade slid his hand from her face into her hair, his fingers gripping the back of her head in a possessive hold that made her lower belly flutter. He nipped ever so gently at her lips, sending a shiver of anticipation through her, then she felt the warm velvet of his tongue soothing the slight sting. Tightening her hold on his shoulders, loving the feel of all that restrained power coiled beneath her fingertips, she sighed in pleasure and opened her mouth more beneath his.

The change in him was instant. He wrapped his free arm around her back and hauled her tight against him as he tipped her head back and penetrated her mouth with his tongue. Erin moaned at the show of hunger and strength, a bolt of sensation shooting through her core. The intensifying throb between her legs grew painful as he held her close to his body, letting her feel the leashed strength that hummed through him and the hard ridge of the erection pressing into her lower belly. On her knees she wiggled closer, wanting more, flattening her breasts against the wide expanse of his chest.

Wade gave a little growl that vibrated in his chest and tangled his tongue with hers. Holding her head still with the hand in her hair, he licked and caressed her tongue so seductively that she shuddered. The potent mixture of hunger and restraint he was using made her feel special and cherished and so damn desperate for more she wanted to tear off his clothes so she could explore all those delicious muscles without fabric in the way.

Unable to get any closer, she gave a frustrated whimper and rubbed against him, parting her legs to get more pressure where she needed him most. Wade made an approving sound low in his throat and shifted her so that she straddled his thigh. She gasped into his mouth as the aching flesh between her legs made contact with the hardness of his thigh. Her head was spinning. She was so wet already, and all he'd done was kiss her. She'd fantasized about him a lot over the past few days, but nothing had prepared her for this wild, dizzying response, the desperate hunger racing through her body now.

Moving her hips as she rubbed slowly against him, she whimpered as pleasure shot outward from where she pressed against his thigh. It was both amazing and frustrating. And as good as it felt, she'd never be able to come like this. She needed skin on skin contact against her clit, his fingers stroking her, or even better, his cock, and coming off the last part of this deployment, she was sick and tired of feeling nothing but her own hand when the need became too much.

She opened her mouth to beg him to touch her, but the words turned into a fractured moan when he slipped the hand on her back around her ribs to cup her breast. Even through her sweater and bra her flesh was sensitive, the nipple hard and straining. Kissing her deep and slow, Wade curved his hand around her and rubbed his thumb across the aching center. She dug her fingers into his shoulders and moaned into his mouth, craving more. Everything he had to give, until he satisfied this empty ache he'd created inside her.

Wade froze at the sound. He broke the kiss and pulled back to stare at her, one hand locked in her hair, the other still cradling her breast. His brown eyes were so dark, the firelight reflecting in them making them appear to glitter. His breathing was slightly unsteady, his nostrils flared and she could feel the heavy thud of his heart against her chest. She licked her lips, feeling dazed as she gazed back at him, unsure why he'd stopped.

Before she could ask what was wrong he bent and pressed a gentle, almost chaste kiss against her lips and slid her off his lap before releasing her. Confused, Erin curled her legs beneath her and licked her lips, tasting him all over again. "Why did you stop?"

He raked a hand through his hair and took a deep breath, let it out slowly. "I shouldn't have done that."

Erin blinked at him. "Uh, I'm not complaining, in case you haven't noticed."

A slight smile curved his mouth, his lips still wet from the kiss. Her body throbbed all over, clamoring for release. "That's good." He lowered his gaze, either unwilling or unable to look at her. "Things are...complicated. Taking this further would be a bad idea."

It took a moment for her to process the words and let them sink in. "Would it?" Because even though she knew he was a trained killer and a skilled manipulator and actor, she also knew that he was an honorable man at his core. He'd protected her at risk to himself, and pulled back from her now to avoid hurting her even though she'd just felt the proof of how much he wanted her. She couldn't deny the insane pull she felt toward him, or how much he fascinated her. She still wanted him despite everything, even though she knew he was everything she'd sworn to avoid since David was killed. "I'll be going back to Bagram shortly, maybe as soon as ten days."

He nodded. "I know. That's another reason why I shouldn't have started anything."

She cocked her head at him, struggling to understand, sensing there was more to this. "I don't expect a commitment from you, if that's what you're worried about. And I wouldn't say anything to anyone about us."

"No, it's not that." He started gathering the plates, seemed to struggle with finding the right words for a moment. "It's been...a long time since I've gotten involved with anyone. And you... you make me lose my head."

Her eyebrows rose, along with a surge of pride. Throwing a man as hard and jaded as Wade off his game? She'd take that as a compliment. "I'm not sorry for that, by the way."

He huffed out a laugh, glanced up at her for a moment before lowering his gaze once again as he reached for the remainder of the cake. She'd never again eat chocolate cake without remembering him and the taste of him on her tongue. "I need to keep a clear head until I know the threat to you is over. I can't do that if I let things go any further."

The threat to *her*. As if he wasn't under the same or worse than she was. "And what about when this is all over? Any objections then?" She wasn't into flings, and even though she knew he'd leave a big scar on her heart when he walked away, it still wasn't enough to dampen her desire. She wanted him, at least once, and was willing to suffer the consequences for it.

He blinked at her and she could tell she'd caught him off guard with that one. "Uh, no, guess not."

What the hell kind of answer was that? The man had gone without sex for the past few years at least, maybe more, he clearly wanted her and she was giving him an official green light. And all he could say was *guess not*?

Unwilling to deal with that head-fuck and recognizing that this was a firm *no* on his part, she got to her feet, though her legs were a little weak and her body was still humming with an arousal so strong that she'd have no choice but to deal with it alone once again if she ever wanted to get to sleep tonight. "I'll take that," she offered, reaching for the cake as she struggled to get her heart rate back to normal. There was no way she could just forget this had happened. How the hell was she supposed to live here alone with him and keep her hands to herself after what he'd just made her feel? He wasn't playing games, she understood that, but wished she could have thought of something to make him change his mind.

"No, I've got it." He glanced up at her briefly, and a shot of satisfaction flashed through her as he raked his heated gaze down the length of her body before looking away again and gathering up the dishes.

"Well, guess I'll turn in then," she said after an uncomfortable pause. Even though it was two hours before her normal bedtime, retreating to her room rather than being forced to endure the torture of looking but not touching seemed like a much more appealing option until she could get her body back under control.

He nodded. "Okay." Was it her imagination, or did he sound almost disappointed? "Have a good sleep."

"Thanks, you too." But she already knew sleep was going to be a long time coming. Now that she'd had a taste of him, she only craved him more. If he could set her on fire that fast with nothing but a kiss, she was dying to find out what he could do with his hands and mouth once they were naked. Except now she wasn't sure if that would ever happen.

Pushing out a breath as she jogged up the stairs, she battled the frustration and disappointment swamping her. And when she slipped beneath the covers after brushing her teeth and changing into her jammies, she stared up at the ceiling, acutely aware of the unrelieved ache between her thighs. He was trying to protect her. She'd made it clear she would settle for just sex, when the truth was she wanted so much more from him, and he'd turned her down anyway.

That honorable core of his. While she didn't want him to lose his focus, she had half a mind to wait until he'd gone to bed and then waltz in there and seduce him. She was pretty sure he'd give in eventually if she pushed hard enough. But she didn't want him to sleep with her because she'd pressured him. She wanted him to take her to his bed because he couldn't keep his hands off her.

So why did it seem like a huge mistake, lying here in the dark without him as the minutes ticked away?

Groaning, she rolled to her side and shut her eyes, convinced she was going to die of sexual frustration before this was all over.

****

Wade was deep in thought about the missing radioactive material as he left his bedroom the next morning, but his mind went completely blank when the bathroom door opened and Erin emerged wearing nothing but a towel. She paused when she saw him, offering a little smile that seemed a bit hesitant as she tightened her fist in the material knotted between her breasts. It ended at mid-thigh, giving him an eyeful of those shapely bare legs and his mind immediately imagined them wrapped around his naked back or shoulders. Her long, dark hair was damp around her shoulders, her face free of any makeup.

She looked fresh and pretty, and her hesitance made something sharp twist inside him. With her standing there looking good enough to eat and the scent of soap and her shampoo drifting from the steamy bathroom, he had a hard time believing he'd actually found the will to put the brakes on last night. He deserved a fucking medal for it. He'd lain awake for a long time before giving into the need and fantasizing about her as he'd taken care of the erection that just wouldn't go away. And God, when he'd pictured her spread out beneath him, naked, her eyes squeezed shut and her mouth parted on a cry of ecstasy as he drove deep inside her and made her come, he'd joined her, barely able to muffle his groans of pleasure as he came.

"Morning," he said, sorely tempted to throw caution aside, walk up to her and yank that towel away. The attraction wasn't going to go away, they couldn't erase the kiss last night, and they sure as hell couldn't avoid each other living in this place together. Fuck. He'd never wanted a woman this much, and he knew it had nothing to do with him coming off a four-year long dry spell. He wanted Erin and no other woman could interest him at this point.

"Morning. You going back into the office today?"

He nodded. "What are you gonna do?"

She sighed. "I dunno. I'll find something to do, I guess."

After another day of this solitary isolation she'd likely be ready to climb the walls, and he didn't blame her. He'd go fucking nuts sitting around here, cooped up all day and night. "I'll talk to the security team. Have one of the guys take you out for a while."

Her gaze sharpened on his. "To do what?"

"I dunno." In all honesty, there wasn't much she *could* do. The boredom would drive him fucking crazy, and he was sure it did her too. He was thankful she was dealing with this whole thing so amazingly well. He respected the effort she was putting forward to make the best of things. "A walk, maybe some local shopping. Something." Anything to get her out of these walls for a while.

"We'll see," she murmured, tucking a damp lock of hair behind her ear, drawing his gaze to the pulse in her throat. He hadn't gotten the chance to taste her there last night. If he sucked on her skin right there would she shiver and squirm? Tip her head back in a silent plea for more, arching those soft breasts toward him? He envisioned her like that, needing him, her nipples hard, begging for his mouth…

God. As his jeans started to get uncomfortably tight again, he shifted. "I was going to—" His phone rang. Pulling it from his pocket, he checked the display and met Erin's gaze as he answered Bill's call. "Hey, what's up?"

"You coming in?"

"Was just about to leave here. Why?"

"Schafer's here. Thought you'd want to talk to him."

Fuck yeah, he did. He had plenty to say. "I'll be there in a while."

"Bad news?" Erin asked softly as he ended the call, and he realized he was scowling.

"The guy I told you about is at Langley for questioning. They're gonna let me talk to him."

"Oh. So that's a…good thing?"

"Dunno yet." He intended to get answers though, and lay this stupid fucking rivalry/grudge thing to rest once and for all. If it turned out his former teammate really had set him up or had a hand in anything involving Rahim, Wade wasn't sure what he'd do, but he knew things would get ugly in a hurry.

He rubbed at the back of his neck, aware that he needed to get going, while at the same time reluctant to leave Erin. His gut said Rahim was up to something big and while he couldn't divulge the details to Erin, he hated leaving her here alone even with the security detail. Not that he wanted her to see him after he'd gone toe-to-toe with Schafer. That overdue confrontation was guaranteed to put him in a piss-poor mood. "You wanna come in with me? You could..." What? Hang out in the staff lounge down in the lobby to wait for him? Helluva lot of fun for her. He tried to think of something she could do, but came up blank. Shit, he hated her being in this situation.

"Nah, it's okay," she said with a dismissive wave of her hand. "I'll just read and putter around. But don't expect another spread like last night. Have to be careful not to spoil you."

He grinned at the wry note in her voice, the weight of guilt and responsibility for keeping her caged up like this easing somewhat. "Too late. Already spoiled."

She flashed him a genuine smile that hit him square in the heart and he had to order himself to stay put and not pull her into his arms. Under different circumstances he'd be going after her with everything he had. Full-on seduction, dates, long, erotic nights in front of the fire together. He'd never thought much about having a relationship again since going undercover, but he already knew he could never just have a fling with Erin. No way in hell he could have her once—or a dozen times, for that matter—and then walk away.

"I'll tone it down then. Wouldn't want to have to live up to those kinds of unrealistic expectations," she teased. "Too much pressure."

"I don't blame you." Though she'd already far surpassed any and all expectations he'd ever had about her and this entire situation. And every minute he spent in her company he felt himself letting her in a little more. She was already under his skin, and truth was, he liked having her there. "I'll text you when I'm on my way back, see if you need anything."

At that a flash of pure heat flickered in her eyes and he knew she was thinking about the same thing he was— them naked together, and, hopefully, what it would be like when he pinned her flat beneath him and buried his cock deep inside her. With effort he unstuck his tongue from the roof of his suddenly dry mouth.

"Okay. Good luck," she murmured.

"Thanks." Tearing his gaze away from her, he turned and headed downstairs. He had to put distracting thoughts of Erin aside and get his game face on. Facing off with Schafer was going to require him to be at his sharpest, something he was definitely not capable of with Erin on his mind. Thankfully she wouldn't be there, so that was one less thing he had to worry about this morning. The woman blew his concentration all to hell by just being in the same room with him. And when he got back here later tonight and they were alone together again, he had no fucking idea how he was going to manage to keep his hands off her.

Chapter Eleven

Wade had expected to find Bill waiting for him when he arrived on the sixth floor, but instead saw the director himself when he stepped off the elevator. Robert nodded to him and gestured for Wade to follow him down the hall. "Bill tell you Schafer's here?" he asked when Wade fell in step with him.

"Yeah. What's he said so far?"

"Nothing, we haven't started anything yet, though he's declined having a lawyer present for his meeting with you. Thought I'd let you take first crack at him."

Wade eyed him in surprise. "Why's that?"

He shrugged. "Figured it'd be best, considering your history, and because the more personal this is the better the chances are that we'll get what we need from him. Unless you'd rather talk to him later?"

"No, I'll do it now." The idea of this betrayal had been burning a hole in his gut for days now. He wanted to gauge for himself whether Schafer had done it—and if he had, why.

Robert's lips twitched as he tried to hide a smile. "Thought you'd feel that way." He led Wade down the hall and turned left down another, stopping at a conference room at the end. The glass windows had been electronically frosted to prevent anyone from seeing in. "He's in here. Go find out what the hell he's been up to."

Wade nodded, waited for him to disappear down the hallway, aware that this was only the illusion of privacy. People would be watching a live video feed of what happened, and everything they said would be recorded and cross-checked. Realizing his heart rate was elevated, he took a moment to slow it down, getting himself in a calm headspace before he twisted the doorknob and pushed it open. He'd spent over three years in one of the most dangerous undercover assignments The Company had. He could do this.

Seated at the far end of a long rectangular table, Schafer looked up when he entered. His brows crashed together immediately and his expression tightened. Wade stilled inside the doorway as it closed behind him and took a moment to absorb the sight of his former teammate. Brady still looked the same, his reddish-brown hair cut short and his deep blue eyes steady on Wade. He folded his arms across his chest and raised an eyebrow. "What the hell's this all about, Wade? They damn near put me in cuffs in Kabul."

Wade resisted the urge to stalk over there and grab the sonofabitch by the throat. He took a breath, let it out silently before speaking. "Must be a disappointment to see me standing here, considering I hear you wanted me dead."

Anger flashed in the other man's eyes, but he shook his head, a muscle twitching in his clean-shaven jaw. "I dunno what the hell happened or how you were involved, but no, it wasn't me."

While he hadn't expected Brady to come right out and admit it, he also didn't expect the clueless routine. Though Wade knew exactly what consummate actors he and his SF brothers were. He strode over and took the seat across from Brady, enjoying a moment's satisfaction when the other man stiffened. "So, what were you doing in Kabul?" he asked as he leaned back against the leather seat and rested his hands on his thighs.

"Working."

"With who?"

"My clients," he said, his voice holding an edge.

"And they are?"

Brady sighed in frustration and unfolded his arms as he answered. "Diplomats. Businessmen. Mostly foreigners. Which you and everyone else in The Company already know. So how about you tell me why I'm really here?"

Wade fought back his anger, determined to stay cool. "Word is you're either working with Rahim, or with someone close to him."

Brady blanched slightly, his jaw muscles flexing as he shook his head. "No," he said adamantly. "Never."

"That's not what I hear. And not what the director heard."

The tiniest hint of doubt entered the other man's eyes. "Well, you both heard wrong."

"That right?"

"Yeah, that's right," Brady snapped.

"So you didn't call someone named Davidson over at Bagram and ask about me? You didn't ask him when I was leaving for Kabul?"

Brady's expression turned eerily blank. "I'd called him about transporting one of my clients down to Kabul with an armed escort, and your name came up."

"How did my name come up?"

"I'd heard through someone at Kandahar that you came in with the Sec Def after he was rescued, and that you'd reported back to Bagram. So I asked Davidson if he'd seen or heard about you and he told me you were coming down to Kabul the next day."

So fucking convenient. Despite his resolve to stay calm and unemotional, Wade's blood began to simmer. "Well that's very interesting."

Brady pushed out a breath. "Look, man, I dunno what happened—"

"So you're saying you didn't pass that information on to anyone? Maybe 'accidentally' leak it to someone in Rahim's network?" he added, using his fingers as air quotes.

"No," he repeated, glowering now.

Fuck this. Wade shoved his chair back and shot to his feet, slamming his palms down on the tabletop as he leaned in and glared at Brady. "Well someone fucking did, because the moment we showed up at the last checkpoint before Kabul, we got ambushed. Me and the two other people in my truck. They came after us, chased us right up into the foothills firing at us, and they almost got us, too." They'd tagged Thompson. It bothered Wade that a former teammate would set him up period, but the way he'd done it and because Erin's life had been endangered—was still endangered—filled him with a rage he couldn't contain. "So don't you fucking sit there and tell me to my face that you weren't involved."

Rather than hold up his hands in self-defense or try to plead his case, Brady rocketed off his chair so fast it slid back and slammed into the wall with a thud. He planted his palms on the table and mirrored Wade's stance, facing off with him across the wooden table. "It. Wasn't. Me," he ground out, eyes narrowed, nostrils flared. "You and I have had our issues in the past, yeah, but even you should know better than to think I'd ever do something like that." He thrust a finger toward Wade. "I'm not only innocent of this bullshit fucking charge you've trumped up—I have no fucking idea what you're *talking* about, man!"

A resounding silence followed the outburst, the only sound their accelerated breathing as they glared at each other while tense seconds ticked by. Finally Wade shoved away from the table and straightened. He whirled and stalked toward the door, running a hand through his hair. He stopped and turned to face Brady again. He'd straightened too, his arms folded across his chest now, and a worried frown creased his forehead. The guy seemed sincere and Wade almost believed him. It was true they'd had problems in the past, yet Wade honestly couldn't see Brady doing something like this. That didn't change the facts before him though.

"Whatever, man. All the evidence points back to you. Better find yourself a good lawyer." He turned to reach for the doorknob.

"Wade, wait!"

Something made him pause. The desperation in Brady's voice. The idea that SF brothers would never betray each other. He looked over his shoulder.

Brady shook his head. "I swear on my daughter's life, it wasn't me."

Wade measured him, the sincerity in his face before responding. "I'd like to believe that, but I can't." He opened the door and walked out into the hall. As the door closed behind him, he was unsurprised to see Bill and Robert exiting Robert's office and striding toward him.

Robert stopped and slid his hands into his pockets. "So? You think he's telling the truth?"

"I dunno. I think *he* thinks he's telling the truth. Or at least whatever version of it he's sticking to." He knew all too well just how many versions the truth had. He'd used every single one of them over the course of his career.

Robert nodded, studied him thoughtfully for a moment. "We'll get a lawyer in here for him and get to the bottom of this. In the meantime, head downstairs and keep working your connections to find out anything about Rahim's recent movements."

"Has anything new come in since last night?"

The director shook his head and Bill didn't respond. Wade gritted his teeth, resenting that he was still being kept sidelined. Until a few days ago he'd been one of The Company's most valuable operatives. Now he was a resource they intended to keep close in case they could exploit something from him. Feeling used didn't feel any better than being on the receiving end of betrayal.

****

By mid-afternoon it was apparent that no one was going to tell him anything relevant about Rahim or Schafer. Wade had exhausted his limited contacts both overseas and stateside, without success, and there was piss-all he could do until the director brought him in on a deeper level or a break came in.

Left with the choice of sitting here twiddling his thumbs until something happened or going back to the safe house to spend time with Erin, the decision was obvious. But he didn't just want to go hang out with her. That would be torture and he wasn't sure how the hell he was going to be able to keep things platonic between them after last night. He'd been thinking about that kiss off and on throughout the day. After the shitty day he'd had, the thought of seeing her seemed like the only bright spot. He wanted to see her smile again, do something that would make her happy.

As an idea came to him, he pulled out his phone and texted her. *What are you doing?*

A few moments later the reply came in. *Nothing. How's your day going?*

Had better, he typed. *Leaving shortly. Feel like going out?*

Where?

How about a horseback ride? There was a stable not far from the safe house that offered trail rides. He'd talk to the owner and see if he could get them to rent a couple of horses out for an hour or two.

YES!!!

Grinning, he texted that he was on his way back, then called the stable to arrange everything as he walked out to meet the security team waiting by the vehicle for him. By the time they reached the safe house, excitement buzzed through him. He'd barely climbed from the SUV before the back door opened and Erin shot through it. She was dressed in jeans, combat boots and a pale pink fleece jacket. Her long hair was tied into a ponytail that fell between her shoulder blades and her face shone with excitement. She looked good enough to eat as she locked the door and hurried toward the SUV. "Are we really going?"

Knowing he was responsible for putting that look on her face made everything that had happened throughout the day evaporate. "Yes, ma'am." He held open the vehicle door for her, couldn't help but eye her ass as she climbed in and slid across the bench seat.

She was still smiling as he settled in next to her, her eyes sparkling with excitement. "Thank you. You have no idea how much I'm looking forward to this."

Yeah, he could, because he was too. Time alone with her on horseback seemed like the best idea he'd had in forever. "I'm glad." If felt good to do something like this for her.

At the stable he spoke to the manager, and after some convincing, managed to get him to allow them to take the horses out on their own for a couple hours. The security team stayed behind at the barn in the vehicle but Wade had the radio with him and a weapon holstered in his waistband. Not that he was expecting any trouble out here, but he wasn't taking any chances with Erin's safety.

Entering the barn, the scents of dust and horses took him back to when he was a kid. Erin went over to greet her horse, a bay mare, and he went to check on the saddle of his chestnut. He tightened the girth a little, watching as Erin put her foot in the left stirrup and effortlessly mounted the horse. She turned the animal toward him, a huge smile on her face.

"You look pretty comfortable up there," he said.

She grinned down at him. "I am."

He mounted, took the reins and returned her smile as they rode out of the barn together. He nodded at the security team as they passed and made their way out toward the pasture and the trails that lay beyond it. The horses snorted, ears pricked forward as they started out. Several others in the fenced paddock next to the barn ambled over to watch them pass.

Wade reached down to extend the stirrups then settled in next to Erin, the creak of leather blending with the clop of the horses' hooves and the trill of birdsong coming from the trees ahead. He pulled in a deep breath of the clear spring air and found himself smiling again. The late afternoon sun cast its warm rays down on them, the golden light catching on the damp leaves and grass, making the rain drops from earlier sparkle like jewels. Everything was so green and lush here—so different from where he'd been living, and it was nice to be able to be himself with Erin instead of constantly living a lie, even though they were still under guard.

Erin tipped her head back and let out a sigh, eyes closed and a smile on her face. "God, this feels good."

"Yeah, it does." He hadn't realized how much he'd missed being in the saddle until now, though he knew a big part of his enjoyment had to do with having Erin beside him. They rode at a walk through the pasture to where the trail narrowed and led into the forest. "You go ahead and take point," he told her.

Erin moved her horse in front of his, giving him a great view of her ass as they wound their way through the trees. The air was fresh and cool here, smelling of damp leaves and earth. Birds and squirrels chattered overhead. Every so often Erin would glance at him over her shoulder and give him a little smile, and every time she did, his heart squeezed a little harder. She was so easy to be with and she appreciated the simplest things. She reacted to the horseback ride the way some women would to dinner at a five star restaurant. He was falling hard for her and didn't even want to fight it anymore. Things were bleak enough in his world; he would enjoy whatever time he had with her while it lasted, as long as she understood and was okay with it ending when one of them left the safe house. He had no roots anymore and no idea what the hell he was going to do with himself once he helped bring Rahim down, and she was going back to Bagram to finish her tour.

Not wanting to think about that yet, he focused on her and the way the dappled sunlight fell on her head and shoulders ahead of him. Her ponytail gleamed as it moved with the rhythm of the horse's gait. She was quiet, obviously enjoying the ride, her head turning to gaze around her and up at the trees with their new leaves basking in the gentle sunlight. Wade stayed silent too, content to just be in her presence and watch her take everything in.

When the trees began to thin and the trail widened as they neared an open field up ahead, he nudged his chestnut forward to walk beside her. "Should we stretch their legs a little?" he asked.

Her lips curved sweetly. "We should."

He nodded and nudged his horse forward. "Come on, then."

He put the animal into a trot where the trail opened up into a large, grassy field that was bordered on all sides by thick copses of deciduous trees. Erin matched his pace and they started through the knee-length grass together. After a couple minutes he glanced over at her with a grin. "Ready to run?"

"Hell, yes," she responded with a gleam in her eyes.

Grinning, he nudged his horse with his heels, let out a sharp, "Hyah!" and took off. Erin gave a whoop of excitement and gave chase, and together they galloped across the field. He glanced over as she came abreast of him, laughed at the smug grin she tossed his way, then she came up in the stirrups a nit to lean low over her horse's neck, urging it to go faster.

They raced the entire length of the field, slowing to a canter when they reached the far side. Both horses were breathing hard but still had a lot of gas left. Wade was tempted to gallop them back the other way, but the look on Erin's face stopped him. She was fucking glowing, nose and cheeks pink as she threw her head back and laughed. "*God* I've missed this!" She righted her head and looked over at him, eyes filled with gratitude and tenderness. "Thank you."

That look on her face made it hard for him to breathe. Before he could respond, Erin sidled her horse closer, reached out to grab the horn on his saddle and stood up in the stirrups to lean over and wrap a hand around the back of his neck. Wade didn't even think about pulling away when she tugged him down and pressed a firm, lingering kiss on his lips.

He cupped the side of her face with one hand and returned the kiss, swallowing the territorial growl that rose in his throat at the feel of her lips parting beneath his. He took her mouth gently, holding her steady as he slid his tongue inside to taste her. She drew in a sharp breath that made the arousal flare even hotter inside him and touched her tongue to his but her horse shied a bit and danced away.

Wade released her, loving that mix of heat and surprise in her expression. What he wouldn't give to be able to pull her from the saddle and tumble her to the ground right here and now, but as much as he was tempted, taking her out here on the rain dampened grass probably wasn't the most romantic setting for her. He already knew she was a bit of a dreamer. She deserved romance, and if they did wind up in bed together, he wanted to make it special for her. Though it was gonna be a damn uncomfortable ride back to the barn with the erection he was sporting.

Erin laughed lightly at him, and he realized he must be staring at her the same way a hungry wolf eyed a raw steak. And there was more color in her cheeks now, either from arousal or a blush. "Shall we keep going?"

Oh, *hell* yeah they should. Until he was buried inside her, listening to her cry out his name while she clenched around him as she came.

Reining in his hunger, Wade nodded and followed her as she turned her horse back across the field. He had no idea what would happen in the coming days or weeks ahead, but there were two things he now knew for certain. Their relationship had just shifted to something much deeper than physical need, and he wanted her more than he'd ever wanted another woman in his entire life.

Unbelievable as it seemed, he was starting to think he'd never be able to walk away from her once this was all over.

Chapter Twelve

T he ride back to the safe house was quiet. Erin couldn't remember the last time she'd felt so at peace and though she wanted to lean over and rest her head against Wade's shoulder, she wouldn't in front of the security team. She would never do anything to embarrass him or make him pull away from her. Not when she wanted just the opposite. Instead she leaned her head back against the headrest in the back seat and closed her eyes to better focus on Wade's scent: clean, crisp air and woodsy aftershave. She was tingling all over at the memory of that kiss and the promise of what might happen between them tonight at the safe house.

Sighing, she shifted against the seat, trying to ignore the buzz of arousal traveling over her skin. This afternoon had done wonders for her mental and emotional state. The ride with Wade and the gallop across the field had exhilarated her.

The SUV slowed a few minutes later and made the left hand turn into the long, winding driveway. Erin stared out her window as the white farmhouse came into view. The last golden rays of afternoon sunlight had been swallowed by dark, leaden clouds that promised the spring storm the forecasters had called for, and the wind had already picked up. The driver pulled around back and Wade stopped her as she reached for the door handle.

"Stay here," he ordered softly, then got out with one of the other security guys in the front passenger seat.

Though she understood they were just being cautious, it was yet another reminder of the predicament she was in and it let some of the air out of the happy little bubble she'd been enjoying for the past couple hours. Wade came out on the back doorstep a few minutes later and waved for her to come inside. A cold gust of wind tugged at her hair as she climbed out of the vehicle, a few raindrops landing on her jacket as she made her way to the back porch. She shut and locked the door behind her then took off her shoes and coat. Her hands and feet were still chilled from the long ride but she was hot as hell inside at the prospect of spending a quiet—and hopefully intimate—night alone with Wade.

As she was hanging up her coat the SUV's tires crunched on the gravel drive as it turned around and pulled away, leaving them alone once again. She let out a breath, releasing the last bit of tension she'd been holding onto. With Wade here she had no reason to worry about her safety and she was looking forward to spending more time alone with him. He was protective and aloof in many ways, yet she had a feeling he'd already let her in farther than he did most other people. She liked knowing he trusted her that much at least.

Heading into the family room, she found Wade hunkered down before the hearth, building a fire for them. He glanced up with a little smile and saw her rubbing her hands over her arms to ward off the lingering chill from the early spring air. "This'll get you warmed up in no time."

She could think of several far more enjoyable things that would get her warmed up even faster than a fire. Hell, the mere thought of them already had heat curling in the pit of her belly. Him stripping her clothes off and unleashing the hunger she'd seen in his eyes. Maybe he'd fist his hands in her hair or pin her wrists on either side of her head the way she'd imagined. She eyed the way his T-shirt stretched taut across his back as he leaned in to light the kindling, imagining running her hands over all those lean muscles as he stretched out on top of her.

Yum.

Not wanting to scare him off, she knelt beside him as the flames caught and held her hands out to the warmth. "Mmm, that feels good," she sighed.

He turned his head toward her for a moment, then cleared his throat and got to his feet. His phone rang. Frowning at the call display, he glanced down at her and walked out of the room and she knew it must be someone from the CIA. Hopefully with no more bad news. Erin stayed where she was and watched the flames dance, exhaling a deep breath as she listened to the low rumble of his voice coming from the kitchen.

Wade appeared in the doorway, slipping his phone back into his pocket. His expression was closed, but she could tell that whatever had been said wasn't happy news. And she also knew he wouldn't tell her what it was. "Should we eat some of those leftovers?" he asked, obviously trying to put whatever it was aside for her benefit.

"Sure." She started to get to her feet but he held up a hand to stop her.

"I'll get them. You stay there and get warm."

Erin watched him go, greedily drinking in the confident way he moved—totally at home in his body, totally in control. So sexy. Turning back to the flames, she debated what to do. She wanted him, badly, and knew he wanted her too, although he seemed determined not to act on it. Should she push him and see what happened? It was tempting.

Wade returned a few minutes later carrying two plates loaded with warmed leftovers. She murmured her thanks and sat cross-legged next to him and they dug in together as the flames crackled in the fireplace. He was always quiet, but tonight more so than usual. Whatever that phone call revealed was bothering him a lot more than he was letting on. Something to do with his former teammate maybe? Cautiously testing the waters, she asked, "How did it go this morning, by the way?"

Wade stopped chewing and for a moment she was worried she'd overstepped her bounds but then he swallowed and sighed. "Not good."

She made a soft sound to let him know she was listening, but didn't push, hoping he'd continue.

A few moments later, he did. "It was weird to see him again, especially like that. And he seemed so goddamn sincere about not being involved in any of it. He was adamant about not even knowing the attack had happened."

He was quiet for a minute, seemingly lost in his own thoughts as he stared down at his plate with a frown. "Do you believe him?" she asked.

His gaze lifted to hers. "Part of me does. The evidence against him looks bad but it could be coincidental. Not that I'm a big believer in coincidence, but…shit, I have a helluva time picturing him doing it. The guy I knew wasn't wired that way."

Erin didn't want to believe a former teammate of his was capable of it either. She studied him as she finished her mouthful of rice. He seemed more upset about Schafer's possible involvement than being pulled off the Rahim investigation. That told her just how much he valued loyalty, something she totally understood. "You're saying it might be a setup?"

He gave a grudging nod. "Can't rule that out at this point either."

"So what happens now?"

He shrugged. "Bill and the director were going to question him, do some more digging to see what they could come up with. If he's clean, they'll find out. And if he's dirty…" He sighed as he let the thought trail off and Erin wanted nothing more than to take the plate out of his hands and wrap her arms around him.

"Maybe he's not," she said to comfort him. Though how else would Rahim have found out about Wade's travel plans in so short a time? Unless someone at Bagram had leaked the info?

He nodded, only his eyes hinting at the torment swirling inside him. "Maybe. I hate being sidelined like this though."

There. This was the crux of it, and she was just glad he was talking about it so she stayed silent and let him continue.

He shook his head. "I was so close to getting what we needed to bring him down. He was just in the critical stages of planning a big operation. If the Sec Def hadn't been kidnapped, I would have had everything I needed within a couple weeks and been able to call a team in to capture him."

But if the Sec Def hadn't been with them, Maya and Jackson would have died.

Erin pushed the terrible thought aside and forked up another mouthful of the rice pilaf, unsure what to say. Wade was such a mystery to her in so many ways, but she knew he was a good man. He'd had to do tough things in order to maintain his cover. Things most people could never contemplate, let alone handle.

As though the conversation had ruined his appetite, Wade suddenly set his plate aside. "And I'm sorry you got dragged into this." He waved a hand to indicate he meant the house, the entire situation. "Having to stay here, with me, when you should be home with your family."

A pang of homesickness hit her as she thought of her parents and how disappointed they'd been that her leave had been "cancelled". That wasn't his fault though. To ease his concern, she put on a smile. "Yeah, but hey, I could've done way worse in terms of roommates." She gave his leg a playful nudge with her hand.

His eyes warmed at her words and touch. The firelight brought out the deep bronze undertones in his hair, flickering in tones of gold and orange. She wanted to run her fingers through it to find out if it was as soft as it looked. He shook his head slightly at her, looking amused. "Why'd you have to be so sweet?"

She shrugged and countered, "Why'd you have to be so damned good looking?" It slipped out before she could stop it.

He stilled and his smile faded, as though her words had shocked him. And if she wasn't mistaken, the man actually blushed as he looked away. Given that they'd kissed twice, she didn't understand his reaction. Did he really not realize how hot he was and how much she wanted him? Did he think himself so unworthy because of who he'd become and what he'd done undercover? Her heart ached to think of him living such a dangerous life the past few years, isolated so long from everything and everyone he'd ever loved. And now that he was stateside again, he had nothing and no one except two siblings he was estranged from. This was just as hard on him as it was on her—no, probably way harder.

Even though Wade hadn't said as much, she could tell he was struggling to find his place here again and knew the uncertainty was driving him nuts. She wanted to pull him into her arms and hold him tight, show him that he was still worthy of being loved, that he was still a good and desirable man despite that remote mask he'd learned to wear so well.

"Sorry," she murmured. "Forget I said that."

He glanced over at her, and her breath caught when she saw the molten heat burning in his eyes before he covered it.

Unsure what to say in the tense silence that followed, she steered the conversation back to where it had been prior to her blunder. "I know you're frustrated about your lack of involvement in the investigation right now, but since you know Rahim best, they'll have to bring you in sooner or later in a more involved manner to get him. And my bet's on sooner. They don't want him out there on the loose without anyone reporting on his whereabouts and activities."

He nodded, seemed to relax at her words, then turned back to the fire. "I need to be the one to get him," he said quietly, staring into the flames. "I need to finish it."

He'd dedicated the last four years of his life to that cause. "I understand. And you will." They'd have to involve him heavily at some point. She didn't understand why they weren't doing so already. He looked so miserable she couldn't stop herself from reaching out to grip his hand and squeezing it.

Wade looked up, his long fingers contracting around hers as the heat returned to his gaze. Then he frowned. "Your hands are still cold." He took both of hers and rubbed them between his to warm them up. The considerate gesture and the gentleness of his touch turned her inside out. "C'mere."

Before she could guess what he meant, he tugged her to his side and set an arm around her back. He tucked her in close against his chest and rubbed both hands up and down her back. Erin closed her eyes and breathed him in, soaking up every bit of contact as she cuddled against him. Her heart was racing, her nipples beading tight. He was warm and hard and more than anything at that moment she wanted to feel his naked body against hers, feel his weight pressing her into the rug as he took her. She shivered.

"You're freezing," he admonished, and she didn't correct his assumption that the shiver and the goosebumps were from the cold instead of his touch. "Why didn't you say something?"

"I'm better now." But rather than move away, she snuggled deeper into his embrace.

His hands stilled on her back. Just when she expected him to withdraw or push her away, he wrapped his arms all the way around her instead and rested his cheek on the top of her head. He squeezed her once, making her light-headed with the feel of all those muscles contracting around her. "I shouldn't touch you, but you make it so damn hard to do the right thing."

"What's the right thing?" she asked, certain she wouldn't like the answer, but needing to understand. There were no rules forbidding them from having sex.

"To get up and walk out of here before I do something I can't take back," he muttered.

At that she tilted her head back to look up into his face. "Why would you want to take it back?"

The words hung there between them as the fire crackled and raindrops pattered against the windows. Wade's eyes darkened with longing, his gaze dropping to her mouth, and Erin couldn't take it another second. She threaded her hands into his hair and brought her mouth to his. Wade made a low sound in the back of his throat, his arms contracting around her, and that was all the answer she needed.

Stroking her fingers through his silky-soft hair, she kissed him with all the hunger and need he created inside her. Her tongue caressed his, tasting him as she ran her hands down his neck and shoulders to explore his ripped chest. One of his hands slid up to cup the back of her neck while the other palmed her ass and pulled her tight to him.

Frustrated by the fabric in her way, she grabbed the hem of his T-shirt and impatiently peeled it up over his torso. Wade released her only long enough to yank it over his head and toss it aside, and she couldn't bite back a moan at the sight of him. His bronzed skin glowed in the firelight, stretched over taut muscle. A few small scars dotted his torso. A dusting of dark hair covered his broad chest and thinned to a trail that bisected his defined abs and disappeared into the waistband of his jeans...right above the thick ridge of the erection straining the fly.

She placed her palms on his chest, felt the muscles contract and the heavy thud of his heart as she petted him. Leaning in, she nuzzled the side of his neck, reveled in his quick intake of breath as she licked him. Wade slid an arm around her hips and hauled her up to straddle his lap. She settled in and resumed her exploration, ignoring the commanding tug on her hair as he tried to urge her mouth up to his. A heavy, drugging throb of arousal pulsed inside her, but she was too hungry for more of him to stop what she was doing.

Big, callused hands slid over her sides, down her stomach to the hem of her shirt. She kept going, shrugging out of her shirt, but paused when she saw the look on his face. He was staring at her breasts, encased in her white lace bra, his expression a mixture of awe and molten hunger. Her nipples beaded tight, tingling in anticipation of feeling his hands and mouth on them. She sat up and reached behind her to unfasten the bra, thrilling at the way his eyes devoured her every move. And when she slipped the bra off and dropped it to the floor, the rank male starvation in his gaze as he stared at her naked breasts sent a surge of primal feminine power through her.

With a low, nearly inaudible growl, he cupped her breasts in his hands. Erin sucked in a breath and arched her back, loving the contrast of his roughened hands on her skin. He squeezed her gently, his thumbs brushing over the hardened centers, sending ripples of pleasure through her body. Her fingers tangled in his hair as he leaned forward to take a nipple into his mouth.

Heat and need swept through her, growing more urgent by the second. She squirmed, reached one hand down to find the button on his jeans as she held his face to her breasts and struggled to breathe. His mouth was a delicious torment, pushing her need higher. She struggled to release his jeans, gasped as Wade sucked and tormented her sensitive flesh with his tongue.

He lifted his hips to help her pull his jeans and underwear down, releasing one of her breasts only long enough to twist his body to the side and yank the jeans down his legs and off. His erection sprang free, dark and thick against his abdomen. Erin let out a needy moan and wrapped her hand around his hot, hard length, still holding his head close. At her touch he tensed all over and groaned, releasing her aching nipple to press his hot forehead against her breast.

He was breathing hard, his breath hot against her, his whiskers prickling pleasantly. One big hand moved up into her hair and fisted there. She tightened her grip and gave him a slow stroke. His spine arched, his head tipping back to reveal the exquisite agony on his face. Erin's heart squeezed. It'd been a while for her, but even longer for him and she didn't want him to have to wait a moment more for this.

Ignoring his firm hold on her hair she scattered kisses over his tightly clenched eyelids, down his nose and over his cheeks to his mouth. She slid her tongue past his lips to tangle with his as she stroked him, enjoying the hitch in his breathing and the way his muscles twitched. The man was dying for more, and yet fighting the pleasure at the same time. She didn't want him to fight it, and told him so with a soft sound of reassurance as she trailed her mouth over his jaw and down his throat, his chest.

When she reached his abdomen every muscle in his body was rigid, tension pouring off him in waves. He released her breast to slide both hands into her hair and seemed to brace himself as she slid her mouth lower. She leaned down to hover over the head of his erection, pressing a soft kiss there that made him hiss and contract his fingers in her hair. The tiny sting only heightened her arousal.

Gripping him in both hands, she let her tongue play gently around the swollen head, absorbing the shudder that passed through him before she finally parted her lips and took him into her mouth.

"Erin. Jesus," he groaned, his voice sounding strangled. The man was strung so tight she kept expecting him to snap. She couldn't wait to find out what happened when he did.

Humming in approval, she took him deeper, wanting to drown him with pleasure until he exploded, and looking forward to finding out what it took to push him there.

Chapter Thirteen

Wade was dying. Had to be.

He couldn't think, could barely breathe at the feel of Erin's hot, wet mouth wrapped around his cock. It was everything he'd ever imagined, and ten times as intense. Her gentleness, the sincere enjoyment she seemed to take in giving him pleasure all but destroyed him.

He fought back the urge to fist her hair in his hands and fuck her mouth until he exploded, but it was a monumental effort and one he was going to lose in the next few seconds if she didn't stop. He was so fucking primed he was ready to come and he'd barely touched her yet. Tugging once on her hair, she made a quiet negative sound and kept sucking until his eyes damn near rolled back in his head.

"Sweetheart, stop," he panted, shaking, desperate to hold onto his control.

She lifted that mesmerizing green gaze to his, and the heated desire there made his cock throb even more.

Lifting her mouth from him for a moment, she whispered, "Want to make you come."

Christ, she would, in about two more seconds. "Not yet," he managed, his voice shaky as hell as he urged her upward and dragged her into his arms. He buried his face in the curve of her neck and held on, trembling all over as he struggled to push away the urge to come. He wanted to please her first. It'd been a long time for him but he still remembered the rules—ladies first, and that was even more important with Erin. He wasn't good with words, never had been, so this was his chance to show her what he felt for her. He didn't want to ruin it.

"It's okay, baby," she murmured against his temple, stroking his back so gently it made his throat tighten. "I want you to let go."

He eased back and met her gaze. The hunger was still there, but tenderness too, and it turned him inside out. She deserved so much better than him fucking her like an out of control animal on this rug in front of the fire, but at that moment that's what he wanted to do more than anything. He lifted an unsteady hand and brushed the hair back from her flushed cheek. "I want to let go together," he rasped out, shaken by his need for this woman he barely knew, yet some part of him protesting being vulnerable while she maintained control.

To get out of his head, he cupped the back of her neck and kissed her again. She opened with a tiny sigh and eagerly met the stroke of his tongue. Wade eased her onto her back and nuzzled her jawline, the side of her neck, then trailed down to her breasts. Her nipples were deep pink and hard and he couldn't resist taking them into his mouth again. She gasped and arched her back, both hands sliding into his hair to urge him on. He didn't need the encouragement though. There was no way he could get up and walk away from her now.

He undid her jeans and tugged them down her long legs as she raised her hips to help him, leaving her in nothing but a thin scrap of black lace that barely covered her mound. As the spicy scent of her arousal hit him, Wade bit back a groan. When he slipped a finger beneath the edge of the lace and found the damp heat of her arousal, his cock surged against his belly. Impatiently he pulled her panties off and flung them aside, raising his head as he got to his knees to better admire the view.

Erin smiled a little and parted her legs. Wade swallowed at the sight of those pink, glistening folds exposed to his ravenous gaze. Knowing she wanted him was one thing. Seeing and feeling it were even better.

Trailing one hand down her side to her hip and over her thigh, he watched her face as he stroked his fingers across her wetness. She hummed in pleasure, her body moved restlessly on the rug, primed and ready for more. He grabbed a throw pillow and eased it beneath her head to make her more comfortable, her tender smile at the gesture making his heart squeeze. With the few functioning brain cells he had left, he suddenly remembered the all-important issue of protection.

"I don't have a condom," he rasped, surprised by how rough his voice was.

Erin reached out to stroke her palm across his scruffy cheek. "I'm clean and I get the shot, so we only need one if you're not sure about you."

He was already shaking his head. "I was tested before I went undercover and there's been no one since before that."

Her smile widened, though he could still see the hunger raging in her eyes. Hunger he was going to thoroughly enjoy satisfying. "Then we're good."

A low, gruff sound came out of him, almost a growl as he leaned down to kiss her and let his fingers resume their exploration of her tender flesh. He kept his touch light at first, but she quickly made it plain she wanted more. She gripped his shoulders tight as she kissed him, then lifted her hips in a clear demand. Lifting his head slightly to watch her reaction, he eased two fingers into her. Erin closed her eyes and moaned, rocking her hips against his hand.

"Wade. More," she whispered, her face awash with pleasure.

She was so damn sexy like this, her muscles tensed, her body hugging his fingers. He curved his fingers slightly and rubbed just inside her entrance. She made an unintelligible sound, one of her hands snaking down to grab his hip and pull him forward. Praying for strength, he took himself in hand and slowly pushed forward. Her inner muscles closed around him in a hot, tight grip that had sweat breaking out across his chest. He paused partway in, waited for her eyes to flutter open. When their gazes met, he planted one hand beside her head and plunged in deep.

Erin's loud gasp echoed in his ears for a split second before her moan echoed around the room. Wade squeezed his eyes shut and hung onto his control by a thread, shuddering.

Oh, fuck. Fuck!

She was so goddamn hot and wet, her inner walls hugging him tight. Pleasure shot through his entire body, leaving him panting and trembling as he fought the urge to hammer into her until he came. He fought it back. Sucking in a breath, he eased back and then plunged forward again. She sighed and dragged him closer, drowning him in the feel and scent of her. The friction was so goddamn incredible he couldn't control the need to move. He came down on his elbow and started a steady rhythm with his hips, dying a little with each drag and thrust.

Over the thundering of his heart he heard the hitch in her breathing and reached blindly between her legs to stroke her clit. Either he didn't do it right or she was too impatient to wait for him to figure out what she liked, because she pushed his hand away and slipped her own fingers to where she needed them. The sight of her stroking herself put him from inside the danger zone to game over.

Helpless against the onslaught of the orgasm gathering at the base of his spine, he jerked his gaze from her fingers swirling over the swollen bud at the top of her sex to her tight nipples and finally to her face. Her eyes were closed, lips parted in ecstasy as she climbed to the crest. The pleasure twisted tighter, higher, and he couldn't fight it anymore. His thrusts grew urgent, almost frantic as he slammed into her. His control was gone, shattered, and he didn't even care.

By sheer damn luck he managed to outwait her. He felt her ripple around his cock, heard her rising moans and her cry of relief as she detonated. A heartbeat later, he joined her, throwing back his head with a roar that echoed off the walls and ceiling. It tore through him in powerful pulses that gradually faded until he was weak and gasping. Turning his face into the curve of her neck, he rested his weight on his forearms and struggled to suck air into his starving lungs.

Erin gave a contented sigh and wrapped her arms around his back, urging his weight down on top of her as she wound her legs around the back of his thighs. He gave in reluctantly but kept some of his weight on his knees, worried he was crushing her into the floor. She ran her fingers through his hair, over his shoulders and spine. Rain and wind continued to lash at the roof and windows. Together with the heat of the fire and the steady thump of her heart beneath his cheek, her touch was hypnotic. He'd never much liked being petted before, but she had him practically in a trance. He could stay like this for hours, breathing in her scent and enjoying the feel of her fingertips wandering over his skin.

"Hmmm," she sighed, kissing the top of his head. "That was worth the wait."

"I can do better," he blurted.

She laughed softly. "It was perfect the way it was."

He raised his head to look down at her. Her eyes held the drowsy, sated look of a satisfied woman, and while that soothed his ego, he also felt a flicker of shame. He'd just taken her on the rug like a fucking caveman and would have come without her if she hadn't taken matters into her own hand. A flush crept up his neck. "No, seriously. I can do way better." She deserved better. Slow and soft and romantic, intense. A different kind of intense than what they'd just shared. Him in full control, all the urgency and desperation locked down until she was thoroughly satisfied, maybe even more than once before he let go. Christ, he'd love to spend hours on end spoiling her in bed. Spoiling her in general.

Unfortunately this whole goddamn situation with Rahim was a serious roadblock though.

She raised an eyebrow. "Yeah? Well, wow then. I can't wait to find out what that entails."

Staring down into her eyes, he felt closer to her in that moment than he had anyone else. She'd never seemed to mind his rough edges or lack of social graces. She lay beneath him now wide open, no shields, no games, and fuck, he didn't want to be the one to hurt her when this was all over, but he didn't see any way around it. She'd be going back to Bagram and he didn't know what the hell he was going to do.

Letting his protective walls down a little more, he bent to kiss her, gently this time, cherishing her mouth rather than claiming it. She made a soft sound of enjoyment and kissed him back, the languid stroke of her tongue against his stirring him deep inside. When he began to slip out of her, he reluctantly pushed up on his hands and withdrew. She raked her gaze over him, a little smile on her lips as she took in the sight of his body and it went straight to his head. "I'll be right back," he murmured, getting to his feet. He cleaned up in the bathroom and brought some tissues back for her, surprised to find her already part way up the stairs.

"I'm gonna grab a shower, then crash," she told him, pushing the dark waves of her hair over one shoulder. "Want to join me?"

The thought of sliding into bed next to her and holding her in the darkness through the night was way too appealing to turn down. He nodded. "I've got a few things to take care of first, but I'll be up in a while."

"Okay."

As soon as she turned and headed up the stairs, he strode back to the fire and pulled on his underwear and jeans, then went into the kitchen. There were no messages on his phone from either Robert or Bill about Rahim or Schafer. He contacted the security team via the radio and received the all-clear. Keeping the radio with him, Wade peered out the kitchen window into the night. The storm lashed the house and it was unlikely anyone would actually be able to find their location, but Wade couldn't shake the feeling that something big was brewing.

After dousing the fire and checking to make sure the house was locked down tight, he went upstairs to his room and found Erin curled on her side in his bed. From her breathing and lack of response as he quietly entered and eased the door shut, he knew she was already asleep.

Wanting to feel her naked body against him, he stripped and slid in next to her. As he drew her into his arms she settled into the curve of his body with a murmur of contentment. Wade absorbed the feel of her cuddled against him and listened to the rain and wind beat against the roof.

He'd fallen for her, hard, and he'd do goddamn anything to keep her safe. The warning hum in his gut told him Rahim was coming. Wade was fully prepared to stand between Erin and any danger that came their way.

****

Somewhere off the South Carolina coast
Pain and cold.

The cold was cruel against his exposed flesh, but it barely registered past the excruciating pain that blasted through him with every breath.

He peeled his blood-encrusted eyelids apart to survey his own personal hell. It was the dead of night, the sky pitch black and the tiny sliver of moon didn't give off enough light for him to see anything except the high walls of the crevice he was lying in. He tried to swallow, gritted his teeth to keep from crying out from the agony and thirst that tortured him. Three days he'd been lying here like this, best he could figure. Three days since that A-10 had unleashed its payload and taken out most of his platoon in a horrific friendly-fire incident. There had been other survivors, but their cries had all faded into silence sometime before dark.

Moving slowly, unable to hold back his own tormented cries as he inched his way forward to the wall of the crevice, he kept telling himself not to quit. He was a fucking soldier. He could make it if he found a way out of here. He'd heard the distant thump of rotors before he'd passed out from sheer exhaustion and blood loss, but the rescue crews hadn't heard his yells for help. They hadn't come back since.

No man gets left behind, *he reminded himself.*
They're coming back for you.

Even as he said it he knew it wasn't true. Three
times rescue crews had combed the area. The operation
would have changed from a rescue to a recovery
mission, and most likely they'd already recovered the
remains of his dead teammates. For months now he'd
been questioning his role in this war. His country had
invaded theirs. Tried to shove its political agenda down
their throats. Left chaos and destruction amongst the
innocent civilians caught in the crossfire, and for what?
They'd never win this war. And when they pulled out,
everything would go back to the way it had been before.
The people of Afghanistan would continue to eke out
their existence in this harsh and ancient land as they had
for thousands of years.

At some point he'd started thinking about defecting,
and even the idea of somehow faking his death to do it.
Was this a sign? Was he supposed to use this moment to
become what he was always meant to be?

Pushing aside his pain and despair, he fought his
way up the steep side of the rock wall trapping him. He
didn't know how long it took him to finally reach the top.
Hours. A day. But when he finally dragged himself over
the edge and collapsed onto his stomach, he realized
how still and silent it was.

He was utterly alone.

He lost consciousness and woke when he heard
voices. He blinked against the sunlight, the clear, blue
sky stinging his eyes. The voices came nearer, nearer,
until he could hear them clearly. Men speaking Pashto.

His heart lurched. They'd see his uniform and kill
him without realizing that he only wore it because he
had no choice. He tried desperately to crawl away, find
a place to hide, but he was too weak, too dehydrated. He
lay sprawled out in the dust with jagged pieces of rock

cutting into him, utterly defenseless. And when the men arrived and he gathered his remaining strength to attack, the Pashto words slipped from him like a prayer.

Please help me.

The four elderly men had gaped at him in surprise for a moment before approaching him. And rather than kill him or leave him to die even though he wore an enemy uniform, they gave him water and tended his wounds. Carried him to their village and took him in. Saving him when his own brothers had left him to die. Giving him the chance to embrace Islam and his true identity.

Rahim.

"Do you need anything else, sir?"

Shaking off the stark memory that had marked the pivotal point in his life, Rahim turned to face one of his men he'd brought on board with him. Traveling by boat wasn't his favorite thing—hell, it was why he'd joined the Army rather than the Navy—but this trip wouldn't last long, and this ship was American. Something he found immensely ironic and gratifying. "No, I'm fine," he replied in English. "What about you?"

"Everything's fine with me, too," the man responded in a heavy Spanish accent, telling him there was no cause for alarm about their identities or plans being discovered. Yet. Rahim had disposed of a few original crew members and gotten him and two of his men on board with the help of some fancy computer work, and all without causing any suspicion.

Rahim nodded and gestured for the man to follow him out of the heavily reinforced iron cargo hold. Stepping out onto the deck close to the railing, he looked back at the container set close against the starboard wall of the cargo area and locked the door behind him. Facing the ocean, he took a deep breath of the salty air as the breeze whipped over his skin. The thrill of freedom and excitement about what he was going to do swept through him. Hidden safely inside that shipping container, the device had passed through security at the port without detection. Now they had only a few hours' sail up the east coast to Virginia, where they'd arrive sometime late tomorrow morning.

Before he passed out of cell reception, he placed a call on another burner phone to Safir, who answered quickly. "Everything looks good on our end," he told the other man in English, wrapping a hand around the iron railing as he gazed at the horizon and the South Carolina coast fading into the distance. "What's going on there?"

"It's been busy," Safir replied. "That location we talked about looks good for sales. The inventory arrived safely at the store today."

He paused, taking in the unspoken code. The hit team had arrived in Virginia. "You've checked out the location?"

"It looks good, yes. Do you want me to make an official offer?"

Officially authorize the hit. "Yes."

"I'll let the agent know right away."

Anticipation lit inside him, a flame given a breath of pure oxygen. "Perfect. When will we know if it's a done deal?"

"By noon tomorrow, I imagine."

Around the same time that the ship would be unloading at the dock at Alexandria. *Perfect.* "That's good news. Great work." A memory flashed through his brain, of Jihad a few days after Rahim had hired him as his personal bodyguard. He'd killed two men sent to assassinate him. Alerted by a gunshot, Rahim had stepped out of the house where he'd been staying to find Jihad standing over the two soldiers' bodies. He'd shot one and slit the other's throat. The bloody knife had still been in his hand as Jihad turned his head and met his gaze.

Thank you, brother, Rahim had said in Pashto.

Jihad had nodded in acknowledgement, his dark eyes burning with a fierce intensity Rahim had mistaken for loyalty.

But now he realized it had been hatred.

Safir acknowledged the compliment with a grunt. "I'll call you tomorrow when the offer is final."

"Sounds good. Have a good night."

"You, too."

Rahim put the phone into his pocket and offered the man next to him a little smile, then nodded for him to leave. Once he was alone, he returned to staring at the endless waves shifting under the ship. He rolled his shoulder, biting back a grimace as the healing tissues pulled, and counted his blessings.

All he had to do now was see that container unloaded and put on the correct truck, then sail back down to Bermuda, where a private jet would be standing by to fly him back to Pakistan. A donation from a wealthy and powerfully connected Pakistani man. From Karachi he would make his way back to the tribal region in the northwest corner and plan his next move in this new phase of the war he was about to unleash.

But first, he wanted to bear witness to the destruction this first attack would bring.

Tipping back his head to breathe in the sea air, Rahim savored the moment. Everything was nearly ready. He'd do what he could to ensure it happened according to plan, then the rest was in Allah's hands. And Rahim had a bone-deep certainty that He would reward his efforts.

Chapter Fourteen

Erin woke to the feel of a hand on her shoulder. It took her a moment to remember she was in the safe house, and that it was Wade's hard body curled around hers.

She rolled to her back, fighting off the haze of sleep. "What?" she whispered.

On his side facing her, he reached out to smooth the hair back from her forehead that felt damp. "You were having a bad dream."

She pushed the covers away to cool her body down, aware that she was perspiring and her heart rate was elevated. "Yeah, guess I was." She grasped at the fragmented images floating through her memory like wisps of fog.

"You were twisting and kicking the sheets away. Bad one?"

Bits and pieces came back to her. Blackness. The sense of being trapped in a confined place and the suffocating sensation it always brought. Screaming at David to stop, to come back as he boarded the

Blackhawk that would take him to his death in the coming battle. "Nightmare, I guess." She hadn't dreamed about David in forever.

"Okay now?"

"Hmmm, yes," she murmured, turning on her side to snuggle back into Wade's hard frame. He wrapped one steely arm around her ribs and settled in close, his warm breath fanning the back of her neck. "What time is it?"

"Little after oh-two-hundred."

She covered a yawn and burrowed back beneath the covers. It'd been a long time since she'd dreamed about the mine. Maybe the uncertainty about Rahim's whereabouts and plans had triggered her nightmare. "I don't like being confined," she admitted. "Fell down an old mine shaft when I was a kid. I broke my leg on impact and couldn't move. It was pitch dark down there. Took my dad over a day to find me, and only because our shepherd mix managed to track me. I've been claustrophobic ever since."

He made a quiet sound to show he was listening, and tightened his arm around her. "Now I'm even more amazed at how you handled yourself in that cave with me."

She snorted. "I hated every second of it, I promise you."

"Maybe, but you still did it."

"Yeah." She was glad he hadn't noticed her fear—or at least that it hadn't gotten the best of her at a time like that. Facing a life and death situation like that, overcoming the claustrophobia had been easier than she'd imagined. Yawning, she cuddled deeper into his embrace. "Funny. I don't seem to mind being confined by you though."

His soft chuckle gusted against her nape. "That's good to know."

"And I was dreaming about David. A guy I dated a few years ago. We were together for seven months before he deployed. I loved him."

Wade was completely still behind her, and she rushed to explain.

"He was killed by an insurgent two months before his tour ended. It was hard." She swallowed, thinking of that horrible, endless ache of grief she'd carried around in her heart. At times it had felt like it would never end. She'd lost not only David, a good, kind man, but also all the dreams of getting married and having a family together. "Took me until about a year and a half ago to finally let him go." To grieve for him and the loss of the life they'd planned.

"I'm sorry," he murmured against her shoulder.

"Thanks. He was a great guy, and while part of me will always miss him, I know he'd want me to be happy. And right now I'm happier than I've been in a long while."

His lips brushed across her skin, sending a shiver through her. "I'm glad."

She drifted off again and woke a while later to the feel of his big, callused hand sliding over her naked back. She started to lift her head but he stayed her by pressing between her shoulder blades.

"Turn over," he murmured against the top of her shoulder, his lips grazing her skin.

Complying with a sleepy sigh, she rolled onto her stomach. Cool air washed over her back as he drew the covers down, then those magical hands were gliding down her spine to her hips. "Thought you were sleeping," she mumbled against the pillow.

"You said you don't mind being confined by me and it got me thinking," he said, his deep, gravelly voice sending a shiver through her.

"Hmm, about what?" she asked, intrigued. The idea of him dominating her in bed sent a wave of arousal through her. A half-dozen fantasies skittered through her mind, all of them involving her pinned beneath him while he teased her until she came.

"'Bout me showing you that I meant it when I said I can do better."

Okay, seriously, the man was taking that to heart too much. "Wade, you don't need to prove anything—" Her words died off when those powerful hands closed around her hips in a firm grip and a heartbeat later she felt the prickle of his whiskers against the base of her spine and a slow, lingering kiss, complete with a tender stroke of his tongue.

Mmmmm.

"Wanna make you melt," he whispered.

Somehow she managed to uncurl her toes and closed her eyes. "Already am."

He made a low sound of male satisfaction and trailed hot, liquid kisses over her bottom and down the sensitive backs of her thighs. His hands tugged backward, urging her up on her knees and she went willingly. The drag of his teeth against the back of her upper thigh made her gasp, then the wet drag of his tongue across the spot made her moan. A hot throb started deep in her belly and spread down between her legs. With her weight resting on her forearms and chest, she kept her eyes closed, waiting to find out what he'd do next.

Still gripping her hips in a tight hold that she wouldn't be able to break easily, he nibbled his way up one cheek, to the base of her spine, and down the other side. Erin shifted and squirmed against the sheets, melting for real. She was slick and swollen already, and so damn needy the anticipation was driving her insane. Her hands fisted the fitted sheet when he tipped her hips up even more and she felt the warm glide of his tongue as he licked at the throbbing flesh between her legs.

Gasping, she arched her back and tried to widen her stance to give him better access but he held her fast and took his time teasing and tasting her. The position should have made her feel vulnerable but instead it only made her hotter. Each soft stroke of his tongue made her legs tremble, turned her into a quivering mass of sensation as he licked and sucked the straining bundle of nerves at the top of her sex.

"Ohmygod, *Wade...*" His name faded out into a whimper as he slid his tongue inside her. She pressed backward, ignoring the commanding hold on her hips, and earned a chuckle in turn. He was so hard, so remote most of the time, she'd never imagined him being such a generous, attentive lover.

His grip was tight, strong enough to likely leave marks later, but his mouth was so tender and he was making it clear how much he enjoyed pleasuring her while having her at his mercy. In and out, he teased her with alternating flicks over her throbbing clit until she thought she'd go mad. When she was writhing and pleading he finally rose to his knees behind her and guided his erection into place. One hand palming her hip, he reached around her belly with the other and stroked her with his fingers. She rubbed back against the hot, hard length pressed against her, the pressure gathering deep in her core.

"Melt for me, Erin," he murmured, then plunged into her from behind.

She cried out and gave into the sensation, her body closing around him in relief. He kept his rhythm slow and steady, working her with that taut, wicked body, each gentle stroke sliding across that hot spot inside her as his slick fingertips circled her aching clit. The orgasm built relentlessly, fueled by his control of her body. It seemed to build forever, intensifying with each thrust, each glide of his fingers, until she was gasping and moaning and shaking all over.

Wade groaned deep in his chest and leaned over her, nipping at the curve of her shoulder. She exploded with a wild cry, a million brilliant colors bursting behind her clenched eyelids. He grew harder inside her, his strokes growing rougher, faster, then a low, throaty growl rumbled in her ear as she felt him tense and release inside her.

She lay curled up on her knees like that until he at last withdrew and eased her down onto her belly once more. Her skin was damp with sweat and her breathing was still erratic, but her heart squeezed tight when he came back from the bathroom with a damp cloth to clean between her legs. He took it back into the bathroom then slid in beside her and eased her into his arms, her back to his chest.

"Okay, you're right," she mumbled, totally destroyed and too weak to move. "That *was* better." So much so she could barely formulate a coherent sentence.

He chuckled and kissed the top of her head. "Yeah." He sounded smug and she didn't blame him. The man was lethal with what he could do to her body. She wasn't ever going to forget him. She just hoped there was a way to make things work between them when she went back to Bagram. Long distance relationships like that rarely worked out long-term, but Wade knew what it was like and she was sure he'd be supportive. If she could just convince him to give this thing between them a shot once their time together here came to an end.

Willing her mind to settle, Erin sighed and told herself she still had time to make that happen. She may have gone into this with the intention of making it a fling, but now she realized her heart was involved way too much for that.

****

Wade's eyes snapped open in the darkness. At first he wasn't sure what had woken him. The house was eerily silent, magnifying the moan of the wind and the lash of the rain. There was no hum from the furnace, no rush of air from the floor vents.

That unnatural stillness must have woken him, and made all kinds of sense when he glanced over to find the digital alarm clock on the bedside table dark. Wind must have knocked the power out. Erin was still fast asleep, curled onto her side next to him. Carefully sitting up so he wouldn't disturb her, he started to push the covers back and his cell phone buzzed on the nightstand. He snatched it up before it could wake Erin, who let out an adorable snuffle and shifted to her stomach beside him.

Frowning at the unfamiliar number, he quickly got up, grabbed the radio, his underwear and jeans from the floor and stepped out into the dim hallway. The phone went silent once more and when he checked, the caller hadn't left a message. He could try tracing the number but doubted he'd have any luck figuring out who it was. The eerie stillness inside the house settled over him. To verify his suspicion he tried the light switch in the upper guest bathroom and wasn't surprised to find the lights didn't work.

As he started for the stairs his phone buzzed again with another incoming call. Seeing a different and familiar number on display this time, he answered, his pulse suddenly thudding harder. The director of the CIA didn't call people at oh-four-thirty for shits and giggles, least of all him.

Wade eased the bedroom door shut on his way past and hit the stairs, his bare feet silent on the carpeted runner. "Sandberg here," he answered quietly.

"It's Robert. Just wanted to give you the heads up that Schafer was cleared and released a couple of hours ago. I was just told, otherwise I would have let you know sooner."

That was fast. Wade frowned as he headed downstairs. The wind moaned against the side of the house, rain drumming on the roof. "They're so sure he was innocent?"

"I'm looking at the report now and I've seen some of the video. His story never once wavered and his polygraphs came back clean. Without any further evidence, there was nothing more we could do, so we released him. Thought you'd want to know."

Yeah, in case Schafer was a lying, backstabbing piece of shit who was now on the loose and a possible threat to his and Erin's safety. Maybe for the second time. "Thanks. Anything further?"

"Yeah." The grim tone and the pause made Wade's gut tighten as he waited for the man to continue. "We located the stolen truck early last night. There's no sign of the material though."

"Where'd you find the truck?" Wade asked. It had to be close to where whoever had stolen it was planning to use it—and his money was on Rahim.

"Just outside of Cancun."

Ah, shit. Right on the Gulf of Mexico. He ran a hand through his hair, mind racing. "What did you find at the port? They had to move it via ship. There's no way they'd try to fly it out—"

"We're looking into every possibility, Wade. There were seventeen ships that left the port over the past three days bound for various locations in the US. So far nothing's tripped our radar and we haven't been able to find any radiological signatures, but you know as well as I do that it could be because the device is small or the signature is being blocked by whatever they've contained it in. I'm letting you know this as a courtesy, but I'm going to need you to come in soon. The moment we get a possible location on this, you're heading up whatever team you want to lock this sonofabitch down."

The hair on Wade's arms stood up as a rush of relief swept through him. "Yessir." And he wouldn't have it any other way. Rahim was his responsibility. "What are the odds Rahim's still in country down there?"

"I'd say slim, but you know him best. What do you think?"

He'd prefer to have this conversation face to face in Robert's office rather than over the encrypted phone, but in the interest of time it couldn't be helped. "I'd say it could go either way."

Robert grunted. "Was afraid you'd say that." He cleared his throat. "Okay, stand by for my call and be ready to go."

"I will." He disconnected and stared into the family room, not focusing on anything as he tucked the phone into his hip pocket. Analysts had narrowed the search to nine possible ships heading into US waters right now, each of them with access to a major American port and from there by ground to a highly populated city like Atlanta or D.C. Robert had sounded calm but the man must be going apeshit right now with so many unknowns to contend with.

Stepping off the bottom stair onto the hardwood floor across from the kitchen, Wade paused and turned his head to look out the small square window in the top of the back door. He'd heard something, and it wasn't the wind.

Striding to the kitchen for a better view outside, he pulled the radio from his pocket and turned up the volume before contacting the security team. The storm lashed the house and surrounding yard with torrents of rain, already standing in great puddles that covered the driveway. Peering outside into the gloom, he saw nothing moving but the branches of the newly-leafed trees waving wildly in the wind.

"Parker, come in," he said, and released the button to await a reply.

Only silence answered.

He checked the volume and the channel again, and tried the other agent, tamping down the curl of dread in his gut.

Nothing.

His fingers tightened around the radio as he lowered it to his side. He didn't like the feel of this, and there was no way the security team would abandon their posts without alerting him first. Not without a damn good reason.

That list of reasons put all his instincts on alert.

Heart drumming a hard tattoo against his ribs, Wade turned and raced back up the stairs. The moment he opened the bedroom door Erin woke and turned her head to look at him. "I need you to get up and get dressed," he told her in a curt tone, wanting to convey his urgency without scaring the shit out of her.

Her eyes widened as she sat up and dragged the sheet up over her breasts. "What's wrong?"

He reached into the top drawer of his bedside table and drew out both his Berettas, checked that the magazines were full. "Power's out and the security team's not answering me. I'm going out to check on them and the perimeter. Keep your radio with you, channel two. I'll contact you before I come back in the house." He handed her one of the pistols, thankful when she took it without protest. "Anyone else tries to get in while I'm gone, shoot them."

Leaving her staring after him in stunned silence, Wade yanked on a shirt and jacket before he turned and stalked out of the room.

Chapter Fifteen

As he stepped cautiously out onto the back of the covered porch, all Wade's senses sharpened. He was hyperaware of everything, each sound and movement around him. He had his phone in his pocket, the radio tucked into his waistband and his Beretta gripped tight in his hands. Already he felt too exposed. He'd called in his concerns to Robert, who was waiting for an update and arranging potential backup. For now, he and Erin were on their own. Normally he'd have barricaded them both in the old cellar beneath the house until backup arrived and they found out what the hell was going on, but he couldn't risk trapping them both.

There was no cover here to offer him protection other than the corners of the house, and no concealment he could use whatsoever once he stepped off the porch. Though he hated leaving Erin here alone, he knew she could defend herself if necessary and he had to go find the security team and find out what the hell was going on.

Keeping his weapon up and ready, he scanned his surroundings before leaving the relative safety of the porch and vaulting over the side of the porch railing. His boots made slight crunching sounds on the wet gravel of the driveway as he hurried across it to the grassy front yard. The tire marks in the gravel weren't fresh and he didn't see any footprints in the sodden grass leading up to the house. He hated moving around in the open in the dawn light like this. Made him feel like he had a fucking bull's eye tattooed across his chest. The back of his neck prickled, his subconscious verifying what the unease in his gut already told him—something was very wrong.

Rain pelted him as he hurried across the grass, the cold wind whipping around him and biting through his jacket. He raced for the thick stand of trees at the far end of the expansive lawn. If a sniper was hidden in there he'd be dead before he reached the trees, but it was the only cover around and he couldn't afford to stay exposed like this.

He paused and pressed up against a thick tree trunk to get his bearings. The branches swayed and trembled in the wind, dripping more rain onto him. Then he smelled it. A faint whiff of iron over the underlying damp earth.

Blood.

Internal radar pinging like crazy, he eased his way around the tree trunk to look farther into the thicket. The tension is his gut remained but that prickling sensation at his nape eased as he stepped deeper into the trees. If anyone had him in their sights right now, he couldn't tell. Walking deeper into the dense foliage, he moved carefully through the tangle of underbrush.

The iron smell grew stronger. Most people wouldn't even have noticed it but he'd spent his entire adult life in combat zones and war-torn countries and he'd recognize that scent anywhere. Pausing behind another thick tree trunk, he reached his left hand down to key the radio. Sure enough, a corresponding squawk sounded off in the distance to his right, where the smell was coming from.

When he covered the remaining distance and peered through the underbrush, he spotted it. An arm lying outstretched on the ground, the hand palm up, the fallen radio lying mere inches from the motionless fingertips. Heart sinking, Wade scanned once more for threats and seeing none, stepped in to see who it was.

Parker. The thirty-one year old former Army lieutenant assigned to the security team. He lay face-down in the mud with his head turned to the side, the whole left side of it blown out. His eyes were half open, staring sightlessly at the forest floor. The blood hadn't coagulated yet; there was no bruising around the wound and rigidity hadn't set in yet. Which meant he'd likely been dead for less than an hour.

Clenching his jaw, Wade looked around for any evidence of who had shot him. He found two sets of footprints leading toward the spot where Parker lay. They began where the far side of the copse met a short grassy area that sloped down toward the ditch separating the property from the road. At the edge of the trees the footprints veered right, toward the driveway. He knew the security team's schedule, but not always the details about who was posted where. Parker and whoever had been with him must have been dropped off by vehicle by some of the others, and headed to their observations posts on foot from there. So where the hell were the others? No one had answered his radio calls and they hadn't alerted him of a channel or frequency change. And where was whoever was responsible for that other set of prints?

Either dead, or on the run after he'd murdered his fellow security agent in cold-blood.

Heart thudding, Wade cursed and hurried back through the trees, careful not to disturb the murder scene so the forensics guys could put the pieces together when they arrived. Whipping out his cell phone, he swiped his thumb across the screen and entered his security code. He paused just inside the tree line and brought the phone to his ear to report everything when he caught a flash of movement in his peripheral vision. He jerked the phone away from his ear and whirled around to see a shadowy figure approaching the east side of the house.

His heart dropped into his stomach.

Cursing, he shoved the phone away and burst from the trees, weapon aimed dead center mass on the fucker. But now he had to get close enough to use it.

He tore over the open ground, not caring about snipers or other threats, focused solely on stopping the intruder before he could get to the house and harm Erin. His boots dug into the soaked grass with every step, the dull thuds matching the frantic pounding of his heart. "Freeze!" he roared when he was within earshot.

The figure—a man wearing a black hoodie, he could see now—whipped around and froze when he saw Wade coming at him.

"Hands in the air, now!"

The man hesitated for a second, then slowly raised both hands in a non-threatening gesture. Wade wasn't placated. "Get on the ground," he snarled, slowing to circle the man cautiously.

Through the driving rain he could make out the tall, muscular build, the short dark hair as the man reluctantly got to his knees. Not one of the security guys. "Right down," Wade growled, watching the bastard's hands.

"For fuck sake, Sandberg, take it easy, it's just me," the man called back.

Surprise jolted through him. He stared in astonishment. "Schafer?"

"Yeah. Put that damn thing away, will ya?"

No way in hell. What the fuck was he doing here? Wade stalked forward and stopped within killing range, the weapon's aim never wavering. "How did you find us?"

Rather than looking cowed or helpless lying stretched out face-first on the soaking wet grass, Schafer turned his head and sent Wade a withering glare. "If you'd answer your fucking phone, you'd know why and you'd have been expecting me."

Wade darted a quick glance around to ensure they were alone before pinning Schafer with his stare. "Who's with you?"

"No one," Schafer gritted out between clenched teeth.

"How did you get here?"

"Drove out."

Wade frowned and risked a quick glance around. The timing was way too damn suspicious. Had he killed Parker? Wade didn't want to believe it. "You alone?"

"Yeah. Now let me up."

"Don't you fucking move," Wade warned, taking a menacing step forward.

Schafer let out a disgusted sigh. "The director released me this morning and said he'd tell you himself."

"So?"

"And so, you should realize that since I've been cleared of any wrong doing in this mess, I'm not a threat to you."

"Or you could have come here to settle the score personally," Wade said, thinking about Parker's body lying in those trees behind him. "Now how the fuck did you find us?" The place was way out in the middle of nowhere, with nothing but farms and horse pastures for miles in every direction. No way he'd been able to follow them, and Wade couldn't see anyone at Langley just handing Schafer the address, verified innocence or not.

"I overheard the address from someone. As soon as they released me I left headquarters and took a cab straight to a rental place, then drove out."

Rage simmered in Wade's blood. There was no way the security team would have let anyone get near here without stopping them or at least alerting him, which meant they were all either dead or dirty. His jaw tensed. If this fucker had killed Parker in the hopes of catching Wade and Erin off guard, he'd—

He forced himself to stop and take a slow, even breath to combat the rush of adrenaline in his veins. "So why are you here?"

"I have to tell you something."

"You could've left a message."

"No, man, not for this, and you know I wouldn't have gone to the trouble of coming here in person if it wasn't heart-attack-serious. Look, let me up, okay? I've got a piece in my waistband and a backup on my ankle, but I'm not gonna reach for either of them. I've gotta talk to you and the woman with you, A-fucking-SAP, and somewhere where no one else is gonna hear it. Feel me?"

Wade's mind whirled as he walked around in an arc, keeping his body between Schafer and the house. If the bastard made a move to reach for one of his weapons, Wade would drop him without batting an eyelash. "Just say what you came to say."

Schafer shot him a baleful glare, then gave in. "I came to warn you."

That awful prickling sensation started up again at his nape. "Warn me about what?"

He shook his head once. "Not here, man. They might be listening."

The driving rain would make that tough, even with a parabolic dish, and there were likely bugs inside that he hadn't located. No, Schafer was going to have to come clean out here. "Fucking say it, asshole."

Schafer's jaw flexed. "I heard someone when I was at Langley, part of a conversation I wasn't supposed to overhear. They said something about recent chatter regarding a possible attack on the safe house. That's how I got the address."

Wade stared at him, a chill skittering down his spine. If that part was true, then Bill and Robert both had to be aware of it. Which meant they either didn't think it was credible enough to warrant alerting Wade, or Schafer was full of bullshit. "What?" he rasped, his pulse echoing in his ears.

Schafer nodded. "I overheard some guy talking on the phone."

"Who and where?" If someone was going to have a potentially treasonous conversation like that, they wouldn't do it at CIA headquarters. Schafer having "overheard" it at all was either a huge damn coincidence, or a bald-ass lie intending to make Wade let his guard down around him. Not happening. Wade wasn't willing to bet his and Erin's lives on either of those things.

"Dunno, I never saw his face. I don't trust any of those fuckers and wanted to come tell you face to face. That's why I came straight out here. I think you both need to get out of here."

Wade didn't know what to believe, but he couldn't stand out here in plain view and keep interrogating Schafer. "Get up on your knees. Put your hands on the back of your head."

Schafer did as he was told, pushing up onto his knees as he held his hands out of reach of his weapons, palms out. Wade rushed forward, keeping his own weapon trained on the man's face. "Don't you fucking move," he warned as he stopped in front of him.

"I'm not gonna move," Schafer snapped, but stayed very still as Wade pulled the Glock from his waistband and tucked it into his own, then reached for Schafer's right ankle and took the backup.

"You carrying anything else?" Wade asked as he frisked him with one hand, watching for the smallest twitch of movement from the other man.

"No." He waited until Wade gave a satisfied grunt and stepped back. "Can I get up now?"

Wade gave a grudging nod. "Yeah." He motioned ahead of him with the barrel of his pistol. "Get in front of me and head toward the house." He was soaked to the skin and already shivering. Whatever the fuck was going on, he needed to call Robert and report everything, and get Erin the hell out of here.

Schafer got to his feet and started toward the house. Wade's heart hammered, his instincts screaming at him to go, *go*. He would already be on the phone to Robert had he not been unwilling to temporarily lose the use of one hand. If Schafer tried anything, he wanted to be ready. "What did they say about the attack?" he pressed, risking a glance on either side to make sure no one else was coming at him. Nothing moved but the tree branches and the quiet country road at the end of the driveway remained deserted. It was dawn now but the dark, forbidding sky and the storm made it feel like it was much earlier.

"I heard him say 'Sandberg', then something about a team being ready to attack the safe house, and the address. Seemed fucked-up, so here I am."

Yeah, it did, and Wade wasn't ready to just accept Schafer's version of the story. He grunted, running through the three most probable explanations. Either Schafer was lying and had killed Parker himself; he hadn't killed Parker but was still part of this whole fucking nightmare; or he was telling the truth.

Wade was counting on it being the third. But he wasn't letting his guard down for an instant until he spoke to Robert and moved Erin to safety. "Move it," he snarled, the sense of urgency making him feel like his skin was suddenly too tight, stretched thin over his muscle and bone.

Schafer broke into a loping run. Wade stayed behind him, close enough to take him to the ground if need be. The house was still dark, so the power wasn't back on yet. He didn't know where Erin was but he knew she was up and waiting and he was glad because they were getting the fuck away from here right now.

Shafer reached the edge of the grass, his feet making crunching sounds on the gravel drive as they headed toward the side entrance onto the porch. He was less than ten steps away from the bottom stair when a bullet buried itself into the wooden siding of the house with a loud *thunk*, shards of wood exploding from the entry hole.

Sniper.

Both of them instinctively ducked and whirled, then hit the ground. The only consolation was that Schafer appeared as stunned by the shot as him. Either the shooter had just gotten into position, or they'd been waiting for him and Schafer to reach the house.

Lying on his belly on the wet gravel, heart slamming against his ribs, Wade lifted his head a fraction to stare up at the side door. He'd never make it. The sniper would take him out with one well-placed shot the moment he tried any of the doors or windows. Maybe even the moment he moved.

Erin.

She had a radio but the channel might be compromised and someone could be listening. He opened his mouth to yell a warning instead, praying it wouldn't come too late.

Chapter Sixteen

U p in her room, Erin wrenched open the top drawer of the dresser, grabbed what was inside and shoved it all into the open duffel she'd set on the foot of her bed. A good fifteen minutes had passed since Wade had issued that gruff command to shoot anyone who entered, then left the house and she hadn't heard anything from him since. Not exactly how she'd imagined waking up this morning. The perimeter around the property wasn't *that* big, so he should have been able to check it by now. She pushed her worry aside and finished packing in case he came back with bad news and the order to leave.

Hurrying to the bathroom, she was shoving all her toiletries into her kit when she heard something, and stilled. The dim light coming through the window behind her was enough to allow her to see her reflection in the mirror above the sink. Her face looked pale, her features pinched as she stilled and listened. Then it came again. The sound of distant male voices, too far away for her to hear what was being said, but it had sounded like shouting. Wade and one of the security team? Her heart thudded against her breastbone as the voices continued, her hand straying down to her hip where the radio rested in her pocket.

Just as her fingers closed around it, the voices faded. She relaxed slightly and resumed packing. Stepping out of the bathroom, she'd taken two steps back toward her bedroom when something slammed into the house. She gasped and instinctively dropped into a crouch, her gaze flying down the stairs toward the front door where the sound had come from. Bits of plaster and wood were scattered on the hardwood floor. Wade's voice shattered the stillness, urgent and taut.

"Erin, sniper! Get down!"

Instantly she went to her belly on the carpeted landing, her eyes traveling up from the debris on the downstairs floor to the silver-dollar-sized hole in the wall beside the front door.

Shit!

She withdrew the Beretta Wade had given her from the back of her jeans. The solid weight of the weapon felt reassuring in her hand. She pulled the radio from her pocket as she made her way to the landing, staying low. Her only thought to help get Wade inside to safety. Crouched down with her back to the wall, she stared at the front door and keyed the radio.

"Wade, are you okay?" she asked, her voice tight and her insides shaky as hell.

Her radio chirped a second later. "Yeah, but we're pinned down. I got Schafer with me."

Relief punched through her at the sound of his voice, immediately followed by suspicion. What the hell was Schafer doing here? "A shot came through the wall by the front door. You'll have to get around back."

"Let us in through the laundry room window. Keep low. I don't know how many more of those bastards are out here."

"Roger." Taking a deep breath, she raced down the stairs and ducked behind the wall separating the family room from the hallway.

"We're heading around now," Wade said.

"I'm almost to the laundry room." She darted down the hall and into the laundry room, had just stepped over the threshold when another shot slammed into the side of the house, somewhere to her left. Cursing, she dropped to her knees and eyed the window above the washing machine. She'd have to stand to pry it open, and Wade and Schafer would not only be exposed while they accessed it; they'd be easy targets once they started climbing through.

"Change of plan," Wade said. "Schafer's coming in the laundry room. I'll come in through the family room window."

He'd have to make it around the other side of the house first. "Roger that. Opening laundry room window now." Heart pounding, she shot to her feet, undid the latch and shoved the sash upward. Moments later she heard boots hit the wooden porch, then a male grunt and two hands appeared on the windowsill.

Another shot rang out just as the unfamiliar man hoisted himself into the window and pushed his upper body through. Erin stood back against the wall, pistol aimed at him as he slid through and landed awkwardly on the floor. He looked up at her and didn't move, a wary expression in his eyes as he took in the weapon and her stance. He must have sensed that she wasn't afraid to use it, because he lifted both hands up and stayed on his belly. "I'm unarmed. Wade took my primary and backup."

She didn't know whether he was telling the truth or not, but she knew Wade would never have let him come in if he'd been a threat to her—though his SF training made him a lethal one, unarmed or not. "I have to let Wade in," she said, and backed out of the room, her gaze locked on him. He slowly got to his feet, hands still up to either side of his head. When he made no move toward her she whirled and ran for the family room.

As soon as she rounded the corner she ducked low and moved as quickly as she could to the window, keeping away from where the curtains concealed the wide panes of glass. Once she was next to the left one she keyed her radio again. "I'm in position."

No answer, but there were no more shots either, and she knew Wade was timing his run carefully. Moving slow so she didn't disturb the curtains and give away her position if the sniper was watching them or worse, following Wade, she reached up and found the lock in the window. "It's unlocked," she told Wade, her Beretta within easy reach beside her knee. "I'll wait for your signal."

"On three," he replied quietly, and she felt a burst of relief that he was still okay. She darted a glance back down the hallway, seeing Schafer as he came out of the laundry room. He no longer had his hands up but he stayed against the wall, watching her tensely.

"One," Wade said. She set the radio down and placed both hands on the side of the window sash. Footsteps behind her had her swinging around in alarm and reaching for her weapon.

Schafer frowned at her in annoyance when she aimed it at him. "You cover him and I'll get the window," he said in a curt tone.

"How do I know you're—"

"You can't cover him and open the damn window, so move aside and let me help," he said in exasperation.

They both knew the pistol was useless unless at close range, but it was all she had and he was right. And if he tried to block Wade's access to the window or make a move to take her pistol, she'd put a bullet in him without blinking. He must have seen it in her eyes, because he grunted, his lips curving in an almost amused half-smile as she moved aside and let him take hold of the window frame.

"Two," Wade said.

Schafer held her gaze, both of them tense and ready.

"*Three*."

The thud of boots reached them as Wade vaulted the porch railing, then running footsteps. "*Now*," Erin urged, moving into position beside him.

Schafer wrenched the window open. Erin had her weapon up and through it just as Wade came into view. His face was tense, body moving in a blur as he took the last few steps toward the window. Another round slammed into the porch, sending up shards of wood from where it impacted the railing a few feet to Wade's right. She ducked back just as he gripped the window ledge and vaulted inside. Another slug came through the open window, burying itself into the wall just inches from where he landed.

Erin shot out a hand and yanked the curtain back in place to give them some concealment just as Wade hit the floor and rolled toward her. He shoved her back flat against the wall, shielding her with his body. Fear and frustration pulsed through her. She didn't want him to shield her—she wanted them all to move away from the window before the sniper got lucky with a blind shot.

"Go, go," she urged, shoving at his wide shoulders.

He eased away and flipped to his belly, crawling for the hallway. She was right behind him, Schafer following her. They scooted around the relative safety of the wall separating the hallway and family room and paused there. Wade shot a glance at Schafer as he spoke. "Think it's only one shooter. We'll hole up in here and call for backup——"

His words were drowned out by a deafening explosion. Erin's gasp was lost in the roar. She hit the hardwood as the floor and ceiling shook, raining bits of plaster down on them. Wade jerked her close and rolled on top of her, covering her with his weight and shielding her head with his arms. When the house stopped rumbling he moved off her and she got a lungful of thick, acrid smoke coming from the family room.

"Jesus Christ," Schafer muttered, coming up onto his elbows to look behind them. Erin followed his gaze. The wall separating the hallway from the family room had holes the size of dinner plates in it and an orange glow flickered over the hall. The crackle and hiss of flames penetrated the ringing in her ears as the silence settled over them.

"What the hell was that, an RPG?"

"Felt like it," Wade answered, his posture and face tense as he glanced from the glow of the flames through the holes in the wall and back to her. The anxiety burning inside her exploded into full-on fear as she realized they'd have to move before backup arrived, before the smoke or another RPG killed them all. "We've gotta get out the back before he can circle around." He scanned her from head to boots. "Grab a jacket."

They had a tiny window of opportunity to exit the house before the sniper repositioned or maybe fired another rocket at them. On her stomach, she crawled as fast as she could toward the foyer, radio in her back pocket and the Beretta clutched tight in her hand. Already the smoke was thickening, stinging her nose and throat, making her eyes water.

Her coat was in the coat closet next to the back door. She hugged the wall and gingerly reached up a hand to pull the door open, careful to keep out of sight through the glass in the back door. Behind her she heard Wade talking on his cell, calling in the situation to who she assumed must be someone at the CIA. Looking back, she saw what was left of the family room completely engulfed in flames. She jerked her jacket down from the hanger and put it on as Wade and Schafer crept toward her down the hall.

Wade's gaze connected with hers. "Let's get outta here." He nodded toward the door.

Any exit was a risk at this point, but the door gave them the biggest opening to go through and trying the window now would stack them up and cost time they didn't have. The smoke would kill them if they stayed in here for more than a few minutes. "Okay." Her voice sounded far steadier than she felt. They had no idea what was waiting for them outside.

He nodded once and started for the back door on his stomach. "Stay behind me. Schafer, you stay on her six." They crouched together at the door. Erin's heart drummed hard against her ribs. Was there only one shooter out there? Where was he now? No way of knowing until they stepped outside, but they couldn't stay here like sitting ducks.

Wade took her chin in his hand, startling her out of her thoughts. His dark eyes were so intense that she shivered. "Run east to the neighbor's place. Don't stop, whatever you do, no matter what."

He meant if he was hit, he was ordering her to leave him and keep going. Well, fuck that. She opened her mouth to argue, but he cut her off with pressure against her jaw and a tight shake of his head. "Don't you stop. Find cover and call for help, or snag a vehicle and get out of here."

Already knowing she wouldn't budge from Wade's side if something happened to him, she nodded anyway. But she couldn't keep from reaching up to lock her hand around his thick wrist and squeezing once, hard. She was scared, but more terrified that she might lose him. He'd come to mean so much to her in such a short time, she couldn't take it if she lost him now. Not like this. Not before they even had a chance to find out if what they had was as powerful as she thought it was.

His hard expression softened for just a fraction of a second, then he dropped his hand. "I'm gonna open the door and hang back a second. On my word, we're all gonna haul ass next door. Got it?"

When both she and Schafer nodded, he rolled to face the door and inhaled deeply. "Here we go," he murmured, and reached for the deadbolt.

It turned with a sickeningly loud snick in the eerie stillness.

His hand gripped the knob. "Get ready." He flipped the knob and yanked the door open while they plastered themselves up against the wall.

No shots. Only the intensified sound of the wind and rain.

Erin swallowed and watched Wade, who was scanning the area he could see outside from their position. He rose slowly to one knee, his pistol gripped in both hands. "Now."

With that he surged upward and barrelled through the back door. Erin felt like she was on autopilot as she shot to her feet and followed. Rain and wind slapped at her face, the waterlogged ground making squishing sounds beneath her boots with each stride. Wade tore across the grass in a zigzag pattern to avoid enemy fire as he led the way. His long legs ate up the distance but she knew he was holding some of his speed back in order to stay close to her.

Scanning the thicket of trees to the south, her breath sawed in and out of her lungs as she waited for the shooter to open fire once more. There could be others, or he could have repositioned already without them noticing. Thudding steps behind her told her Schafer was sticking close behind her as Wade had ordered.

It felt like it took hours instead of minutes to cross the lawn. Wade hesitated at the split rail fence separating the property lines and looked back at her. A spray of mud and grass kicked up a few feet to Erin's left. She yelped and veered right, terror streaking through her. The lack of body armor made her feel even more vulnerable.

Wade turned away from the fence as though he was going to come back to her. She opened her mouth to yell at him to run just as another round slammed into the grass between them. The continued misses told her the shooter wasn't very experienced, but that did nothing to dull the knife-sharp edge of fear.

She veered left, desperate to avoid the sniper's crosshairs and kept on running. Wade grabbed her around the torso when she reached him and flung her over the fence. She sailed over it, arms pin-wheeling as she landed, but it was no use. Her feet came out from under her and she hit the muddy ground on her belly with a hard grunt.

Scrambling to her feet, she risked a glance over her shoulder in time to see Wade and Schafer both vaulting the fence. Another bullet took a chunk out of the top railing. Schafer yelled in pain, his face contorting as he fell head-long on the sodden grass. Wade instantly lunged for him, jerking him up by one arm as he pinned Erin with blazing dark eyes. "Run, goddammit!"

She turned and ran, heading for the small, red barn about fifty yards away. Her legs felt strangely numb, her muscles rubbery with fear. Almost to the barn, she heard a pained grunt and whipped her head around.

Wade.

He'd fallen face-first into the ground. She skidded to a stop, her heart lurching, certain he'd been hit. Before she could take a single step toward him, he got up and reached for Schafer, and Erin realized the other man must have been hit again. He was barely moving as Wade hauled him upward and tossed him over his shoulders.

Using the adrenaline still coursing through her body, Erin sprinted for the barn. When she'd reached the far side of it she crouched down and rapidly sucked air into her starving lungs. Wade shot around the corner moments later, dropped to his knees and slid Schafer off him, revealing the trail of blood streaking his side and jeans.

"Hit twice," Wade panted as he settled his former teammate onto his back. He looked up at her. "See what you can do for him while I find us a way out of here."

She nodded and turned her attention to the wounded man as Wade got up and disappeared around the back of the barn. Schafer's face was pinched, his jaw locked tight against the pain. Erin bent over him and pulled his hands away from the wound in his side, slipping into medical mode.

"I'm a nurse," she told him, ripping his shirt open. Something had penetrated his chest wall just beneath his left armpit. A bullet fragment or a shard of wood, most likely from the size of the entry wound. "Can you talk to me?" She couldn't find an exit wound anywhere, but he did have another hole in his left calf. That was the least of her concern right now though.

"Hard to...breathe," he panted, his breaths short and rapid. Frothy blood oozed out of the small wound. A sucking chest wound. Extremely serious and potentially lethal if he didn't get proper treatment in time.

"I know, but try to stay calm. I'll be here with you until help arrives. Just focus on staying calm, keep your breathing as slow and shallow as you can." She had nothing to treat or dress the wound with and he would lose too much body heat if she stripped his shirt off in these temperatures. The last thing they could afford was him going into shock. Instead, she took off her jacket and peeled her own shirt off then put the jacket back on.

Balling up her shirt, she pressed it to the wound, ignoring his hissed breath, and pulled his arm down to lock the shirt in position. Just as she was applying pressure to his arm to help staunch the bleeding, an engine fired up nearby. Seconds later an old blue pickup barrelled around the corner and Wade emerged from the cab.

He took in Schafer with a single glance. "How bad is it?"

"He needs an ambulance or an E.R.," she told him.

Wade's mouth tightened at the announcement. "Can't wait here." He hurried forward and carefully lifted Schafer over his shoulder, sliding him into the rear bench seat of the cab. Erin climbed in next to him as Wade got behind the wheel, slammed the door and put the truck into gear. The vehicle skidded around in a slew of mud and gravel, then shot down the driveway toward the road.

Schafer was struggling to breathe, his face pale and sweaty. She had to stop the air from leaking into his chest cavity, or his lung could collapse and send him into cardiac arrest. Since he'd stayed behind her to protect her during the run to safety and she was pretty sure he wasn't involved in any of this since he'd been the one who was shot, she didn't want him to die.

She scrambled over the console and leaned in to wrench the glove box open. Rifling through it, she tossed aside a couple maps and a flashlight, then spied the insurance papers and a roll of duct tape.

Jackpot.

She grabbed the tape and tore off a large piece of the thin plastic envelope holding the papers. Lifting Schafer's arm, she pressed the plastic tight over the wound to seal it and prevent any air from entering, then used her teeth to rip three pieces of duct tape. After wiping the blood away, she taped the top and sides of the plastic tight to his skin, leaving the bottom open to allow for a one-way valve.

Once she was sure it was staying in place, she pressed his arm against it and turned him slightly onto his side to ensure optimal function in his undamaged lung. "Better now?" she asked him, using her thigh to anchor him in place. It was the best she could do under the circumstances, and she hoped it bought him enough time for them to reach a hospital.

"Little," he managed.

She braced a hand on the roof to steady herself as the truck bounced and jostled its way down the gravel driveway.

"Here." Wade reached back to offer her his jacket. She took it and covered Schafer, then put pressure on the wound in his calf and met Wade's eyes in the rearview mirror. There was nothing more she could do for Schafer. He needed a chest tube and a trauma team, STAT, to protect his lung and get the bleeding under control.

Wade looked away, back to the road in front of them, expression grim. "Hold on tight," he warned.

Erin braced herself and Schafer as Wade slowed the truck at the end of the driveway then made a sharp, quick left and gunned it.

Chapter Seventeen

Wade pinned the accelerator to the floorboard. The ancient truck—beast had to be damn near forty years old—grudgingly responded, slowly gaining speed but not as quickly as he'd like. Adrenaline surged through him, the urge to escape intensified because of Erin. She was innocent in all of this and those fuckers had tried to take her out anyway. Raw fury burned through his veins.

He sped down the country road in the opposite direction of the safe house. In the rearview he could see the bright orange flames licking up the siding and onto the roof, but luckily, so far no one seemed to be following them. His mind raced as fast as the struggling engine as he sped down the road, wipers swishing fast to clear the torrential rain. A sniper and an RPG?

A stop sign appeared through the gloom up ahead. He glanced in the rearview at Erin. "How's he doing?"

"Hanging in there. How long to the nearest hospital?"

Too fucking far. "Not long," he lied for Schafer's benefit, though even through his shock he had to realize it.

"My wife," Schafer wheezed. "Daughter."

"Shh," Erin said. "Don't talk now, just concentrate on taking those small, shallow breaths like you were doing. As soon as we can get you to an emergency room we'll get you a decompression and you'll be able to breathe easy again."

Wade's jaw tightened as he slowed to make the right turn that would take them toward the highway. Whatever Erin had jury-rigged seemed to have worked for now, but it might not be enough. He was convinced Schafer was truly innocent now, but it still didn't make any fucking sense. No way could anyone have found their location without either being dirty, or getting help from someone on the inside. Robert had sounded tense and grim when Wade had talked to him on the phone earlier and promised to assist them in any way he could. By now he'd already be at headquarters. Local cops would be on their way out, Robert would be assembling a response team and digging into what the hell was happening.

Wade hit the brake to slow for the turn. "Hang on." The bald tires squealed and slipped on the wet pavement as he cranked the wheel. The back end of the truck swung out in an arc as he took the corner hard and straightened it out. Thick stands of trees and field flashed by. An amber light flashed up ahead at the next intersection where a gas station and convenience store stood on one corner. Beyond that it was a straight one mile shot to the highway.

The old engine revved with a high-pitched whine as the vehicle picked up speed once more. He didn't let up on the gas when he neared the intersection, barely saw the dark SUV hurtling toward them at a ninety-degree angle before it shot through the light and wrenched into a hard right turn.

Wade swore and veered to the side just in time to avoid impact. Erin gasped and slammed back into the window. A second SUV screeched around the corner and gave chase behind the first one. Was this the backup he'd been counting on? Sweat bloomed on Wade's face and chest when the second vehicle remained behind the first. More bad guys. Must have been watching during the sniper episode and followed when they'd run. There was nowhere to go but forward and the old truck was too slow to evade the SUVs, which were already gaining on them.

"You okay?" he asked tightly.

"Yeah," she muttered, rubbing the back of her head as she repositioned herself over Schafer to brace him and looked out the rear window. "What are we going to do?"

He hated the thread of fear in her voice because he couldn't do anything to stop it. "Buckle up tight. This is gonna be close."

She didn't say anything, just scrambled to buckle Schafer in before doing up her own seatbelt and leaning low over him.

Wade scanned the terrain around him, willing the truck to go faster. Ditches ran on either side of the two-lane road. There were no more places to turn until they hit the on-ramp. If he tried a one-eighty now he'd likely roll the truck and kill them all. The shrill pitch of the engine grated on his tautly stretched nerves—

The rear window exploded in a shower of glass, the bullet tearing through the windshield mere inches to the right of Wade's head. Erin cried out. He ducked and swerved, the back of the truck fishtailing before he regained control. Wind and rain blasted through the fist-sized hole left in the windshield, the safety glass already fracturing outward from it in a huge spider web. *Fucking hell.*

"Stay down," he snapped at Erin, just as another round impacted back in the bed somewhere. He stuck his head out the driver window so he could see. The sign for the highway appeared on the shoulder. A quarter mile.

Keeping his foot pinned to the floor, he steered the truck back and forth to try and avoid any more shots. When the on-ramp finally appeared up ahead, the SUVs were less than fifty yards behind them. Wade took the ramp at full speed and cut in front of a semi, barely avoiding its front end. The rig let out a blast from its horn but Wade ignored it, desperately trying to weave his way through the light traffic and buy them some distance and time.

In the rearview the two SUVs were forced to slam on the brakes to avoid colliding with the semi. Wade seized the opportunity and cut into the far left lane, zipping in and out of slower traffic amidst the angry blare of horns.

The SUVs were still back there, but having trouble following now. Wade got into the center lane, waiting until he had enough distance to give them a shot at losing the SUVs to veer across two lanes of traffic and take an exit late—cutting off yet another car. The driver hit the brakes and fishtailed on the wet pavement, swinging it around in a wide arc. The car behind it did the same, causing the semi to jack-knife and block the exit ramp behind them, providing a temporary traffic snarl.

Thank you.

Pulling his gaze away from the rearview as the two SUVs skidded to a halt back at the exit, Wade blew the red light at the bottom of the ramp and turned right. He sped through the residential neighborhood, zigzagging his way through the streets toward another on-ramp. As he merged onto the highway once more, he didn't see any sign of the two SUVs behind them and pulled in the first deep breath he'd taken since that sniper had opened fire.

There were two routes to the highway from the safe house. Too much coincidence that the two crews of gunmen had both guessed right. So how the fuck had they followed them? Were they tracking them somehow? If so, this reprieve was temporary. His and Erin's phone were clean, he'd checked them himself.

His gaze cut to Erin, still leaning over Schafer in the backseat, her eyes wide as she stared back at Wade. "See if he's got a phone on him," he told her. He wasn't worried about a wire, since Erin would have noticed it when she examined and treated Schafer's wounds. Without a word she sat up and checked Schafer's hoodie and jeans, and pulled out a cell phone.

"Here."

Wade grunted. "Open it up and check for anything weird with the SIM card and battery."

"Hold on a sec." She fiddled with it for a few seconds before popping open the back compartment. He caught her frown. "There's something on the card." She glanced up at him, worry lacing those big green eyes. "About the size of a grain of rice, either metal or plastic." She pried it off and held it up between her thumb and forefinger for him to see.

Fuck. "Open the window and chuck the phone as far as you can."

Schafer made a sound of protest but she ignored it as she straightened and cranked the window down. The whistle of the wind increased and once it was open fully, she cocked back her arm and hurled the phone through it. Wade watched in satisfaction as it hit the shoulder and bounced off into the long grass.

So long, assholes.

"Didn't...know," Schafer gasped, and Wade believed him.

"Save your air, man," he told him, allowing himself to relax slightly even as a new knot formed in his gut. "Gonna get you help real soon." Someone at headquarters must have bugged the phone. Someone connected to the hit squad. And he had a sickening suspicion who it was. "Just another fifteen minutes or so."

While Schafer was getting treatment, Wade was getting some fucking answers.

****

Erin walked out into the waiting area to find Wade talking on his cell phone, likely to someone at the CIA. Soon after they'd arrived, the hospital had been flooded with federal agents and local police to secure the area and take their statements. Wade spotted her the moment she entered and gave a nod, but kept talking and didn't approach.

Not wanting to intrude, she stayed where she was. Wrapping her arms around her waist, she leaned against the wall, feeling uncertain. She didn't know who Wade was talking to though she knew it had to do with everything that had happened this morning. God, it wasn't even ten o'clock yet and it felt like she'd been up for twenty-four hours straight. Rubbing at her tired eyes, she drew in a deep breath and let it out slowly. So many things had gone down she didn't even know what to feel anymore.

"Hey."

She looked up as Wade stopped in front of her. "Hi." She tried a smile but it must have fallen short of its mark because he wrapped his arms around her and pulled her close to his chest. Shuddering, she returned

189

the embrace and buried her face in his neck, savoring his scent and the rasp of his whiskers against her skin. Up 'til now she'd held it together fine but it was like everything had hit her all at once and she couldn't find her footing.

"It's okay," he whispered into her hair.

She didn't know if he meant it was okay to cling, or if he was giving her permission to lose it here in the middle of the waiting room, but she knew he didn't mean everything was going to be okay. Thankfully he just held her while she pulled herself together and she relished every second of him holding her. When she felt steady again she raised her head and he relaxed his hold enough to shift her until she rested her cheek against his chest.

"How's Schafer?"

"Stable. As soon as they got the chest tube in and drained all the blood his vitals bounced back almost right away. They did x-rays and an ultrasound and nothing else showed up so he only needed minor surgery to stop the bleed in his chest. They're doing some stitches in his calf right now. They want him to stay at least overnight but he's refusing."

"Good, because he's not staying here."

At that she lifted her head and met his eyes. "Why not?" Were the gunmen still after them?

"We're going in to headquarters. I've got something I need to take care of there."

The hard gleam in his eyes sent a shiver of foreboding up her spine. "You think someone set us up?"

"I'm gonna find out." As he stared at her, his expression softened and he lifted a hand to stroke a thumb along her jaw. "You're amazing, you know that?"

A delighted smile tugged at her lips. "Yeah?"

He nodded. "Way tougher than you look, that's for sure, and you're quick on your feet. That was fast thinking with the duct tape and plastic. Bought him enough time to get us here."

She looked away, her face heating up at the praise. "Just lucky it worked." She rubbed her hand over the center of his chest, feeling his heartbeat steady beneath her palm. "You're the one who got us out of there and away from those guys."

He didn't answer, only slid a hand into her hair to gently explore the back of her head. She covered a flinch when he touched the lump from when she'd hit the truck window and his eyes darkened with anger. "I'm gonna find out who did this."

Erin swallowed at the buried rage in his voice, the black expression. "Please don't do—" She stopped talking when Wade looked to his left and she noticed the young nurse standing there.

"Miss Kelly? Your friend is asking for you. He's still insisting on leaving AMA."

Against medical advice. Big surprise. "I'll be right there." She looked up at Wade, raised her eyebrows. "You really want him to leave here?"

Wade nodded and released her. "For the best right now. Come on."

She followed him back to find Schafer in the process of pulling his bloodstained hoodie over his head. He grimaced as it pulled at his wound, that startling blue gaze landing on Wade the moment he stepped into the room. "Find out anything?"

Wade gave a mute shake of his head.

Schafer grunted and eased the hoodie down the length of his torso, covering the bruises and the bandage on his right side. "Still think I'm involved?"

"No." He said it so emphatically that both she and Schafer looked at him in surprise.

Schafer's shoulders lowered a bit, as though he'd been expecting the opposite answer. "So what now?"

"We go in and I talk to Robert."

Schafer seemed to weigh the words for a moment. "Sure that's a good idea?"

"I'm sure. You up to leaving?"

"Hell yeah," he answered with a scowl. "I wanna find out who shot me and nail the fucker."

One side of Wade's mouth curved in an approving grin. "Let's get the hell outta here then, huh?"

A couple Feds drove them to headquarters, where the guards at the gate called inside to verify their identities before letting them through. Once they entered the building and passed through security, Wade immediately took them down into a medical area located in the basement and told them to wait there.

Erin jumped up and grabbed his arm, following him out and shutting the door behind her to give them some privacy. He was leaving her here, just like that? "Where are you going?"

"Upstairs to talk to someone."

His voice was so grim, his expression so remote that it alarmed her. Were they even safe here? For all they knew someone in this very building had set them all up. "We don't know who was behind it. What if—"

He stopped her with a gentle finger against her lips and he looked her dead in the eye when he spoke. "I would never leave you here if I didn't think it was safe. Schafer's not in any shape to be up and about, let alone confront anyone, and he could still develop complications. I need you to stay here with him until I get back." The finger wandered across her mouth to trail across her jaw, his touch almost reverent, as though he couldn't get enough of touching her skin. "Okay?"

Everything he said made sense. Erin licked her lips and nodded. "You'll be careful?"

"Yes." He cupped the side of her face with his hand and leaned in to kiss her. His lips molded to hers in a tantalizing caress that belied the tension she could feel humming in his body. "I'll be back soon."

Watching him go, Erin couldn't help but think about how close they'd both come to dying today. She felt so much for him—more than she'd ever felt for anyone—and she didn't want to hold back anymore. He was absolutely worth the risk. The moment all this was cleared up, she was going to lay it all on the line.

And pray her heart wouldn't get shattered in the process.

Chapter Eighteen

With Erin as safe as he could get her for the time being, Wade rode the elevator to the director's floor and got off. After receiving instructions to wait for Robert in his office, Wade passed through security and strode down the office-lined hallway, his anger growing with every step.

People stopped and stared when they saw him and his bloodstained shirt. Wade barely paid them any notice, all his focus on the upcoming confrontation. Once he confirmed who was behind all this, he was going to rip him apart.

Robert's office was at the far end of the hall. Wade didn't make it that far.

He stalked to the fourth office on the right and threw the door open. Seated at his desk on a phone call, Bill's eyes widened as Wade stormed in and slammed the door shut hard enough to rattle the framed diplomas on the walls.

"I'll call you back," Bill muttered, and set the receiver into the cradle on the desk. He eyed Wade warily. "Problem?"

"Yeah." He took two menacing steps forward and planted both hands on Bill's desk, bending at the waist to glare down at him. "Did you set me up?"

Bill hesitated the barest second, a subtle tension taking hold of his frame. "I don't know what you're—"

He slammed his fist down on the desk, hard enough to make it vibrate. Bill's expression tightened. "Did you *set* me *up*?"

His mouth tightened and resentment flashed in his eyes. "Not in the way you think."

The fuck did that mean? "What the hell did you do? You were my goddamn handler. I got you everything you ever wanted—"

"Except Rahim."

Wade absorbed that for a second then shoved back from the desk. He would have given him Rahim, too, if not for the situation with the Sec Def, and Bill knew it. Wade folded his arms tight across his chest and forced in a calming breath, afraid he might vault over the desk and beat the ever living hell out of Bill before he got to the bottom of this. "Did you send a hit team?"

"No."

He wasn't convinced. "Did you send Schafer?"

"Yes."

"Did you bug his phone?"

"Yes."

The admission surprised him. "Why? You knew where I was." Then a disturbing thought occurred to him and the rage built again, yanking against the chains holding it back. "You wanted to set it up so it looked like he was the one behind everything?"

Bill's face and neck were slowly turning red, either from humiliation at being called out or anger from the accusation. Knowing him, probably both. "You don't know shit," he growled.

"Don't I?" He clenched his jaw, counted to three before responding. "I know somebody sent a hit team this morning with a fucking lousy sniper who had to resort to hitting the house with an RPG. I might've believed it was Schafer who'd orchestrated all that because of the timing when he just showed up like that, except for what happened afterward. He's downstairs recovering from a couple bullet wounds, by the way, one of which was nearly fatal, so I know it wasn't him."

At that, Bill's face seemed to pale slightly and the hostile gleam in his eyes turned to wariness.

The tiny bubble of hope that he'd been wrong about this burst inside Wade's chest. "Didn't count on him being alive and talking, I take it?"

Bill didn't respond, but he didn't have to. The lying, traitorous sonofabitch was behind at least some of this. "You fucking *asshole*," Wade snarled, and the tenuous hold on his temper snapped. He lunged forward. Bill shot out of his chair and hastily backed up out of range, putting the length of the desk between them.

Before Bill could say anything, the door flew open behind him. "What the hell's going on?" the director demanded, then stopped when he saw Wade facing off with Bill.

Wade straightened but didn't take his eyes off his handler. "That's what I was just asking Bill. And so far he's had some pretty interesting answers you might want to hear."

Rather than seem surprised, Robert grunted and stepped back. "Both of you in my office. *Now*."

In all his dealings with the director, Wade had never heard that tone from him before. Dark. Deadly. The back of his neck prickled with heightened awareness as he watched Bill round the desk and go out into the hall. He never took his eyes off the man, not even when they reached Robert's office.

Wade stood by the left hand wall, his back to it, gaze pinning Bill as the man sank into a chair positioned in front of Robert's desk. The director snapped the door shut and crossed to his desk, but didn't sit. Instead he stood next to it and folded his arms across a chest that was still plenty impressive despite him being in his early fifties, and darted a glance at Wade before turning his full attention on Bill.

"So where were you last night and this morning?"

Robert's question threw Wade as much as it seemed to throw Bill. Wade quickly focused on his handler, gauging his reaction.

"I stayed the weekend at my cabin," Bill replied tightly. He didn't fidget or sweat but Wade could tell from the tightening around his mouth and eyes that he didn't like where this was going.

"I don't think so." Robert's voice was even colder than his frigid expression as he stared down the man who had been one of his best officers.

A knock sounded at the door and it cracked open when Robert told the person to come in. Wade was surprised to see Erin and another man standing there with Schafer. Bill rose from his chair, slowly, and mimicked Robert's posture. Except instead of being intimidating, it was defensive.

Wade spared a glance at Erin, who helped Schafer into the other empty chair and stepped back toward Wade, casting him an uncertain glance that told him she had no clue why they'd been summoned here. Wade curled an arm around her shoulders and pulled her next to him, not giving a damn that the move was possessive or what anyone thought of it. He hated that Erin was about to witness the dark, ugly side of the covert world of espionage.

"I wanted them both present to hear everything, since they both almost died today," Robert continued. He glanced again at Wade then went back to glaring at Bill, who stood frozen in place, looking like a trapped animal. Wade realized that his pulse was racing, aware that they were all about to hear the unthinkable.

"You're close to retirement, Bill, and the Rahim case was going to be your send-off. But everything went to hell when the Sec Def got captured and Wade made the only call he could have. You couldn't let it go, couldn't stand the thought of not being the one to break the case and bring Rahim in. And when leads weren't turning up fast enough, you got desperate. So you decided to stop trying to bring Rahim in, and let him come to you instead." His eyes cut to Wade. "Using the bait you knew Rahim couldn't ignore."

Erin's gasp sliced through the deathly quiet in the room. Wade tightened his arm around her, taking comfort in her presence even as the truth of it exploded inside him. He'd trusted Bill—as much as he'd ever trusted anyone in this business, for a long time, and that's why it hurt so much.

You mean the same way Rahim trusted you?

Wade shoved that thought aside. They were two different things entirely.

Bill let out a short, humorless laugh. "You don't know what the hell you're talking about."

Pinning him with a withering glare, Robert called out to someone waiting outside. "Aaron."

At the mention of the name, Bill's face paled and he swallowed. Wade glanced at the door in time to see a young guy in his early twenties step into the room, looking nervous. He shut the door behind him and leaned against it, casting a guilty look at Bill.

"This is Aaron, one of Bill's hand-picked interns. Bill's had him making some interesting phone calls over the past few days, hasn't he, Aaron?"

The young guy swallowed and looked around helplessly, and it was obvious to Wade and probably everyone in the room that Aaron hadn't realized the magnitude of what he'd been doing, let alone the illegality of it.

"Turns out Aaron didn't think the calls were that secret though, since someone overheard one of them," Robert continued.

Wade's gaze shot to Schafer, who frowned and nodded in confirmation. "Yeah, I told Wade already." Schafer glanced up at him for affirmation, and Wade nodded to Robert.

The director cocked his head and studied Bill, who at last looked uneasy. "You had him call someone in Rahim's network, but you didn't tell him who it was. You had Aaron pass on little tips the network might find useful, knowing they'd eventually funnel up to the top of the food chain because they had to do with Sandberg, the agent formerly known as Jihad. Things like his travel itinerary from Bagram to Kabul and the location of the safe house here. You made Aaron believe he was passing on that info to someone on the security team, when in fact you were using him to help dangle the lure you knew would bring Rahim out of hiding."

In the taut silence that followed, all eyes were glued to Bill. He stood with his arms folded across his chest, face pale, body tense. He knew he'd been caught, but he wasn't going down that easily. Wade ground his back teeth together, careful to keep from squeezing Erin too tight as his muscles bunched.

"I didn't know if anything would come of it or how it would pan out," Bill muttered defensively. "I didn't know how they'd use the information, or if it would—"

"Shut the fuck up," Robert barked and Bill fell silent. A muscle jumped in the director's jaw and he seemed to struggle to regain his composure for a moment. "I'm not really interested, but anything else you wanna say? Maybe to the three people in this room you nearly killed this morning?"

Bill's nostrils flared but he didn't look away from Robert. "Not without my lawyer present."

Robert made a sound of disgust, picked up the handset on the desk and dialed a number. "Come get him." He'd just placed the handset back into its cradle when two Special Protection Officers came in to read Bill his rights as they cuffed him. In the vacuum of silence that followed after he was taken from the room, Aaron spoke up.

"I'm sorry," he said, looking at each of them individually. "I honestly thought I was telling the security team." He swallowed, took in the blood on Wade's shirt and Schafer's hoodie and jeans. Turning his gaze back to Robert, he frowned. "The security team. You said—"

"All dead," the director confirmed. He met Wade's stare. "Found the three others dead in one of their vehicles about a half mile west of the house."

Aaron sucked in a ragged breath and dragged a hand through his hair, looking shaken. "Jesus, I'm sorry. So, so sorry, I…" He trailed off, looking sick to his stomach and Wade actually felt bad for the kid.

"Go down to the conference room," Robert told him. "We'll need an official statement from you. And you, if you're up to it," he added, looking at Schafer.

"Yeah, of course," Schafer said, though it was clear from the looks of him that he should still be lying down in the medical area.

"Okay, then let's head down to—" Robert paused when someone else knocked on the door. "Come in."

The door edged open, revealing another employee Wade recognized but couldn't remember his name. The man nodded at Wade before speaking to Robert. "Something just came in. It's big."

Robert eased onto the corner of his desk and waved the man in. "Shut the door. This is Chris Pollock," he told everyone. "One of the heads of our covert ops division."

Pollock closed the door behind him and looked questioningly around the room, his brows drawn together in a frown.

"Go ahead. This involves all of them, so they deserve to know."

Pollock raised his eyebrows at that and cleared his throat, clearly surprised to divulge this kind of intel in front of civilians. "Probable hit on Rahim's location."

Wade stiffened and released Erin's shoulder, took a step toward Pollock before he realized what he was doing. "Where?" The word came out low, raspy, a surge of raw adrenaline punching through his bloodstream.

Pollock met Wade's gaze. "You Sandberg?" When he nodded, the man continued. "Intercepted a phone call about thirty minutes ago. From a ship entering a harbor here in Virginia, not far from DC. Low level radioactive reading on board from what we can tell, but the call was between two men speaking in English, and the voice print is almost a dead match for Rahim. Port authorities have been alerted and we're getting teams together."

Excitement raced through Wade's veins. Rahim was finally *here*, within reach. Wade could feel it. He wasn't letting the bastard slip through their fingers again. Not this time.

"How sure are you it's him?" Robert asked.

"Eighty percent," Pollock answered.

"What about you? You ready?"

Wade turned his head and met the director's cool stare. The man knew exactly how much he wanted this, what it meant to him, and that despite the fucked-up way Bill had gone about it, Wade was indeed the best bait for this shark. "More than."

Robert stood and nodded as though he wasn't surprised. "Come with Chris and me. Schafer, you go down to the conference room with Miss Kelly." He strode for the door. Wade hung back. Erin was bending to help Schafer up, but Wade took her by the arm.

She looked up at him, and the pain and fear he saw there hit him like a kick to the solar plexus. "Give us a minute," he said to Schafer, and pulled her out of the room. This far down the hallway it was quiet, and while they didn't have complete privacy, it was as much as they were going to get. The moment he closed the door behind him she stepped back and wrapped her arms around her middle in a gesture of self-comfort. Wade set his hands on his hips and tried to think of what the hell to say. There were no good alternatives.

"You're really going after him?" Her voice sounded small, uncharacteristically shaky.

He nodded, not knowing how to explain it to her. This thing between him and Rahim had always been personal. Now that he'd ordered a hit on Wade that had nearly cost Erin her life, it was even more so. "I know him best. He wants me almost as much as he wants to wage war on American soil. If he's here, I'm the strongest currency the agency has to bring him out of hiding."

She swallowed, blinked quickly a couple of times and it twisted his heart to know she was battling tears on his behalf. "So you're going to what, sacrifice yourself? Stand out there and offer yourself up as human bait so they can bring him in—"

Wade stepped up close and curved a hand around the back of her neck to silence her. She bit her lip and lowered her gaze, hitching in a ragged breath that tore through him. "It has to be me. Can you try to understand? The risk he poses outweighs everything else." Even his life, if necessary. He tightened his fingers slightly, desperate to get through to her, to make her see why it had to be this way. But goddamn it, he hated leaving her, hated going with all this uncertainty left between them.

He pushed out a breath and leaned his forehead against hers as the emotions bombarded him. Anxiety. Longing. An overwhelming sadness that this might be the last time he got to touch her. He didn't know what to do with it all. "I never expected to fall for you," he whispered, his throat tightening.

Her head jerked back and she stared up at him with those huge green eyes swimming with tears.

"I didn't," he insisted, feeling awed and bewildered at the realization that this woman meant so much to him. "You've made me feel things I never thought I'd—" He broke off, swallowing. Caressing her nape with his fingers, he cradled her cheek in his other hand and stared into her eyes. "It didn't matter to me before if I lived or not, so long as I got him, but it's different now. You matter to me, and I'm going to do everything in my power to come back for you. Okay?"

A tear slipped down her cheek, followed by two more, and his heart squeezed so tight that for a moment he couldn't breathe. Erin took his face in her hands, gently shook him once. "I love you, Wade. Do you understand that? I fucking love you, and I don't care if it's too soon to say it or if it freaks you out. It's how I feel, and if you don't come back I don't know how...I don't know how I'll..." She made a choked sound and flung her arms around him, burying her face in his chest as the silent sobs shook her.

Silently cursing at himself, Wade crushed her to him and pressed his nose into her hair. She was no doubt thinking about David and how he hadn't come back, and panicking that Wade wouldn't either.

He'd never expected her to say she loved him, but fuck, it filled him with such a fierce possessiveness that he thought his heart might explode. He'd only had two of what he'd classify as serious relationships before going undercover, and what he'd felt for both those women didn't even come close to what he felt for Erin. He wrestled with his own feelings, struggling to make sense of them all. If love meant wanting to protect Erin from anything and everything that tried to hurt her and wanting to wake up next to her every single day... If it meant not being able to envision a life without her in it and being willing to stand by her through everything that came at them, including taking a bullet for her, then yeah, he loved her. The realization shook him to the core.

"I'm coming back for you," he whispered fiercely. Part of him called himself out for being a chicken shit and not saying the words back to her, but he'd already bared his soul to her in a way he never had with anyone else. And he didn't want to say them now in case he didn't make it back from this. It would only make it harder for her to let him go. "I swear I will."

She nodded and clung harder, the strength of her grip surprising him. He loved the feel of her holding him so tight, pressed up against him like this, and wished they had more time.

"Sweetheart, I gotta go," he murmured, regret in every word.

Erin squeezed him one last time and leaned back to cup his cheek. Her eyes were still wet, her dark lashes spiky with tear stains on her cheeks. She was the most beautiful thing he'd ever seen.

I love you, sweetheart. His heart pounded with the fierceness of it.

Reaching up to take his face between her hands, Erin leaned up and gave him a tender, hungry kiss. Wade met it eagerly and drove his tongue into her mouth to taste her, caress her in this intimate way, hoping it wouldn't be the last time. When he heard voices behind them down the hallway, he eased back and brushed the tears from her cheeks.

"You look after Schafer for me," he told her. "I'll be back as soon as I can."

Biting her lip, she nodded, her eyes haunted by shadows he couldn't erase. "Hurry back."

"I will." If he survived the coming battle, he'd move heaven and earth to get to her side, and spend the rest of his life earning the right to stay there.

Chapter Nineteen

The rig rolled away from the docks with a rattle of its trailer and exhaust streaming from the stacks on either side of the cab. From his hiding spot amongst some pallets stacked behind a medium-sized warehouse on the busy wharf, Rahim watched it cross the railroad tracks and make the turn onto the access road. The two-lane strip of asphalt would take it directly to the highway and onward to its final destination. Letting out a relieved breath, he lowered the binoculars.

Port security had been every bit as tight as he'd expected. He'd purposely had the device hidden in a container full of medical equipment to lower suspicion if the authorities happened to check inside or scan it with their mobile x-ray unit for radiation. By now, someone had to know he was trying to get into the U.S. Luckily, his container hadn't been chosen for random inspection, likely because the importer the container was assigned to wasn't flagged in the U.S. database. And they definitely wouldn't be looking for a device in the food delivery truck he had waiting a few miles away. Some of his most trusted men were overseeing the transfer. He'd planted them months ago to work at the delivery company to ensure everything was in place. And now it was.

He checked his watch. Less than an hour from now, the tide of this war would shift. By then he'd be out of the port and on his first leg of the journey back to Pakistan.

And by then, Sandberg would be long dead.

He tugged his ball cap down low on his forehead and looked around, pulling in a deep breath of the cool, salt-tinged air. The docks were alive with activity, the cranes busy loading and unloading cargo from the four container ships docked here. Longshoremen drove forklifts as they moved cargo and supervised the loading of containers onto trucks. In the leaden sky that promised more rain, gulls and terns circled, their cries carried by the damp wind.

Stepping out from behind the pallets, he paused to let a forklift pass by, its driver barely sparing him a glance. Rahim smiled to himself. Everything had gone smoothly—far more smoothly than he'd ever dared hope. Customs officials had come aboard to check passports and do a search of the ship with sniffer dogs looking for drugs and bombs. Thankfully the container of medical equipment hadn't been flagged.

It had been a ton of work behind the scenes to get what he needed to pull this off. His network had outdone themselves this time, hacking into various sites to get him the necessary documentation to pass through the tight security, then digging into employees' backgrounds. They'd found someone here willing to take a bribe and look the other way while Rahim oversaw the loading of the container onto the truck because the man's daughter had leukemia and he needed the money for medical costs his insurance didn't cover.

There'd also been luck involved that the container hadn't been one tagged to be searched at random—luck he knew had come directly from Allah. It was His hand alone guiding Rahim from this point onward.

He glanced down the length of the dock at the ship he'd come in on. It was already unloaded and refueled, about to leave port. Originally he'd planned to sail with it into international waters, but he'd since changed things so that a private helo would pick him up aboard a different ship once they were an hour out of port.

His boots made hollow thuds on the wooden planks as he strolled down the length of the dock. When the burner phone began to ring in his front pocket, he pulled it out and answered it, careful not to look around or do anything else that might cause suspicion.

"It's me," Safir said in English.

Anticipation tightened his muscles. "What's up?" He turned sideways to squeeze between another forklift and a stack of pallets.

"How did the unloading go?"

"Great, no problems. How are things on your end?" He assumed that's why Safir was calling.

"Couple things have come up."

His focus sharpened on the conversation though he still maintained an awareness of what was going on around him. Safir must have news about the assassination. "Really?" A heady sense of anticipation bubbled up inside him.

"Heard back from a guy on the other crew. Apparently they missed the shipment."

Rahim stopped walking as dread sliced through him. "All of it?"

"Yes. But there was a lot of damage. Emergency crews are at the house trying to put out the fire. And there was someone else involved, apparently. A man."

Rahim frowned. "They don't know who he was?"

"No, he just showed up at the start of everything. He left with the other two.'"

The hit team had missed *all* of them? How was that possible? Where was the rest of the crew while the sniper had been engaged? He might not have had many options to choose from, Rahim had still hand-picked the crew, all American-born former military, and all willing to carry out the hit for the amount of cash Rahim had offered.

"Where are they now?" he asked, unable to keep the frustration out of his voice. He'd personally checked their backgrounds and credentials. There was no way all four of them could have let Sandberg, the woman and the stranger slip through their fingers, unless they were completely inept. For God's sake, he'd made sure they'd been supplied with a top-of-the-line sniper rifle and a rocket launcher. How hard was it to hit a house with an RPG? A freaking twelve year old could do it.

"The shipments? No idea. The crew's likely scattered, I would think."

Because the cops and likely some Feds or CIA employees were combing the area for them, now that Sandberg and the others had reported everything. Rahim's heart rate quickened and he resumed walking toward the waiting ship. "Is that it?" The bitter sting of disappointment filled him. He'd wanted Sandberg to die before this new phase of the war began. But maybe it was Allah's will to let him live to see it.

"No, there's more. I got an interesting phone call from our source a few minutes ago."

"What did he want?"

"They know where you are. The main shipment is on its way to the docks right now."

Rahim stopped and whirled, scanning the leaden sky above as his bravado evaporated. The cries of the gulls and sounds of the port surrounded him as he strained to listen for the thud of approaching rotors. Jihad—Sandberg, he corrected angrily—was coming *here*? In the wake of the shock of that piece of intel, the quick burst of elation he felt was smothered by a layer of fear. He hadn't expected this. Hadn't even anticipated it. Was that why Sandberg had escaped death this morning—so Rahim could deliver it by his own hand? Was this Allah's will at work?

"I've already contacted your driver," Safir went on, meaning the helo pilot. "He left about ten minutes ago and should be showing up within the half hour. I told him to keep the same pickup point."

Rahim heard the words but his mind was racing. If what Safir had been told was true, the port would be swarming with tactical teams by then. Even as he thought it, he noticed a group of security personnel dressed in black step out of a building partway down the adjacent dock. One of them was a dog handler, his big Belgian Malinois waiting calm but alert at his side. The men were looking at a piece of paper together, and Rahim knew it was an APB about him.

"I'll talk to you later," he said to Safir, and quickly disconnected. They could only trace his phone if it was on so he turned it off and shoved it back into his pocket in case he needed to call the pilot directly and change plans again. For now he needed to get out of sight and hunker down.

Tugging the brim of his cap even lower, he put his hands in his pockets and made for the ship waiting second-to-last in line. A sense of urgency drove him, made his heart thud in time with his rapid steps. He didn't see any security personnel at the ship yet, but the tingling at the back of his neck told him the danger was increasing. At least the truck had left port without any problems. Even if authorities suspected what was happening and were searching for radiation signatures throughout the city, the bomb's reading should be low enough that it was unlikely they'd find it in time to disarm it.

Everything hinged on that. If he died, so be it, but not until the bomb detonated. And not by some random bullet fired by a stranger. No. If he died here, it would be while taking Sandberg with him.

He showed his fake credentials at the ship and received permission to board. Other crew members—a mix of mostly Americans and Puerto Ricans—went about their business as he passed them on the way to his locker where he stopped to pick up a backpack before heading up to the cargo deck.

Once up there he found a good vantage point and hid himself behind the corner of a container to take another look with his binoculars. Sure enough, security teams were sweeping the port, slowly working their way from the access road toward the docks. Though he might be able to sneak past if he left now, it was unlikely he'd make it to the access road and find a vehicle without being noticed.

His chances of escape were dwindling by the second, yet he couldn't bring himself to run. More and more, this seemed like a test. As if Allah was testing his loyalty and how devout he was to Islam. He'd passed every one of those tests placed before him. This was his chance to truly prove how dedicated he was to this cause.

The security teams had a lot of ground to cover and a whole hell of a lot of places to check before they reached the ship, but he knew there would be more men coming, and once they fanned out he wasn't sure how much time he had before they boarded his boat.

No sooner had he thought it than an announcement came over the ship's PA system, announcing that all crew members were being ordered to go ashore while a security check was conducted. Rahim's mouth tightened as he hung there, deciding what he should do. Seconds later men began streaming down the ship's gangplank, and when he checked, he could see the same thing happening in the neighboring ships. Security agents dressed in dark fatigues converged in groups on the dock, assembling to begin the hunt.

Time to find a better hiding spot.

He was partway down an access ladder when he caught the faint throb of rotors in the distance. He froze, training his gaze on the sky. The thumping became louder and louder until the unmistakable silhouette of a helo broke through the low hanging cloud deck in the distance. Rahim stayed where he was as it came closer. Too early for it to be his ride out of here. Coast Guard? He watched it take shape, the sleek outline of a military-issue Blackhawk.

Hidden in the shadows, he pushed back the anxiety clawing at him and watched as it flew toward the ship, hovering over a clear spot near the bow on the main deck. Strong gusts of wind battered him from the powerful rotor wash. Shielding his face with one hand, he squinted as four men dressed in black fast-roped from the belly of the helo and slid to the deck. Rahim focused on each man in turn, and when the first one turned around, he held his breath.

Jihad.

His betrayer said something to the others then waved the helo off. Even though they couldn't possibly see him up here, Rahim shrank back against the cold, steel ladder, breathing fast. How had they known he was on this ship? Bracing his shoulder against the ladder, he shrugged off the backpack and took out the pieces of the rifle. His hands were slightly unsteady as he put them all together and loaded a full magazine into it. He shoved the four spares into the various pockets on his cargo pants and slowly climbed down toward the deck, ready to begin the hunt.

But first he had to find a way to isolate Sandberg from the others. This had to be between only the two of them. It was clearly what Allah wanted. Then Rahim would send him to hell where he belonged.

****

Wade knew Rahim was here. He could feel it.

Where are you, you slippery bastard?

They'd traced the cell phone signal from the dock, and based on the direction he'd been heading, this was the analyst's best guess as to what ship he'd boarded. Agents on the ground had already spoken to the crewman in charge of checking credentials, and he'd confirmed that someone matching Rahim's description had come aboard less than half an hour before. Teams of Feds and SWAT guys were already on scene, along with snipers and field agents from a half dozen other government agencies. HAZMAT and military personnel were being dispatched also.

He was horribly aware that he was acting as human bait. Robert had had Aaron call his contact within Rahim's network again, to "leak" the intel that U.S. authorities knew where Rahim was and that Sandberg was part of a team being dispatched. They were all counting on that being enough motivation to make him stay and fight.

Standing on the deck of this ship with his three teammates, Wade felt like he had a neon sign blinking over his head.

Here I am, Rahim. Come get me.

They'd kept his team purposely small in the hopes of lulling Rahim into a false sense of security. All the guys were former Tier-One operators from either the

SEALs or Delta, and two of them were currently serving on the FBI's Hostage Rescue Team. They all knew the score: provide backup and assistance where necessary, but give Wade enough room to lure him out into the open. Upholding standard policy, Robert had been adamant in his instructions to Wade before boarding the Blackhawk with the others.

The CIA wanted Rahim captured alive, but that was laughable and they all knew it, so Wade hadn't made any promises he didn't intend to keep. The bastard would absolutely put a bullet in his own brain before allowing himself to be captured, and he'd take out anyone he could before then.

If it came down to either dying in order to bring Rahim in or taking him out and walking away to get back to Erin, he wouldn't even have to think about what his decision would be.

Knowing he couldn't afford to let thoughts of her distract him, Wade locked the door on his mental vault and focused on his quarry. He knew Rahim better than anyone. If he were in Rahim's shoes, where would he hide? It'd been a long, long time since Wade had trained to take down a ship. Even though there were teams already checking out the lower parts of the ship, Rahim currently held the advantage. He could be fucking anywhere on this monster of a boat.

Wade signalled to the others. They split into two-man teams and began methodically moving their way along the cargo hold. The containers were arranged in horizontal rows, each placed tight to the one next to it with no room for a man to hide between them, leaving only narrow corridors between the rows. Snipers positioned up on the crane platforms and other observation points had eyes on the ship and its cargo, and would alert him if they saw anything suspicious.

That didn't do much to ease the buzz of unease in Wade's gut.

He and his partner moved their way cautiously from row to row, receiving occasional updates from the teams sweeping the interior of the ship. Intel came in that the bridge was clear, as were the mechanical, medical and crew areas. Two other teams were moving up to the cargo deck to assist in the search, where they'd move toward the bow.

Wade and his team kept moving toward the stern. With the butt of his M-4 tucked firmly against his shoulder, he swung around and checked each alley created by the rows of containers.

"I got movement," one of the snipers suddenly said via the earpiece. "Eighty meters to your two o'clock. Zeroing in on that position now and will advise. Over."

"Copy that." Wade took a deep breath and continued forward, his muscles drawing tight as he braced himself for what was coming. The tactical vest he wore wouldn't save him if he was slower on the draw than Rahim. Wade had never seen him miss anything he aimed at. And right now it could be Rahim who had his crosshairs lined up on Wade's face.

His boots made hollow thuds against the steel deck despite his effort to walk softly, and to him they seemed to echo far too loudly.

"Sniper at your one o'clock!"

Wade instinctively dropped to one knee and swung the barrel of his rifle around just as a shot rang out and buried itself in the deck a foot away from his left boot.

Chapter Twenty

"**S***hit*." Wade jerked back and took cover behind the container.

"I don't have a clear shot, but he's pinned down in there," one of the other snipers reported. "You gonna move in and trap him?"

That would just end badly for everyone. Rahim would kill any and all of them he could before he died, but it was *him* he wanted more than anything. Even more than the chance of escaping alive. "No, give me time to draw him out," Wade ordered him. These guys were all pros and would hold off on taking a kill shot unless it was the only available option left. Wade prayed it wouldn't have to happen. They needed to know where the bomb was. Time was running out. "Anderson, you see him?" he asked one of the guys who'd gone around the other side of the containers.

"Negative. Has to still be in that corridor though."

"Copy." He spoke to the man behind him. "Cover me, but give me some room to flush him out."

"Roger that."

Even though he had plenty of backup and even though he'd mentally prepared himself to face this, forcing himself to move out into the open went against every one of his instincts. His mind and body were screaming at him to stay behind cover.

His sense of duty wouldn't allow it. Rahim was *his* responsibility and no one else's.

Taking several deep breaths to psych himself up, he got to his feet and mentally reviewed his next move. Calling on every bit of strength and speed he had, he overrode the warnings blaring in his brain and burst out from behind the container. He took two running strides and dove. Bullets thudded deep into the steel deck as he rolled and scrambled behind cover of the next container.

"Are you hit?" one of his teammates demanded over the earpiece.

"Negative," he panted, though it had been damn close. His heart was pounding like a jackhammer against his sternum and the adrenaline was pumping fast and hard through his bloodstream. Only two more rows of containers separated him and Rahim.

He got to his feet again, ignoring the tremor in his muscles as he made his way quickly down the corridor to the other side. "Coming out on your end, Anderson," he whispered. Rahim could only cover one end of the corridor at a time. Wade could only hope that he hadn't anticipated his latest move. *How do you want this to go, brother? Just you and me?*

He was putting everything on the line, betting that Rahim would be unable to resist the lure of going one-on-one with him. Too much hinged on this capture. Wade was ready to finish this.

On another desperate burst of speed he tore out from behind cover and sprinted for the next row of containers. Sunlight and shadow flickered past as he ran.

A burst of rounds blasted the air. Two tore past him close enough for him to hear the whistle of them and plowed into the container inches above his head. He was focused on the edge of the next container, timing the moment he would dive behind it when a sudden flash of movement came ahead of him from the shadows.

"He's at your twelve o'clock," a sniper reported.

Everything went into slo-mo.

Rahim emerged out of the shadows, his silhouette outlined against the rust-colored containers for a split second as he jumped to the deck. His boots hit with a solid thud. He turned slightly toward Wade, his expression hardening when they made eye contact. Both of them had their rifles up. Rahim fired as he whirled. Wade ducked but not in time to avoid the bullet that slammed into the lower portion of his vest. The round punched into his body armor like a sledgehammer, knocking the air from his lungs and dropping him to his knees. Pain tore through him as he let the momentum carry him to his belly. Fighting to drag air into his starving lungs, Wade brought his rifle muzzle up and fired two rounds at Rahim's running legs.

His aim was off slightly but he still managed to wing him in the calf. Rahim crashed down face-first on the deck. Over the roaring in his ears, Wade hauled himself to his feet and raced after him. Everything slowed even more. His focus narrowed to his quarry and the weapon in his hands.

Forcing himself to stop to steady his aim, Wade tucked the stock into his shoulder and pushed out a wheezy breath as he squeezed the trigger. A metallic ping rang out. Rahim yelled in pain as the rifle fell from his grip and clattered to the deck. Wade skidded to a stop and dropped as Rahim spun back to get it, his right hand bleeding from the bullet wound.

"Put your hands up," Wade called out in Pashto.

Rahim's vivid blue eyes flashed with raw fury.

"Holding on target," the sniper added. Wade blocked out the distraction and the knowledge that his teammates were all waiting for the order to engage, dying to get into the action.

"You're surrounded," Wade continued, his voice a breathless rasp as he fought past the pain throbbing in his belly. Only a few dozen yards stood between Rahim and the stern of the ship. The bastard knew he was surrounded, that his only option for surviving was to surrender.

They both knew he'd never do it. Still, Wade had to try.

They'd narrowed down the bomb's location to one of seven possibilities. But they didn't know which one, and they didn't know how long they had to find and disarm it. If Rahim planned to do the suicide by cop routine, Wade had to somehow get that vital piece of intel from him first. "There's no way out. Give it up, brother." The last word came out by habit.

Rahim stared back at him, pure hatred in that familiar, chilling gaze. His lips peeled back over his teeth in a feral smile that said he was looking forward to what would happen next. "Just you and me finish this," he rasped back. "And you're not my *brother*."

A chill snaked down Wade's spine at the venom in those words. Before he could take a single step Rahim's uninjured hand flashed down and came up with a pistol. Wade reacted instantly, dropping to one knee to get out of the line of fire. A searing pain hit his left forearm a split second before he squeezed the trigger again, knocking off his aim just enough that the bullet skimmed Rahim's right upper arm as he whirled and raced for the stern.

He distantly registered the blood trickling down his arm and dripping from his wrist. A taunting shot. Rahim knew the leverage he had over Wade and the others, and that all the firepower in the world couldn't get it from him if he died.

Rahim wanted this up close and personal, the two of them locked in a death struggle. And as it was the only way Wade could get what he needed, he had no choice but to give it to him. Erin's face flashed through his mind. Her warm, loving smile lighting up the darkest parts of his heart and banishing the ghosts and regrets he carried with him. The sooner he got this over with, the sooner he could get back to her.

Rage and icy determination filled him as he stared at Rahim.

Let's do this.

Letting out a guttural roar, Wade surged to his feet and tore after his enemy.

****

They needed him alive.

They'd confirmed it the moment Rahim had taken that first shot and no one had returned fire. They needed him to find out where the bomb was, and he was the only way to make that happen.

Grim resolve curved Rahim's lips into a smile as he ran. Even if he survived what came next, he would never reveal the bomb's location, not under any form of torture.

It didn't matter that he was outmanned and outgunned. Even as they congratulated themselves on cornering him, he had still won.

With that burden lifted from him, he felt suddenly lighter, stronger. His boots pounded against the steel deck, the reverberations ringing up through his wounded leg, in time with the throb in his bleeding hand. He barely felt the pain. He was more than ready to die and become a martyr for Islam. And Allah was rewarding him by ensuring he would get his final wish—a battle to the death with the man who had betrayed him.

The thud of rapid footfalls behind him told him Sandberg was close and gaining. It didn't matter. They weren't going to shoot him in the head. Weren't going to risk wounding him badly enough for him to die. They were willing to allow Sandberg to sacrifice himself, and likely many others, in the hopes that they could capture him. The hairs on the backs of his arms stood on end as goosebumps raced across his skin. Sixty feet away, the stern of the ship loomed. He raced straight toward it without slowing, anticipating the moment when Sandberg caught up to him.

Another shot rang out. Pain exploded in his left shoulder. The impact knocked him off his feet. He gritted his teeth against a cry of pain as black dots swarmed his vision. His chin glanced off the deck as he sprawled out on his stomach. Rising above the agony, he rolled onto his side and reached for the pistol he'd dropped. A heartbeat later, a heavy weight slammed into him. The back of his head bounced off the steel, momentarily stunning him.

He distantly heard the clatter of a weapon then Sandberg was on him. All his reflexes kicked in, his body in full survival mode, giving him an almost supernatural strength he'd never felt before. He grabbed hold of the powerful forearm shoved against his windpipe and twisted to the side in time to avoid a hook to the jaw. Sandberg hissed in a breath as his fist connected with the deck instead, and in that split second Rahim went on the offensive. He drove his knee up, hitting Sandberg where the round had impacted the vest.

Sandberg grunted, his forearm slipping sideways off Rahim's throat. Rahim bucked and flipped them over, reversing their positions. His weight landed hard on Sandberg and he used it to his advantage, pressing his left elbow into the wound on Sandberg's forearm. Face turning red from the pressure around his throat, his enemy's eyes filled with silent fury and a resolve Rahim had to respect. They heaved and twisted, bodies deadlocked as they grappled for superiority in this desperate struggle.

The pain began to bleed through the haze of rage and adrenaline. Rahim's muscles shook with the strain.

"Where's the bomb, asshole?" Sandberg growled in English.

It was the first time Rahim ever heard him speak it. He gritted his teeth and let out an answering snarl, enraged all over again that this man had duped him for so long. He'd trusted him, implicitly and without reservation. The pain and humiliation of it was more than he could bear. He was going to inflict it all back and then some before he died. "Fuck you," he managed past the sudden restriction in his throat.

Feeling his strength beginning to wane, he dug down deep and twisted with all his might. An angry roar tore out of him as they rolled. Sandberg scrambled to stop them, his boots slipping on the deck. Rahim kept pushing, inching them closer and closer to the side. Finally they reached the tipping point and went over the edge. A moment's freefall, then they hit a small platform on the rear starboard part of the ship. The impact knocked them apart and squeezed the breath from his lungs.

Move, move!

He narrowly avoided the elbow to the head as he jerked to the side. Lashing out with his boot, he connected with Sandberg's kneecap, a spike of elation flashing through him at the man's pained shout. Sandberg lunged for him and again Rahim rolled them, ready to take Sandberg over the edge and into the freezing gray-green water below.

The veins in Sandberg's temples stood out as he struggled to hold him down, nostrils flared and mouth pinched into a flat, white line in the midst of that dark beard. Rahim flailed in the unbreakable grip, the pain of his wounds and the fatigue sapping his remaining strength. Sandberg's powerful arms contracted even harder, squeezing against his windpipe, obstructing the flow of blood through his carotid arteries.

"Tell me where it is!" Sandberg demanded, his whole body quivering from the effort of holding him down.

The bomb should be close to the target already. Only minutes until it detonated.

Rahim laughed and went lax in the brutal grip.

Sandberg stilled in surprise for an instant. He shifted his weight off him, giving Rahim just enough time to snatch the knife from the sheath at his hip.

He watched Sandberg's eyes snap toward the matte black blade, widen. He flashed out a hand to ward it off, but Rahim drove the KA-BAR upward, slicing through clothing and flesh as it ripped through Sandberg's thigh and hip. The man yelled and caught Rahim's wrist, wrenching it backward in a brutal grip until the bones snapped. His own howl of agony rent the air.

With his remaining strength he twisted once again. He lost his grip on the knife. Ignoring it, he focused solely on pushing Sandberg the remaining few inches off the platform. Their gazes locked. Rahim read the determination in Sandberg's face, the rage and the unexpected flash of regret.

Too late for that. "I *trusted* you!" he bit out, glaring up at him. Rahim was going to send him to hell where he'd suffer endlessly for his betrayal in ways Sandberg couldn't even imagine.

Baring his teeth, steeling his resolve to meet his death bravely, he bellowed his rage as he wrenched his body sideways, yanking Sandberg with him. Sandberg's eyes widened, the knowledge of his death registering there an instant before his arm flashed up in a desperate bid to find a handhold. A deep, hideous pain exploded low in Rahim's belly. They both froze as his agonized scream ripped through the air. It paralyzed him, suffocated him.

Sandberg shoved him onto his back and scrambled to his knees, his gaze cutting to the handle of the knife protruding from low in his abdomen. "Fuck!" he snarled.

He couldn't let them take him. Refused to be locked up for the rest of his days. Suffering a few minutes' more of agony was far better than what he'd have to endure if he allowed them to take him alive.

Staring at the knife handle, Rahim battled through the haze of agony and gathered his remaining strength. In one last, desperate move, he grabbed it and tore it out of his body before Sandberg could stop him, tearing it sideways to slash through his bowel and as many arteries as possible.

"You fucking crazy bastard," Sandberg snarled, immediately pressing both hands to the wound and pressing down with his body weight to slow the bleeding.

The gesture was futile, and they both knew it.

Blood pulsed out from beneath the restraining hands. Already he could feel his body growing cold, weak. He didn't have enough strength to shove Sandberg overboard. A chilling fear began to take hold. He'd failed to kill Sandberg and now he was dying, before the bomb could go off.

As his mind floated he heard Sandberg snapping orders to the others, asking for paramedics and an airlift to the hospital. The pressure on his abdomen remained solid, and he jerked when strong fingers gripped his jaw, forced his gaze upward. Sandberg's bottomless brown eyes stared down into his. "Where," he pleaded. "Just tell me where, damn you."

His answering laugh turned into a pained wheeze and he let his eyelids drift shut. "Never."

Sandberg cursed and issued more orders. Running footsteps. Urgent voices. Someone tearing open his shirt and pulling away the tactical vest. He barely felt the cool air washing over his bare skin, too immersed in the pain to care.

A hard hand gripped his jaw again. "*Gary*. You look at me, goddammit."

His eyes snapped open to find Sandberg still there above him, dark eyes boring into his, willing him to live. *Gary*. The name and identity he'd abandoned when he'd crawled his way out of that pit and into the light. Hatred and resentment swelled, enough to override the pain. "My name...is *Rahim*," he rasped, shaking all over. The paramedic next to him had the defibrillator ready. His heart would fail soon. Only a few more minutes...

He didn't know how much time passed before Sandberg sucked in a sharp breath and his head snapped up. "*What?*" The word came out strangled, his face paling beneath the dark stubble as he stared toward the dock. Then his eyes snapped to Rahim's, full of horror and disbelief.

And in that instant, he knew.

A slow, satisfied smile spread across Rahim's face. He wanted to laugh in joy but didn't have the strength. "I...win," he whispered. Victorious, despite their every effort to prevent it.

Cold swept through him in an arctic blast, obliterating the temporary warmth of victory. His heart lurched then stilled. He felt his eyes bulge, his mouth opening as his throat worked, desperate for air. As though from a great distance he heard the urgent voices around him, felt the paddles placed on his chest. In that last moment of consciousness he stared up at the clouds, where his spirit would soon soar to meet the God he'd served with such devotion.

Chapter Twenty-One

"You're gonna wear out your lip, doing that."

Realizing she was biting her lower lip again, Erin glanced up from the dial of the sphygmomanometer and offered a guilty smile at Schafer. "Sorry."

"Don't be. Was just an observation."

She squeezed the bulb to re-inflate the blood pressure cuff and went back to studying the gauge. A few moments later she pulled her stethoscope from her ears and draped it around the back of her neck. "One-oh-five over sixty," she said, tearing the Velcro apart and removing the cuff.

He looked pleased about that as he sat up, albeit gingerly and with a wince as he put a hand over the bandage on his side. "Not bad, considering I've got a hole in my chest and a lot less blood than I had a couple hours ago."

"Yeah, but you should still be lying down."

"Nah. Besides, it hurts less when I'm upright."

She bent to peel the edges of the tape away from the bandage covering his right side. "Sutures are still holding nicely." She straightened and smoothed the tape back into place. "Just don't overdo it, okay?"

He gave her a devilishly charming smile that made his blue eyes sparkle. "Okay."

Though she doubted he'd do what he was told—she'd learned long ago that alpha males were the very worst patients in the entire world for compliance—she nodded and set her hands on her hips with a sigh. "Now what?" His vitals were all surprisingly good and there was nothing else she could do for him. Someone had escorted them both to the medical area here at headquarters after Schafer had given his official statement in the conference room earlier. Since then they'd been stuck in here while Schafer had rested and she'd checked his vitals every half hour.

"Might as well sit down and make yourself comfy," he said.

She couldn't sit—she'd explode. It'd been over two hours since Wade had left her outside Robert's office. No one had told her anything, except to say they'd update her when they could. Meaning they weren't going to tell her anything until it was all over. She understood why, she just didn't like it. Cooped up here and worrying about Wade heading into a deadly situation was slowly driving her insane.

She dragged a hand over her face, fighting back the memories of losing David that kept slamming into her brain. But no matter how much she told herself that this time would be different, she couldn't shake the sick, helpless feeling inside her that she'd never see Wade again.

"Hey. Come on and sit down over here," Schafer coaxed, patting part of the cushioned table next to him.

Giving in, she scooted up beside him and idly swung her feet back and forth.

"So how long have you known Wade?"

She glanced up at him in surprise. "Not that long. Why?"

He shrugged, winced as it pulled at his wound. "Never seen him like this with a woman, that's all."

She frowned. "Like what?"

He met her gaze. "He's seriously into you, in case you hadn't noticed."

She'd noticed. She was still tingling inside from the urgent tone in his voice when he'd told her he'd fallen for her, and hoping there was more to it. "Yeah, well, I'm seriously into him too."

Schafer's dark eyebrows rose. "So, how long have you known each other?"

"Less than a week, actually."

He let out a low whistle. "Wow, that's...wow." Then he chuckled as though he found that incredibly amusing.

She frowned harder, feeling suddenly defensive. "I know it's fast and maybe it sounds unbelievable, but it's what I feel."

He held up a hand. "Hey, not bashing you for it. Just never thought I'd see the day when Wade went all territorial alpha over a woman, that's all. Pretty cool to watch it happen, to tell you the truth. I know how fast it can happen." His wide shoulders moved in a shrug. "My wife and I met at a wedding and eloped three weeks later."

She smiled, glad he wasn't judging her and that he was providing her with a badly needed distraction. "Really?"

He nodded. "My friends and family thought we were insane. This line of work is hell on marriages, but it's been nine years and we're still together. Our daughter turns seven this year. I'd been planning to make a point to be home more and cutting my overseas time starting next month. This just pushed the timeline up, is all." He nodded toward his bandaged side.

She loved how his whole face softened when he talked about his family. "I love hearing that." Because if she and Wade made a go of things after this, they'd be facing a lengthy separation almost right away, and God knew where Wade would land up after this op or what he'd wind up doing in terms of his career once this was all over. Certainly undercover work in the Middle East was out for him after this deadly drama with Rahim.

He's coming back, Erin. He had to come back. She couldn't go through that again, and what she felt for Wade was already way more intense than what she'd felt for David. Swallowing, she changed the subject. "What about you, how long have you known Wade?" She knew their relationship hadn't exactly been easy over the past few years, but she was still curious. Wade thought enough of him that he'd believed Schafer's innocence, and he'd risked his life to get him to safety.

"We met during SF selection," Schafer said, shifting a little on the table. "We were close, but we had a solid rivalry going. Somewhere along the way it went from friendly to not so friendly." He stared at the opposite wall as he spoke, as though he was lost in memory. "I don't know what he's told you about me, but I wasn't always an asshole."

"Well, no, not if you used to be friends," she teased, nudging him lightly with her shoulder, careful not to jar him.

A half-smile curved his mouth. "We used to one-up each other every chance we got, but on a mission we were tight. Real tight," he added, an almost wistful note to his voice. "It was afterward, when we got out of the Army and started contract work that it all turned to shit."

Erin stayed quiet, not wanting to interrupt him. She was curious to hear Shafer's version of it, see if it meshed with what Wade had told her.

"There was this one night mission in the tribal region. We got in a tight spot. I was team leader on that security detail and I...made the wrong call. Guys died. The client, two of our guys. Others were badly injured. Wade took over and got us out. I resented the hell out of him for that later." He paused, a muscle flexing in his jaw. "It took me a long time to admit what I knew deep down was the truth—I'd screwed up. I didn't want to have those guys' deaths and injuries on my conscience, but yup, the fault lies with me and no one else. If Wade hadn't gotten us out we'd have all died out there that night." He looked down at his hands, clenched tight around the edge of the table. "I'm gonna tell him that when he gets back. It's long overdue."

Erin looked away and swallowed, fear thickening her throat. Wade was out there right now risking his life to bring Rahim in. *Please let him stay safe.* She glanced up at Schafer when he laid a hand over hers, the comforting gesture taking her by surprise.

His face was solemn. "He's good. As good as operators get. He's so fucking talented, Erin, and in so many ways I could puke from jealousy." He smiled when she laughed at that, but then his expression sobered. "He knows what he's doing, and he'll be watching out for himself. He's gonna do everything he can to do this and get out of there."

Yes, and Rahim was also the most lethal enemy Wade had ever faced. The whole situation was emotionally intense for him. She hated that he was the one being forced to draw Rahim out. "But he won't let this go until it's over, one way or another." She knew it without a doubt. It was what he wanted, needed, what he'd worked for so hard and so long.

Schafer conceded the point with a nod. "Yeah. But you wouldn't want him to be any other way."

No, she wouldn't, Erin realized. She'd seen that steely, honorable core in him almost right away, and it was a big reason why she'd fallen so hard and so fast for him. She drew in a deep breath, let it out slowly. "You're right."

"I know," he said, and she couldn't help but smile at his smug tone.

"Thanks, Schafer. I appreciate you talking me down from the ledge. It's just that I…lost someone a few years ago who meant a lot to me. The situation was totally different, but he was a soldier too, and he didn't come back."

"I'm sorry."

She lowered her gaze. "Thanks." Expelling a breath, she looked over at him and offered a smile. "When this is over and you're healed up more, I think you, Wade and I should have a night on the town together. For old times' sake. And new ones."

His eyes warmed as he smiled at her. "I'd like that. And I've already told you three hundred times, call me Brady."

"Fine, Brady it is. So, since you seem up to it, wanna make that call to your wife now?"

"*Love* to," he said, his expression earnest.

Happy to give him at least this, Erin slid off the exam table and handed him her cell phone that they'd already received clearance to use. She pointed her thumb over her shoulder at the door. "I'll just…"

"Thanks."

"I'm gonna grab something to eat." The thought of food wasn't appealing when she was so worried but she hadn't eaten since last night. "You want anything?"

He paused in the midst of dialing the number. "Sure, whatever you're having would be awesome. Appreciate it."

"No worries." Pulling the door shut behind her, she headed down the brightly lit hallway to a coffee bar she'd seen earlier. It only reminded her of when she'd found Wade standing puzzled in front of one upstairs, and when she'd poured him a cup in the safe house kitchen. A sudden lump lodged in her throat.

Deep breath, Erin. He's gonna be fine.

She was a third of the way down the brightly lit hallway when a loud roar shattered the silence and the world suddenly exploded around her.

****

Wade straightened on his knees and stared out at the dock, his whole body rigid with denial at Robert's unexpected announcement over the team earpieces.

The bomb had detonated. Where?

Erin.

His heart had shot up so hard and tight in his throat it felt like he was choking on it. Rahim would have chosen an important target, one that would make the biggest statement and have the biggest impact. A government building maybe, or something strategically important. Had the bomb gone off anywhere near her location? Had the radioactive material contaminated anything, and was she in the fallout zone? Next to him the paramedics were using the defibrillator again but he knew Rahim only had seconds left, his half-closed blue eyes already staring sightlessly up at the leaden sky.

Too late. You're too late to stop any of it now.

He'd failed on every level. He hadn't been able to bring Rahim in alive or find out the bomb's location or intended target.

Closing his eyes, Wade dropped his head and exhaled a ragged breath as a crushing sense of defeat slammed into him.

"Is he still alive?" Robert demanded in a curt tone, jerking Wade back to the present.

He didn't need to get the paramedic's confirmation to tell him what his gut already knew. "No."

"God*dammit*. All right, pull back and let the clean-up crew in."

Wade pushed to his feet on unsteady legs. He was bleeding from the slice in his thigh and the furrow in his arm burned like hell but the pain barely registered above the guilt and fear engulfing him. How big had the blast been? In a highly populated area, even a relatively small device could rain devastation. He turned away and frantically scanned the dock. Security and medical crews were swarming the area. The radiation threat scared him even more. He was trapped on this fucking boat with no way to get to Erin and it iced up his insides. He needed to hear her voice, know she was okay and tell her to stay put until he could get to her.

Putting a hand to his earpiece, he searched the crowd for a familiar face and spoke to Robert, needing answers before he fucking lost his mind. "What's happened? What have you heard?"

The director responded a moment later. "We've confirmed that a bomb went off outside CIA headquarters a few minutes ago."

His heart stopped beating. "*What?*" *No.* It couldn't be.

"It was hidden in a food truck. It stopped in a loading bay and the driver detonated it. Heavy damage to the lower floors on the south side of the building. Mass casualties reported. No idea yet if the radiation leaked or not. Crews are responding now."

The medical area was in the basement on the south side.

His stomach pitched and rolled, bile burning the back of his tight throat. Oh, fuck, he was gonna be sick. "Erin," he croaked, aware that he was breathing too fast, that he was shaking all over and couldn't stop it. She needed him, might be hurt, and he couldn't fucking *get* to her. He sucked in an unsteady breath, forcing back the panic clawing at him. "I need you to call her—"

"Already had someone try and there was no answer," Robert said. "I've got a helo inbound to pick us up, ETA twelve minutes. Meet me at the bottom of the gangplank. The pilot will fly us in as close as possible to headquarters, but everything's gonna be shut down tight. With the radiation threat I can't guarantee we'll even get near it."

"You gotta get me in there." Wade didn't care how the director made it happen, just as long as he did. Wade had to get to Erin *now*.

"I'll do whatever I can, but I can't make any guarantees. Now move your ass and get down here." Robert disconnected.

Everything faded out. The noise around him disappeared. Frozen inside, Wade cast one final glance down at Rahim's body before turning away, a curious sense of numbness stealing through him as he looked at the man he'd protected with his life for the past few years. There was nothing. No grief, no regret that Rahim was dead. Only the horror and regret that he hadn't been able to protect Erin and prevent the bomb from going off. Oh, Jesus, he couldn't handle the thought of her hurt, maybe dying or even—

A wounded sound tore free of his chest, terror and grief crushing his lungs and heart.

One of the medics caught his arm as he turned away. "You're bleeding pretty badly. Let me take a look and get you bandaged up."

Wade shook him off with a warning snarl and limped away as fast as his wounded leg would allow, hurrying through the stream of people rushing toward the stern. Two of his teammates caught up with him. They each banded an arm around his waist and hustled him through the crowd, down the gangplank. Wade spotted Robert immediately, standing with his own security team as he spoke on the phone.

The director's gaze dropped to the blood streaming down the leg of Wade's fatigue and he put a hand over his phone long enough to say, "Get that patched up before the helo gets here."

He didn't want to get patched up—didn't want to waste a single fucking second waiting here when Erin needed him—except there was nothing he could do but wait for the helo, and he needed to stop the bleeding if he was going to be any help in the rescue effort. But inside his head, his mind screamed.

He prayed silently, an endless litany in both English and Pashto. Since getting kicked off the case he'd felt lost, a man between worlds without a home, but now he knew exactly where his home was. With Erin.

Don't take her. Please, anything but that.

"Here, use this."

He looked up at Anderson, who handed him a phone.

"Hope you get through to her."

Right. His teammates would have overheard everything he and Robert said. Wade thanked him and dialed Erin's cell number. It rang and rang then went to voicemail. He tried a text, waited endless minutes for her to answer while the medic stitched up his hip and thigh. The gash was deep but he was bleeding way worse on the inside. Dying little by little as the seconds ticked past with no response. The repeated prick of the needle was nothing compared to the torture of wondering what had happened to her as he waited for her to reply.

But no answer came.

His pulse drummed a hard, terrified rhythm in his ears. *Come on, sweetheart. Give me something. Tell me you're okay.*

He didn't think he could live with the alternative.

Wade looked up from the phone when Robert pushed his way through the circle of emergency responders a few minutes later. His face was grim, his dark eyes unflinching as they locked gazes. A block of ice settled in Wade's gut, every muscle in his body snapping taut as his instincts screamed in denial.

"Damage is bad," Robert told him. The distant throb of rotors rose over the noise on the dock, mixing with the roaring in Wade's ears. "The lower portion of the south side has collapsed, and the entire area's been contaminated with radiation. No one's getting in or out until HAZMAT can clear the area."

Chapter Twenty-Two

Disoriented, Erin opened her eyes to find herself locked in a waking nightmare.

Dark. Trapped.

It was pitch black and she couldn't move. Something was pinning her in place. *Hard, cold.* Sealing her in a concrete tomb.

No! Panic blasted through her, robbing her of the ability to think or breathe. The terror was all consuming, paralyzing. She automatically struggled to break free of her prison when a sudden jolt of pain tore through her left forearm in a vicious, searing bolt that stopped her cold. Her breath froze in her lungs.

Through the blazing pain, her brain slowly came back online. Other things began to register.

Her head ached, her ears were ringing and she was pretty sure her left arm was broken. She didn't know how long she'd been unconscious, she only remembered heading for a coffee when the walls had suddenly imploded.

Trapped. Think. Have to get out.

Pulse racing, she tried moving again. She was wedged between what felt like two slabs of concrete. Being unable to see or move intensified the claustrophobia. Her mind instantly took her back to that cold, black mine shaft, immersing her in a suffocating panic. All her old fears came up to haunt her, closing her throat off as though someone was choking her.

No. Stop it. You have to think.

After some wriggling she managed to pull her legs up and use her feet to push her body into a better position. Her heart was slamming so hard against her ribs it made her nauseous, her breath rushing in and out of her starving lungs in a constant hiss of air that seemed overly loud in the unnatural silence. She ached and throbbed all over, the worst of the pain in her left arm and the back of her head. "Hello?" she called out in a shaky voice.

No answer. Only a faint echo. Nothing moved.

She swallowed, fought back the terror that threatened to drag her back into screaming mindlessness. "Hello!" Her shout was absorbed by the debris around her. "Can anyone hear me?" Her voice shredded on the last word, tears of horror and fear flooding her eyes. She couldn't go through this again, trapped and alone in the dark. Craning her head back, she frantically scanned her surroundings. There was no light, not even a sliver of it to give her some bearings. She was trapped alone underground with no way out.

"I hear you!"

She froze at the muffled shout that seemed to be coming from her right. "Where are you?"

"Medical room."

She sucked in a breath. "*Brady?*"

"Erin! Thank God. Are you okay?"

She licked her lips, the rush of relief making her light-headed. She wasn't alone down here. They'd work together to find a way out. "I think my arm's broken. You?"

"I'm...pretty banged up."

His words made her go even colder, because for him to admit that meant he was hurt bad. "Can you move?"

"Not much. You?"

"No, I——" She wiggled around, using her right arm to feel her way along the seams of concrete. Her fingers found a gap. She traced its edges, cradled her busted left arm against her chest as she struggled to maneuver her way toward the hole. "I'll try to come to you," she called back. Had he damaged his lung more? "Can you keep directing me with your voice?"

"Yeah. Take it slow—no telling when something might shift."

She shuddered at the thought of being crushed to death by a slab of concrete, or worse, lying pinned beneath it while she died of internal bleeding. "Slow's all I can do anyway," she answered back. "Can you see anything?"

"Can't see jack. You?"

"No." She had no idea how much of the building had caved in around them. And they might be completely sealed off from the outside, which meant these pockets of air might be all they had. If the air ran out... *Stop it and move.*

Digging down deep for her mental discipline, Erin inched her way along the rough concrete wall beside her. She had to twist onto her back to push head first into the opening she'd found and squeeze through, the whole time terrified she'd become trapped or be crushed in the rubble. Every movement hurt. Jagged shards of pain splintered through her broken arm with each shift of her body. The uneven edges of the concrete scraped against her clothes and tore through her skin. She hissed in a breath when a sharp piece of rebar sliced into her leg as she dragged her way along.

"Say something so I can follow your voice," she called out. The pain and terror would overwhelm her if she let it. Keeping it at bay right now was the hardest thing she'd ever done.

"Think I'm to your right."

Sounded that way to her, too. She crawled closer, feeling her way. The debris angled up sharply for a few yards. She inched her way up, used her feet to feel a route down. A shower of dust rained down on her, small bits of concrete pelting her. She coughed as the dust hit her lungs, squeezed her eyes shut. "Have you got my phone still?"

"Dropped it. My arm's pinned...can't move it."

His voice was getting closer, even though it was still muffled. She slipped and wriggled her way through whatever opening she could fit through, moving blindly through the darkness and praying she wouldn't fall into a hole or bring anything more down on top of them. "Brady?"

"Still...here."

The strained quality of his voice registered. *Oh, shit, his lung.* "Okay. Don't talk. I'm coming. Just hold on."

"Yeah."

Her foot hit another barricade. Her right hand felt along the wall, finding another gap. She drifted her fingers along its edge, snatching her hand back when she unexpectedly encountered human flesh. Immediately she grabbed for it again. Fingers. A hand. Still warm. She gripped it, gave it a little tug and recoiled when it came loose in her hand.

"Shit!" She flung it away in reflex, her skin crawling with revulsion. Not even all her medical training could have prepared her for a grisly shock like that, here in the stygian darkness. Her stomach rolled. How many others were dead or dying in here?

"What's...wrong?" Brady demanded.

"Body," she answered, gritting her teeth and pushing herself forward. *Body part.* She knew there had to be many more trapped in this mess. "I'm getting closer. Your voice is clearer."

She knew she and Brady were lucky to have survived the explosion at all, let alone the collapse. Officials obviously hadn't found the bomb in time. Had Wade found Rahim? Was he okay? Did he know headquarters had been hit and was he coming for her? Holding firm to the hope that he had, she pressed onward.

Fresh cuts and scrapes stung and burned all over her, the pain of her fractured arm covering her in a cold, clammy sweat. She edged over another broken wall and slid down it on her backside like a ramp. Too fast. Afraid she was going to plunge to her death, she shot her right arm out to grab at whatever she could find to slow her descent.

She winced as she caught something, its sharp edge slicing her palm open. She'd stopped, but the blood made her grip slip, making it impossible to hold on. Swallowing a cry, she fell and plunged to the ground. Her feet hit something solid, her legs crumpling beneath her. She landed on her hands and knees, a thin scream ripping from her as the fractured bones in her left arm buckled under the impact.

"Erin!"

She rolled to her side and cradled her left forearm against her body, the pain stealing her breath. It consumed her for long moments until at last it ebbed enough for her to suck in a shallow, shaky breath.

"Erin...answer me!"

"H-here," she called back, trembling all over. Fighting through the haze of agony enveloping her, she refocused on the direction of his voice. It had been close. Almost directly beside her. And below her. "I'm close."

"Up and...to my left."

Turning onto her back, she used her legs to drag herself down the slight incline to where his voice seemed to be coming from. It wasn't pure black anymore. Some tiny light source was still getting through because there was just enough illumination for her to make out the faint impression of the jumble of debris in the area. Lots of concrete, but plaster too, and what she thought was office furniture.

"How about now?" she asked.

"Close." It came from under her, close to where she was standing.

Crouching down, she felt around as her eyes adjusted, hungrily drinking up that tiny bit of illumination. With her feet she shoved the moveable bits of debris away.

"Dust," Brady managed, and she understood she'd shifted something that was raining dust down on him. He was right beneath her.

Hope rose so hard and swift it formed a painful knot in the center of her chest. Her right hand sifted through the rubble, searching for a gap. And found one. "Can you lift your arm up?" she asked, lying on her side to stick her arm through and move it around. Seconds later, she made contact with warm flesh. And this time when her fingers curled around the hand, it didn't come loose. "Gotcha," she told him, closing her eyes in relief.

"Hey," he said, giving her hand a squeeze. "How...deep are...we?"

Holding tight to his hand, she turned her head and squinted above them. A long slab of concrete lay directly overhead, the broken and twisted spikes of rebar sticking out of its edges. Moving anything more risked bringing the rubble down on top of them. "Can't tell. It's lighter here than it was where I started from, but I can't see daylight."

Brady grunted in reply but didn't answer.

Stretched out on her side, cold and hurting more badly than she ever had in her life, Erin clung to that hand and prayed a rescue crew would find them. "Let me know when your arm gets tired," she told him, grateful when he squeezed in reply. Having him close helped take the edge off the claustrophobia.

She didn't know how long they stayed like that. Her right arm was completely numb and Brady's had to be too, but he didn't let go. Every so often one of them would squeeze the other's hand as a reminder that they were still together. Erin suffered through the pain, trying to escape somewhere else in her mind. She thought of her parents, her friends, but mostly she thought of Wade. If he was alive and knew about the bombing, he'd be frantic to get to her.

"Wade'll find us," she mumbled, shivering from shock and pain.

A firm squeeze around her hand answered her.

She was so deep in her own thoughts as she struggled with the pain that it took her a few moments to realize the voices she heard were coming from above them. The muted wail of sirens had never sounded so beautiful.

She raised her head, a renewed surge of hope flooding her as she stared above them. "Rescue teams," she told Brady. She could definitely hear them, hear a low rumble up there. She licked her lips. "I'm gonna let go now, so I can try to get their attention." When he squeezed in reply she let go and painfully climbed to her feet, every muscle protesting the movement.

"Can anyone hear me?" she shouted, craning her head back to direct her voice at the ceiling of debris. "There are two of us trapped down here!"

No answer.

Frantic, she searched around her for something to make noise with. Her fingers landed on a loose piece of rebar. Grabbing it, she carefully climbed her way up the few feet she needed to reach the bits of rebar sticking out of the concrete slab above them. She hammered at it, using the metallic clang to signal anyone above ground. Three rapid strikes, three spaced ones, three more quick ones. Over and over she repeated the pattern.

SOS. SOS. SOS.

She kept going until her arm ached and her fingers were numb from the grip around the steel rod. Desperation drove her, kept her going long after her muscles had exhausted themselves. *Please hear me. Someone please hear me!*

Something wet dripped onto her cheek. At first she thought she was crying, but then another drop landed on her forehead. She stilled, tilted her head back as yet another drop hit her face. Not tears. Rain.

Knowing that daylight had to be just above the slab overhead, she swung the rebar with renewed strength.

SOS. SOS. SOS...

A shaft of light suddenly appeared above her. She dropped the rebar, raised her hand to shield her eyes even as a cry of relief broke from her. "I'm here!" she screamed.

"We hear you!" a voice shouted back, much closer than she'd even dared hope. "Are you alone?"

"No, there's a man here too. He's trapped below me and badly injured."

"What's your name?"

"Erin. Erin Kelly."

"Stay where you are, Erin. We'll come down and get you. Everything's gonna be okay now."

Erin dropped to her knees in the rubble and let the tears come. Sounds of people and heavy machinery moved around above them. She went back to the hole and laid down to put her right arm through it. "You still with me, Brady?"

His hand found hers, locked tight. "Good...job," he managed.

She gave a watery laugh and held on to him. The shaft of light became brighter and brighter, and then scuffling noises reached her.

"Erin?"

She released Brady's hand and stood. "Over here." Straining to see in the darkness, her heart leapt when the beam of a headlamp flooded the space.

"She's here," the man called back to whoever was outside.

More shuffling, the rattle of bits of concrete as they fell through the rubble, disturbed by whoever was moving around up there.

"*Erin!*"

Her breath snagged in her throat at the sound of that familiar, deep voice. "Wade?"

She heard his exhalation of relief. "Sweetheart, I'm coming to you. Stay there, okay?"

She reacted without thinking. A sob tore free and she launched herself toward the opening above her. Her feet scrambled over the slippery layer of debris overlying the concrete. A figure dropped down through the opening, the silhouette backlit against the bright daylight streaming in from outside. She reached for him. Strong arms caught her, came around her and pulled her to a tall, hard body.

Wade.

"Fuck. Oh, God, baby, it's okay now," he whispered raggedly as he held her close, his voice strangely muffled.

Two things registered at once through her dazed mind as she tipped her head back to look at him. Wade really had found her.

And he was wearing a HAZMAT suit.

Chapter Twenty-Three

Wade was frantic by the time they got Erin up and out of the rubble. He lifted her through to the emergency worker above ground and quickly scrambled through after her. She was covered in blood and a fine powdery gray dust, cradling her left arm against her body. The skin was split wide open halfway up, the jagged end of a bone showing through.

Shit.

Boosting himself through the hole in the rubble, Wade took Erin from the man holding her and bundled her up against his chest. He ran for the nearest medical tent, cursing the damn suit they'd made him put on before entering the scene. "You're okay," he panted, the stitches in his wounded leg burning as he raced to the tent.

Her eyes were dilated, her entire body shaking from shock and cold as she took in the scene of utter chaos and devastation around them. People dressed in HAZMAT suits were everywhere, along with heavy equipment and armored vehicles. Military and civilian units alike had converged on the scene. Victims were being dragged out of the rubble from the remains of the building and the surrounding blast area. Already a row of bodies had been laid out beside one of the medical tents, covered in plastic tarps. Survivors were streaming in for treatment, needing decontamination and medical care for blast and crush injuries.

"Brady's still down there," she mumbled against his shoulder.

"They'll get him, don't worry."

"He's hurt b-bad." Her voice was hoarse.

"They'll get him out," he repeated, focused only on getting her help.

"Is there radiation?" she managed through chattering teeth.

He couldn't lie to her. "Yes."

"Oh God." She curled tighter into his chest and closed her eyes.

"It'll be okay." He'd goddamn *make* it okay.

She remained silent as he burst into the tent and a team descended on them. Though he hated to let her go, he handed her over and let them take her into a decontamination area while someone checked his suit. He stood with his arms out and his legs apart while they looked him over.

"You've got a hole here," the woman said to him, brown eyes worried as she looked up at him through her plastic mask.

He glanced down and behind him to see a tennis ball-sized hole at the back of his leg. Ah, shit. Must have caught it on a piece of rebar on the way down to get Erin. Resigned, he headed back to the shower stall and started stripping off the protective suit and his clothes.

A blast of cold water hit him and two people entered the stall to scrub him down with strong soap and water. His wounds stung but he didn't care, too busy worrying and caught up in his fear for Erin. Nobody knew how much radiation had been leaked with the initial blast. He could still lose her if she'd been exposed to a high enough level of it.

Terror punched through his chest and wrapped around his heart, squeezing it in a relentless grip. He forced it back, reminding himself that she didn't appear to show any symptoms of radiation poisoning yet, so the exposure might have been minimal.

Someone handed him a towel. He dried off as they scanned him for radiation, the Geiger counter giving a low-level reading. After throwing on some scrubs, he hurried to the back of the tent where they were treating Erin. They'd wrapped her up in a blanket after washing her and laid her on a cot amidst several other patients.

A restraining arm blocked his way. "Sir, you'll have to wait out here."

"I'm going in with her." He shoved past the man without hesitation, intent on getting to Erin.

Her face crumpled when she saw him. Wade cursed and knelt beside her bed, grasping the hand she reached out for him. They'd bandaged her left arm to slow the bleeding and started an IV, but he knew she needed surgery to repair the severe fracture. She had to be in agony and it tore at him.

He caught the back of her head in one hand and cradled it to his chest, bending to press his cheek against her wet hair, feeling helpless. The sting of antiseptic soap burned his nostrils. "It's gonna be okay now, sweetheart. I'm staying right next to you."

Her fingers gripped the front of his scrubs as sobs ripped through her. Unable to do anything, he closed his eyes and stroked her hair as he held her. He didn't know how much time passed before they finally rounded up an ambulance to transport her to the hospital, but when they arrived there it was clear the facility was completely overwhelmed by the large influx of patients.

Minutes after entering, staff took Erin away for more treatment and tests, and a doctor ordered a battery of tests on Wade. He submitted because he had to, and because it was the quickest way for him to get clearance and access to Erin. After his tests they told him she was being prepped for surgery, so once he was done with his blood work and given medical clearance he went and sat in the hallway outside the O.R, as close to her as he could get.

While he was waiting, he got word that they'd brought Schafer into the E.R. Wade found him, standing back as the team examined him and did some initial treatment. Both his legs were busted up bad, and he wasn't breathing well, but he was conscious and alert. A nurse snapped the curtain around his bed closed. Moments later, a guttural cry of pain emerged from behind it. When it opened, Wade stepped inside.

Schafer was pale and sweaty as they bandaged up the hole in his right side again. "Fuck I hate chest tubes," he muttered, wiping a hand over his glistening face.

Wade stood beside him and set a hand on his shoulder. "How are you otherwise?"

"Beat to shit, man." He focused on Wade, scanned his body quickly before meeting his gaze once more. "You get him?"

"Yeah."

"Good. Hope the fucker burns in hell."

That made two of them.

Schafer looked down at his bandaged legs where the blood had seeped through. "Ah, fuck. Guess I won't be taking Penny dancing when I get home."

"Not for a while," Wade agreed. "Anything I can get you?"

"Yeah, a phone. I was talking to Pen when the bomb went off. She's gotta be freaking out."

"I'll call her for you. Anything else?"

Schafer nodded, reached up a hand to wrap his fingers around Wade's wrist. He squeezed tight. "Your girl's fucking amazing, man. She held her shit together through all that, crawled her way to me through all that mess and banged out Morse code with some rebar to get the rescue crew's attention." Admiration glowed in his eyes as he shook his head. "Tell her I owe her."

Wade's throat tightened at the thought of her doing all of that while trapped in the darkness. It had to have been hell on her, reliving that old terror. "Tell her yourself later. She's on the operating table right now getting the orthopedic surgeon warmed up for you." He patted Schafer's shoulder and the other man released his wrist. "Gimme your number and I'll go call Penny. I'll check on you later."

After making the call and assuring Schafer's wife that he was going to be okay, over an hour passed before someone came out to tell him Erin was finally in recovery. He insisted she be taken up to a room to recover and after some arguing, he got his way. They put her in a semi-private room they'd equipped with plastic barriers to prevent further radioactive contamination. When she opened her eyes, he was right beside her.

"Hey, sweetheart." He smoothed the dark tangle of hair back from her forehead, struggling against the urge to cry as he gazed down into those beautiful green eyes. "Doin' okay?"

She swept her tongue across her lips and glanced down at her casted arm, then around the room. Seeing the plastic visibly rattled her. "How bad was the exposure?" Her voice was raspy from the intubation, but he heard the edge of fear in it.

He pulled a chair over and lowered himself into it, took her right hand in his. "Minimal. The bomb was dirty, but more explosives than radioactive material, and the prevailing winds carried most of what was released out to sea within a few minutes. Being underground when it happened protected you from the worst of the blast wave and the radiation. Your levels measured at point eight grays, so you're good."

The furrow between her eyebrows told him she wasn't convinced. "What about you?"

"My levels were even lower than yours."

She seemed to sag in relief at that, her eyes closing as she pulled in a slow, shaky breath. Then her eyes snapped open in alarm and she swallowed hard, putting a hand to her stomach.

"You gonna be sick?" When she gave a jerky nod, Wade frantically looked around for something to use and grabbed a pressed cardboard tray from a shelf over her bed. He handed it to her and she latched on with both hands, her grip made awkward by the cast covering half her left one. Before he could do more than put a hand on her back to support her she starting retching. And retching. And retching, until there was nothing left to come up and she was dry heaving.

Finally she stopped and dragged in a gulp of air. He dumped the tray into the garbage and found a facecloth to dampen in the sink. He got some water for her to rinse her mouth with, wiped at her face as she trembled and gasped for breath.

Finally she relaxed and allowed him to help her back against the thin pillow. Her skin was pale and sweaty, her eyes wide and full of terror as she stared up at him. "What if it's radiation sickness?"

Her fear cut through him like a white-hot blade. He slid a hand beneath her nape, squeezed gently as he held her gaze. "Even if it is, you're still okay. Your levels were low. It's been five hours since the bomb went off, so if the exposure had been severe the symptoms would have started a long time ago. The vomiting could be from the minimal dose you received, but it could be the anaesthetic and shock, too."

She absorbed all that for a moment and nodded. "You're right, and I know all of that, but...God. I can't stop jumping to the worst possible conclusion." She exhaled and seemed to sink back into the bed, clearly exhausted.

She'd also been through hell, and no one could blame her for fearing the worst. "You should sleep."

Her eyes opened. She ran her gaze over him in a thorough way he recognized, paused when she noticed the bandages on his left forearm. She'd flipped straight into nurse mode. Tensing visibly, she sat up, her eyes full of worry as they flashed up to his. "Oh my God, I didn't even ask—What happened? Did you find Rahim—"

He stopped her by laying a finger against her lips. "Yes." He didn't want to talk about it or think about it right now. All that mattered was her, and keeping her calm and safe through this.

She searched his eyes, kissed the pad of his finger before curling her hand around his and holding it to her chest as though she was afraid he might get up and leave. He had no intention of budging from her side until he knew for certain that she was going to be okay. "What's that, then?" she asked, nodding at the bandage.

"Flesh wound. It's nothing, I'm fine."

Frowning as though she didn't believe him, she met his gaze once more. "And Rahim?"

"Dead."

She didn't flinch at the blunt delivery but her eyes filled with sympathy. "Were you the one who…"

He nodded, dropped his eyes to their joined hands because he couldn't bear to hold her gaze any longer. "It was…intense." His emotions were a roiling mass in his chest. Guilt. Regret. Anger. Bitterness.

Shit, his throat was starting to tighten up again.

"I'm sorry, that must have been awful," she said softly. "But I'm so glad you're okay. Come here."

Knowing she needed the comfort, he didn't protest when she slid an arm around his shoulders and pulled him down so that his head rested against her shoulder. But then a strange thing happened. As he lay there, some of the tension melted away and he realized he'd needed this as much as she did. The steady thud of her heartbeat reassured him. She was alive and safe and that's all he cared about. Except until now he hadn't let himself think about what had transpired on that ship, the deadly struggle on that platform; he'd been too worried about Erin. Now everything flashed back to him like a movie on fast forward. He closed his eyes and pressed his cheek harder into her, tears burning the backs of his eyes.

"I couldn't get it out of him," he whispered roughly. "I had him pinned underneath me and still couldn't find out where the bomb or the target was." And she'd paid for it, along with many others. "I'm sorry I couldn't stop it." He'd done his best but it hadn't been enough. The guilt was already eating him alive.

"Hey." She squeezed him once, then pressed a kiss to the top of his head before stroking her hand over his hair. "Wade, it wasn't your fault. *He* planned all this, not you. You did everything you could to stop it, including risking your own life in a way I don't even want to think about because it'll give me nightmares for the next ten years. I'm just glad you're safe."

He let out a hard exhale, letting her words flow through him. She might not blame him, but he wasn't sure if he could forgive himself. He'd brought all this down on her. Twice today she'd nearly died. She'd suffered too much.

"They brought Schafer in while you were in surgery," he said, knowing she'd be worried about him. Her soft heart was one of the things he loved about her most, and it also scared the shit out of him because it made her vulnerable. He wanted to protect her from everything and everyone.

Yeah, great job you did at that.

"That's great news."

Wade nodded and slapped away the derisive voice in his head. "I think he'll be going into surgery soon to get his legs set. They were both busted up pretty bad. He told me what you did, said you were amazing and asked me to tell you he owes you."

"He doesn't owe me anything," she grumbled in annoyance, still stroking his hair.

Wade hated to think of her trapped beneath all that rubble, scared and alone. "That must have been really hard for you down there."

She swallowed audibly. "Yes. But I kept thinking of you, and I knew you'd come for me if you could."

Meaning, if he lived through the op to bring down Rahim. Which he almost hadn't. "When I heard the bomb went off at headquarters, I—" He paused to wrestle his emotions back under control before continuing, soaking up the tender way she held him. "I've never been that scared before in my life. Ever. Because I didn't know what I'd do if I lost you."

"I felt exactly the same way, waiting for word about you. And after the explosion when I woke up in the darkness and was freaked out of my mind, thinking about you gave me hope." Her voice caught on the last word.

Raising his head, Wade met her gaze, his heart squeezing when he saw the tears standing in her eyes. He brushed them from her lower lashes before they could fall. That they were both still alive after everything that had happened today was a fucking miracle. He didn't intend to waste a moment more of it.

"I love you."

Her expression softened and the tears spilled over, faster than he could catch them. She wrapped her arm around his back and buried her face in the side of his neck. "I love you too. And don't you ever scare me like that again, running off to save the world by offering yourself up on a silver platter to the most dangerous terrorist on the planet."

No, he wouldn't be doing a repeat of that anytime soon. Once the dust settled he'd be in some intensive debriefings and meetings. Hell, he didn't know what he'd be doing after this was finished, but he knew he wanted it to include Erin.

Smiling, thanking God that she was alive and in his arms, Wade hugged her tight. "Deal." No matter what happened next, he knew he could never let her go.

Chapter Twenty-Four

Five days later

Erin sank onto her parents' leather couch in the family room and let out a tired sigh. It was only a little after nine but it felt like it was two in the morning. Considering she was still running on Eastern time, that wasn't far off. The familiar, comforting sounds and smells of home surrounded her. She was finally where she'd wanted to spend her leave…except it didn't feel right now that she was separated from Wade.

Her parents' nine year old shepherd-lab mix, Hairy, hopped up on the couch and curled up on top of Erin's feet. Idly she reached down to stroke the dog's soft ears, earning a contented sigh from him in return. She'd always adored him but ever since she arrived home this time he'd seemed to pick up on her inner turmoil and stayed close, as though to comfort her.

"Sure you're up to a movie?" her dad asked, ensconced in his favorite recliner across from her.

"Yes, just don't be offended if I nod off partway through." She liked having company around. The night before, all alone in her room in the guest cabin, she'd barely slept. It had been stupid to stay alone after what she'd gone through but she'd hoped the solitude would help her unwind. In reality, it had done just the opposite.

Her arm had bothered her despite the pain killers she'd taken, but it was the nightmares that were the worst. They were more like flashbacks than dreams, and so vivid they'd jerked her out of her fitful sleep a handful of times, leaving her heart pounding and her body soaked with sweat. Tonight she didn't want to be alone and planned to camp out on the couch once her parents turned in.

Her mother came in from the kitchen with a bowl of fresh popcorn and a glass of iced tea. "Move over." She nudged Hairy aside and curled up on the opposite side of the couch, her feet touching Erin's.

Erin laid her head back against the buttery soft leather and tried to focus on the movie, but she was too tired to concentrate. The stress of the past few days had finally caught up with her and combined with the lack of sleep and uncertainty about her and Wade's future, she knew she was crashing.

It had taken two days to finally get clearance to leave the hospital, and another to travel here to Montana. Wade had to stay in DC for debriefings and other security clearance protocols, then he had a whole bunch of meetings to attend about Rahim and his network. She didn't know when he'd be finished or what he'd be doing next, let alone when they'd see each other again. That didn't help the constant buzz of anxiety in her stomach.

They spoke on the phone every night, and though he played it cool she could tell he was physically and mentally exhausted. It still wasn't easy for him to open up to anyone, not even her, but he was gradually letting her in even more, little by little. The latest intelligence Wade had relayed to her said the immediate threat from Rahim's network was over, but the ongoing one was not.

Now that the war had been brought back to U.S. soil, the tide had shifted irrevocably. Everyone was on edge. The cleanup effort at the bombing site was an enormous undertaking and very expensive. Officials had rushed to downplay the danger and the threat level to the public. But Rahim's operatives and others like him were out there, actively looking for an opportunity to strike.

Sighing, she snuggled deeper under the throw quilt her mother always kept draped over the back of the couch. A gentle hand rubbed up and down her calf. "Need anything?"

"No, thanks," she murmured, and let her heavy eyelids drift closed. It felt good to be home, and awesome to spend time with her parents again. They'd listened patiently to everything she'd told them about Wade and the bombing, though certain things about Wade's past and his job she'd kept to herself for security reasons. Her mother had fussed over her and Erin had been more than happy to let her.

The nausea she'd experienced that first day at the hospital had continued right through until morning, then dissipated. It hadn't bothered her since, but now she was constantly fatigued. The doctors said it was likely more from stress and exhaustion than mild radiation sickness, and she hoped they were right. Thankfully her levels were normal, her body having already absorbed or shed any of the radioactive particles she'd been exposed to, and she hadn't experienced any other symptoms. Right now the worst thing was that she missed Wade so much it hurt.

Hairy sighed again and rested his chin on her thigh. Shifting her cast against her hip to make her arm more comfortable, she let herself drift, secure in knowing that she was safe and surrounded by her family.

She woke sometime later when Hairy let out a low woof. Erin sat up, blinking groggily. The TV was still on but her father had paused the movie. "What's wrong?" she muttered, rubbing at her eyes. Hairy jumped down and ran to the window, ears perked, tail up.

"Someone's here."

Fully awake now, Erin leaned back to peer through the gap in the curtains behind the couch. A pair of headlights swung around as the vehicle parked at the top of the driveway next to the garage. Her father got up and went to the door, opened it with Hairy at his side. She couldn't see who it was, but she could hear their footsteps crunching against the gravel at the base of the porch steps.

"Evenin'," her father called out.

"Hi, Mr. Kelly."

Her heart leapt. She'd recognize that deep voice anywhere.

"Wade!" Vaulting off the couch so fast her mother gasped and spilled popcorn everywhere, Erin raced for the door. Her father stepped aside, a big smile on his face, but she barely noticed, her eyes all for the man coming up the porch steps. He was dressed in a dark leather jacket and jeans, and the grin he flashed her in the midst of the heavy stubble made her heart stutter.

"Hey, sweetheart."

With a glad cry, Erin flew across the porch and threw herself into his arms. Her cast thunked against his back, sending a flare of pain up her arm, but she ignored it. Wade caught her with a good-natured grunt and chuckled, his arms closing tight around her. She thought she might burst from happiness as she clung to him, drawing in the scent of leather and spicy soap. "What are you doing here?" she asked against his neck.

"Finished up early this afternoon, told Robert I needed a few days and caught a flight into Billings. Surprise."

Lifting her head, she beamed up at him. "Best surprise *ever*. Come in." She snagged his hand and drew him into the house. After introducing him to Hairy and her parents, his mother insisted on feeding him and they sat around the family room while he ate. He seemed perfectly at ease with them, which surprised her, given how tense and uncomfortable he'd been when they'd first come stateside a week ago. Already the adjustment was becoming easier for him. Unless he was just putting on a good show. Either way, she loved him to pieces for his effort.

Her parents must have guessed how much she wanted to be alone with him because they both bid them goodnight and headed upstairs to give them privacy, even though they were both nighthawks like her and usually stayed up until at least one. As they hit the stairs, Wade looked uncomfortable all of a sudden. "I should…probably head to a hotel now."

She almost laughed. He was so adorable, worried about offending her parents by staying with her. "Wade, I'm twenty-six, not sixteen, and they know how I feel about you. You can stay with me at the cabin."

His eyes lit up. "Cabin?"

"There's a guest cabin I use whenever I come to visit, about a half mile away. You can drive us there and save me the walk back."

Smiling, he reached up to cup her cheek in one broad hand and she leaned into his touch. "Missed you."

"Prove it."

"I plan to." Grinning, he pulled her to her feet. "Come on. You ride shotgun and navigate."

Though the idea of jumping him in the cab of his rental had its merits, Erin contented herself with pressing against his side and gliding her right hand all over him as he drove, mapping every muscular curve and dip she could reach. The pain in her left arm wasn't nearly as bad as it had been a few days ago but the cast was awkward and covered part of her hand. She was so damn hot for him already, her body achy and tingling at the thought of his mouth and hands all over her.

"You're playing with fire," he warned, his amused tone belying the hungry glint in his eyes when he looked over at her.

"I'm *stoking* the fire," she whispered back, coming up on her knees to nibble on his earlobe. They had lots to talk about and plenty of uncertainty to tackle, but that could wait. Right now she wanted to feel him naked against her, feel him slide deep and hard inside her and know she was his.

"Trust me, the fire doesn't need stoking." He caught her hand and pressed it to the rigid length of his erection jutting against the front of his jeans.

She'd left the kitchen light burning. The moment the front door shut behind them she grabbed him by the shoulders and pushed him back against the wall, ignoring how the cast encumbered her as she lifted up on her toes to capture his mouth with hers.

Wade gripped the back of her head with one hand and her hip with the other, jerking her tight against him as they devoured each other. She moaned into his mouth at the feel of his tongue gliding against hers, at the press of that hard, hot body. In between deep, searching kisses they peeled off each other's clothes, dropping them on the floor on the way to the stairs that led to the bedroom in the loft.

Naked, Wade swung her up in his arms and carried her upstairs to the queen-size bed set under the eaves. He laid her down on the sheets and came down on top of her, and in the light streaming in from downstairs, she saw the jagged gash on his hip and thigh. She gasped and pushed him upright with her good hand to see it better. The wound looked deep, and over a foot long. The stitches were red and raw looking. "What happened?"

"Knife," he answered, tugging her back up with a hand in her hair and seeking her mouth once more.

She opened for the erotic glide of his tongue, a delicious somersaulting sensation curling low in her belly as she ran a gentle hand over his hip. "But—"

"Just kiss me," he muttered against her lips, and she heard the desperate edge of need he'd kept buried until now.

Though she wanted him just as badly and longed to soothe that desperation she sensed in him, she didn't want him to feel even a second's discomfort when they made love. She pulled back slightly and pushed against his shoulders. "Let me on top this time."

He hesitated for a moment, searching her eyes in the dimness. Finally he gave in and allowed her to help roll him onto his back. The faint light streaming into the room outlined the lean, sexy lines of his powerful body and the hard, thick erection she couldn't wait to feel inside her.

Tingling all over with anticipation and desire, Erin straddled his hips, careful not to touch his stitches, and bent to kiss him. He fisted one hand in her hair and held her fast as he kissed her so deep and hard it made her dizzy. Tearing her mouth free to drag in a breath, she trailed a line of kisses down his jaw and neck, over his chest and belly while her right hand snaked down and curled around the rigid length of his cock.

Wade bit back a groan and wrapped his hand around hers, holding her still. She looked up the length of his body and their eyes locked. She could see him battling with himself, fighting back the urge to take. But there was no need. Smiling, she reached up to stroke her fingertips, exposed at the end of the cast, across his bristly cheek. "Let me love you, Wade."

His eyes flared at that but he didn't protest and after a moment he relaxed his grip, releasing her hand to let her do as she wanted. And what she wanted was to show this man everything he made her feel, and everything she felt for him.

****

Wade's heart was pounding almost as hard as it had when he'd pulled her out of the debris after the bombing. He was strung so tight, so desperate to claim her, he didn't know if he could handle giving her control right now. But she'd made it clear how much she wanted this and there was nothing he'd deny this woman if it was within his power to give it to her.

Pulling in a deep breath, he consciously made himself relax and gave himself up to her.

Her hand was like warm silk as it flowed over him, her touch loving and reverent at the same time. She was so damn gorgeous on display for him like this, her perfect curves illuminated from behind, those round, pert breasts with their tight pink nipples rising and falling with each breath. The grip on his cock was pure, perfect torture, a slow glide down and up, combined with a squeeze and twist around the head. Groaning at the pleasure of it, he set an arm around her back and lifted his head to capture a nipple in his mouth.

Erin moaned and awkwardly cupped the back of his head with her casted hand, still stroking him with the other. "I want you so much," she whispered, shifting to rub his rigid cock against her damp slit. The soft, wet sound of it ramped his need even higher.

He switched to the other breast and rocked up against her, adding to the pressure and heat. It thrilled him to know how much she wanted him. These past few days without her had felt like a fucking eternity. He needed to be buried inside her, to feel her grip him tightly as her inner muscles fluttered around him and she came undone in his arms.

Suddenly he couldn't wait another second. "Baby, ride me," he gritted out, needing her so much it shook him. He'd take her slow and sweet next time, wake her with soft kisses and languorous caresses until she was begging for more. Right now he needed her hard and fast to take the edge off this unquenchable need before it killed him.

Humming in agreement, she managed to grip a fistful of his hair despite the cast and twisted his head up to meet her kiss. She licked and sucked at his tongue, swallowed his guttural growl as she stood him up and slowly eased him inside her tight, wet sheath. Her hips shifted, did a little circle that almost blew the top of his head off before she finally sank all the way down and took him deep.

Wade struggled to breathe and dug his fingers into her hip, held on tight as she began to move in a slow, torturous rhythm that was as hypnotic as it was agonizing. She was the fucking sexiest thing he'd ever seen as she rode him, those green eyes heavy-lidded with growing pleasure and the certainty of her feminine power over him.

She guided his mouth back to her tight nipple and he obliged her, making love to the sensitive bud as she rocked and swayed atop him, drawing out the pleasure for both of them. Her little gasps and sighs added to the heat, bringing out the intense possessiveness she made him feel. She was *his* and he wanted her to know it in every fiber of her being. He felt the climax coiling low in his belly, his muscles drawing tight as the release built deep inside.

Riding him harder now, she widened her knees a little and slipped her right hand between her legs to stroke her clit. Her throaty moan of enjoyment wrapped around him, her inner walls squeezing and caressing him until he couldn't hold back anymore. He seized control. Gripping her hips tight in both hands, he lifted her slightly and held her in position while he thrust into her.

She moaned his name and dug her nails into his shoulder, stroking the fingers of her right hand faster between her thighs. Over and over he plunged deep, reveling in her growing cries of pleasure, the slight sheen of perspiration on her skin as she climbed those last few steps to orgasm.

Her breathing hitched, a thin cry of need spilling from her parted lips. When he bent to suck on a tight, pink nipple, she shattered. Her inner muscles contracted around him, increasing the heat and the friction. White-hot ecstasy burned him. He held her firmly in place and let himself go, pumping his release into her body, his ragged groan of relief muffled against the soft cushion of her breasts.

Gasping, hearts pounding, they clung to each other as the waves gently faded. Erin sighed in contentment and kissed the top of his head, her hands gliding over his damp shoulders. Feeling totally relaxed for the first time in over a week, he drew her down to lie full-length on top of him, still buried deep inside her and wishing he could stay there forever.

He ran his fingers through the long, silky strands of her hair, basking in the sense of peace and rightness he felt with her. She was safe and sated in his arms, giving him what he'd so desperately needed since he'd first heard about the bomb going off at Langley. She'd seen him at his best and worst, and still loved him despite everything, warts and all. To him it was nothing short of a miracle.

"Spoke to my sister today," he said.

She turned her face up to his. "How did it go?"

"Better than I expected. There's still so much I can't tell her or my brother about my job, but they both still wanna see me. I was thinking I'd drive down there tomorrow and stop in for a visit." He ran his fingertips up and down the valley of her spine. "Come with me?"

At that she lifted her head and smiled at him. "I'd love to be there when you see them again."

"Good, because I have a feeling we're gonna need a buffer, and you're about the best people-person I know."

She snuggled back against his chest, that little smile still in place. "I'll be happy to act as your buffer, but I bet I won't need to."

They lay together for long minutes until their heartbeats returned to normal, until all the unanswered questions between them crowded his brain. "How long until you go back to Bagram?" he finally asked.

She sighed, the sound sad. "Probably as soon as my cast comes off in another six weeks."

With his chaotic work schedule and her staying in Montana, those six weeks wouldn't give them much time together. He didn't like knowing there was a hard deadline coming up. "How much longer do you have left in your tour and contract?"

"Seven months on the tour, and eleven months in my contract."

He let the quiet spread between them for a minute before continuing. They hadn't talked about the future or anything about continuing their relationship, but since they'd already admitted they loved each other, he figured that meant there *was* a future. "What will you do after that?"

A subtle tension crept into her muscles. "I don't know. I guess it depends on what happens with us."

He cupped the side of her face, turned it toward him so he could see her eyes. "What do you mean?" He needed to know exactly what she wanted, what she envisioned happening before he laid everything on the line.

She lowered her gaze, focusing on her fingertip as she drew a gentle pattern over his chest. "Will there be an *us* when all that's over?"

He drew back to scowl at her, stunned that she'd even question that. "There better be."

She glanced up, as though startled by the warning tone, and a relieved smile curved her mouth. "What about you? What are you going to do after all this is over?"

"Robert's offered me a consulting job. Minimal travel, most of it stateside. Pay and benefits are good. Helluva lot better than my last stint with The Company. And I could do a lot of it via conference call or video meeting. Which means I could work from Montana as easily as anywhere else."

Her face lit up. "You'd do that?"

He tried not to be offended by the surprise in her voice. "Hell yes, I would. But what do *you* want? I mean, after you're done with the Army."

"I'll get a job at a hospital here. And I want to do some riding therapy with wounded vets. It's something I've dreamed of for a long time."

He could easily see her doing something like that. And she'd be damned good at it. Maybe he could even help from time to time. "That it?"

She shrugged, not meeting his eyes.

Uh-uh. Putting a finger beneath her chin, he tilted her face up until she met his gaze. "What about weddings and stuff?"

She narrowed her eyes. "Define 'stuff'."

"You know, kids and whatever." She'd be a fantastic mother to some lucky kids.

"Someday, yeah. Wedding first though. You?" She seemed almost hesitant to ask him.

Wade had done a lot of thinking about everything over the past few days. The Army and his service to his country had been his entire adult life until two weeks ago. He'd never imagined wanting to be a father, had never really thought he'd find someone he wanted to marry and have a family with but now that the undercover chapter of his life was done and he could move forward, he could actually see it with Erin. Hell, he craved the idea of creating that solid foundation for them and their family, the sense of security it brought.

"Two kids. Boys. Because I wouldn't have a clue what to do with a little girl." The thought scared the hell out of him, actually.

Laughing softly, Erin pressed her lips to the center of his chest. "Oh, I dunno. I think you're better with the ladies than you realize. And I have no doubt that a little girl would have you wrapped around her finger in about three minutes flat."

"If she's anything like her mother, then probably," he said with a grin, a pang hitting him square in the heart when he saw the way her eyes went all soft and tender at his words. "All that's at least a year out though."

Her expression turned glum. "I know. It's a long time for us to be apart. A lot of relationships don't make it through a deployment that long."

"Yeah, but they haven't faced what we already have." And nobody understood what it took to get through a deployment better than him. He smoothed a hand over the length of her spine. "Done a few myself, sweetheart, so I might be willing to wait for you if you asked me to."

Those gorgeous green eyes lifted to his. Held. He could see the hope there, and the trace of uncertainty. "Would you wait for me?"

He planned to banish that uncertainty once and for all. Where his feelings for her were concerned, he never wanted her to have a moment's doubt about them again. "Yes," he answered simply. "For as long as it takes."

Her answering smile seemed to light up the room. "Then you've got yourself a deal."

Cupping her face between his hands, he lifted his head from the pillow to cover her mouth with his, sealing that vow with a long, slow kiss.

Epilogue

Fifty-four weeks later

Shouldering her heavy duffel, Erin stepped off the jetway and into the waiting area at the gate with a mixture of excitement and anticipation humming inside her. It had been almost five months since she'd last seen Wade and now that she'd officially completed her contract with the Army and her honorable discharge was in the works, they could finally begin their life together.

The Billings airport was surprisingly busy considering it wasn't even six in the morning yet. Most of the waiting lounges at the gates were full as she passed by. She walked at a fast clip, winding her way through the slower moving foot traffic on the way to the baggage claim area.

The crowd all gathered in a bottleneck at the doors and she impatiently lifted up on her toes to scan the area around the luggage carousels. Lots of people stood waiting for their loved ones, but she didn't see any sign of her parents or Wade. Her flight had landed a bit early though, so she supposed she couldn't be disappointed they weren't here yet.

Once inside the baggage claim area she made her way to the correct carousel and went back to scanning the crowd. Still nothing.

A little bummed out, her excitement faded as she stopped looking and went to stand beside the carousel. Ten minutes later the bags started loading onto the conveyor. Hers was practically the last one out. She grabbed it and turned to face the exterior doors.

And broke into a huge smile.

Her parents, both grinning back at her, stood by the exit holding a big banner that read *Welcome Home Lt. Kelly!*. Hairy sat patiently next to them wagging his tail, a bandana with an American flag motif tied around his neck. She rushed straight to them and grabbed them both in a double-armed hug while Hairy leaned against her leg, his whole body wriggling in excitement.

"God, it's so good to see you guys," she said as she stepped back to give Hairy a proper petting. Even better to know she was moving forward with the next chapter of her life and getting to spend it with the man she loved. "Have you heard from Wade? I thought he was—" She broke off when her father nodded meaningfully behind her.

Turning around, she stared, almost didn't recognize him for a moment without the heavy facial growth she was so used to. One hand flew to her mouth.

Wade stood beside her luggage holding a huge bouquet of red roses. Her heart rolled over in her chest at the sight of him.

He was dressed in a black button-down shirt and dark jeans that hugged his long muscular legs, and, lord have mercy, the black Stetson pulled low over his forehead nearly did her in. Dropping her hand from her mouth, she raced over and flew into his arms. Chuckling, he lifted her clear off the floor and kissed her. She distantly heard people clapping, knew they were staring and didn't give a damn, elated to know Wade felt the same.

Winding her arms around his sturdy neck, she broke the kiss to stare up into his deep, dark eyes. "Hi."

"Hi, sweetheart," he murmured. "You miss me?"

My God, that hat on him. He was a dark and dangerous cowboy commando, the snug shirt molded to a powerful body that could dish out pleasure or pain in equal measure. He was straight out of her hottest fantasies and it was so hard to comprehend that he was all hers. The past five months since her last visit home when she'd gone overseas again had been almost unbearable. "More than you'll ever know." True to his word, he'd waited for her through the rest of her previous deployment and the entirety of this one. She loved him even more for that.

One side of his mouth tipped upward and he arched a dark eyebrow. "Talk is cheap. Prove it."

She tugged on the brim of the Stetson, unable to wipe the smile off her face. "Oh, I will later, handsome."

He led her out to a shiny new black Ford pickup and drove her to the restaurant to meet her parents for a long breakfast. By the time it was over, she was more than ready to get to her cabin and spend some quality alone time with Wade, naked.

"So, you said you had a surprise for me?" she said as he drove down the highway.

"I do."

She couldn't get over how different he looked without the beard. Younger. His face all hard angles and planes. She was looking forward to exploring every inch of it and the rest of his body with her hands and tongue. "What is it?"

"You'll see." A secret smile played around his mouth but he didn't say anything else.

Leaving it for the moment, she filled him in on everything that had happened since their last Skype call eight days ago. Ace, Ryan, Jackson and Honor were still over there. That Night Stalker pilot, Liam, was as well, but whatever had broken them up had hurt Honor so badly she'd kept her distance from him ever since she'd found out he had returned to active duty after being wounded in that mission last March.

Erin stopped talking when Wade took an exit two miles before the one to her parents' ranch. "Where are you going?"

"Someplace I want you to see."

Her surprise? She tried to puzzle out what it might be as they drove away from the highway and south to the rolling ranch land. At a driveway marked by a bright red mailbox, he turned up it and a tidy, two level log house came into view. The property was beautiful and well maintained. "What's this?" she asked him.

Wade parked in front of the house and killed the engine. "Come on."

She hopped out and followed him up the front steps, excitement flaring through her. Fishing in his hip pocket, he came up with a key and handed it to her. "Open it."

She smiled, took the key and pushed open the front door. "Ohhh…" It was beautiful. Dark wood, tall windows and what appeared to be a newly renovated kitchen with granite countertops and stainless steel appliances.

"Barn's out back, and there's a creek about a half mile to the south. You can see it from the master bedroom window upstairs. Property's twenty-five acres." He walked up and slid an arm around her shoulders. "Whaddya think?"

She turned, realized she had her hands on her cheeks. "Is it ours?"

"If you love it, it is."

Oh my God. A lump formed in her throat. "It's beautiful. Oh, man, I love it. But how can we afford it?"

"I've got plenty socked away in investments. My cost of living was pretty low when I was living in Afghanistan all those years," he said dryly, "so I've got enough saved up. And my new salary's not too shabby, either."

She didn't know whether to laugh or cry. "Seriously? We could have this?" She was already mentally decorating the place and imagining her in the kitchen while the kids—a boy and a girl, because she was certain Wade was meant to have a daughter as well as a son—sat at the island and did crafts or homework.

"Yeah," he said with a grin, bending to nuzzle the sensitive spot just below the edge of her jaw, making her shiver as a tidal wave of heat roared through her. "Want to check out the master bedroom?"

"Later," she managed, grabbing him by the shoulders to kiss the hell out of him.

Wade groaned and seized her by the hips, lifting her as he walked her backward and set her atop the island. Erin wrapped her legs around his waist, rubbing the hot glow between her thighs against the ridge of his erection. She grabbed the halves of his shirt and yanked, sending buttons flying.

He laughed against her mouth and cupped her bottom to bring her up even harder against his groin, then shrugged the shirt off. "Sure you don't want to christen the bedroom first?"

"No, later," she repeated on a gasp as he reached beneath her T-shirt to cup her breast, his thumb rubbing over a hard nipple. "Right now I want you to strip down and do me right here on this island." Her heart pounded at the thought of feeling him inside her again after so long. Just looking at him made her want to jump him, but knowing he'd waited so long for her and had planned all this as a surprise...

All of her dreams were coming true, and all because she had him. Now he stood there before her in nothing but his Stetson and a pair of jeans. She licked her lips in anticipation. Damn, she'd never get tired of that view.

Wade reached up to push the Stetson off but she stopped him and shook her head. "Nuh-uh, cowboy. The hat stays on," she ordered, and dragged him back down for a scorching hot kiss.

—The End—

Complete Booklist

Titanium Security Series (romantic suspense)
Ignited
Singed
Burned
Extinguished
Rekindled

Bagram Special Ops Series (romantic suspense)
Deadly Descent
Tactical Strike
Lethal Pursuit
Danger Close

Suspense Series (romantic suspense)
Out of Her League
Cover of Darkness
No Turning Back
Relentless
Absolution

Empowered Series (paranormal romance)
Darkest Caress

Historical Romance
The Vacant Chair

Acknowledgements

A big shout out to my readers, who encouraged me to write this story in the first place. I loved writing about Wade!

As always, Katie Reus and Julieanne Reeves, you are both fantastic and I appreciate your help and support so much.

To my long-suffering husband and amazing proofreader, you rock on with your eagle eye!

And last but not least, to my editor at JRT Editing, a thousand thank yous for helping me strengthen the story even more.

About the Author

NY Times and USA Today Bestselling author Kaylea Cross writes edge-of-your-seat military romantic suspense. Her work has won many awards and has been nominated for both the Daphne du Maurier and the National Readers' Choice Awards. A Registered Massage Therapist by trade, Kaylea is also an avid gardener, artist, Civil War buff, Special Ops aficionado, belly dance enthusiast and former nationally-carded softball pitcher. She lives in Vancouver, BC with her husband and family. You can visit Kaylea at www.kayleacross.com